The Black of Space

J W Murison

Copyright ©JWMurison.2020

All rights reserved.

ISBN-13: 9781657696624

DEDICATION

To George Trowbridge and his wife Mary. Avid reader, friend and old comrade in arms.

CHAPTER 1

Steven looked over the gathered crowd and felt the nervousness grip.

Komoru squeezed his arm, 'You have stood on galactic stages Steven, there is no need for you to be nervous.'

He cast his eyes over the gathered crowd, 'This lot are far more frightening.'

'How so?'

'Because they refuse to believe what is right in front of their eyes. That's what makes them dangerous.'

'You are going to be nice, aren't you?'

He was surprised by her remark. 'Yes of course I am.'

The room was still filling up, but already there were those who were crying out for attention.

'God will punish you for your lies!' Seemed to be the most common phrase that was thrown at them. 'You will burn in the fires of hell!'

'Earth is flat!'

'There are no such thing as aliens!'

By the time the room was full, Steven could feel his temper start to rise. An usher hailed for quiet and announced Steven's name. He received a roar of disapproval.

A small plan started hatching in the back of his mind as he took the podium.

'How many of you still believe in a flat Earth? Stick your hands in the air.' At least a dozen people raised their hands. 'All it takes is a cheap flight around the world to prove how wrong you all are. I will presume you don't have enough money to procure a flight, so let me oblige...' he had already been in touch with Babes and Buzz, everything was ready. Those who had raised their hands began to disappear. Some of those who were left started to cry out in alarm.

'Don't worry, they are all fine. I have just beamed them aboard my ship, and we are giving them a free once around the world. It should only take a few minutes. Now the idiots are out of the way, let's deal with the rest of you.'

The room went deathly quiet as he looked around them, all aware that they were being televised.

'Would those of you who believe that I am an actor and that my ships are all part of some great government tax hoax please make yourself known.' No-one volunteered. 'Really? Are you sure? According to my information there are at least twenty of you in here. The flat Earthers will be back any time now. We have plenty room on board the ship. Would you like a trip to the Moon or Mars? If that doesn't satisfy you, we can always toss you out of a fucking airlock once we get there.'

There were cries of alarm. Here and there individuals began to move towards the doors. 'It looks like we have a few believers now,' Steven waved. 'Goodbye folks, please come again anytime.'

He looked back over the crowd. 'So, who does that leave... ah! The religious people. Aliens do not exist right? It is all make believe, that is what you are telling people, isn't it?'

There was a sudden commotion as the missing people were beamed back into the room. Many of those already standing there began to hold their noses. Abuse was hurled at Steven as yet more people made their way towards the exit.

'Do we still believe the world is flat people?'

'You are a fucking bastard!'

'I know, did you shit yourself as well? Never mind... do you still believe the world is flat? Would you like to go again?'

The exodus ended. 'Now, where was I?' The silence was deathly. 'Oh right, the religious freaks.' That did not receive a response. 'Now I know for a fact that many religions have had practitioners out there in space. They comforted many during the campaign against the city ship. They saw aliens. Where are they now?' Steven held up a hand. 'It's alright, I know. You defrocked them. Threw them out of your churches. I believe even a few were stoned to death in some backward countries, places in which I built schools and hospitals with alien technology. Some of which have been attacked, burned, the doctors and nurses hurt and abused. Tomorrow I am going to reduce those places to dust and have the staff return home to a decent society. From here on in, you will get no help from me, or my people. You can live in the rat-infested shitholes you call home and dream happy, happy thoughts all day about your God, or Gods.'

That elicited a response from the crowd. One cried out 'God is great,' and three others around the room took up the chant. One ran forward to within a few feet of Steven and Komoru. He held up a device and pressed the plunger. Nothing happened.

Steven shook his head and looked down his nose at the bearded man.

'Did you really think we wouldn't detect the explosives? We replaced them with plasticine. It weighs about the same. No go boom boom though. There are people waiting to interview you outside. Goodbye.' The bearded man promptly vanished.

Now there was an even greater outcry. 'What, no thank you?' Steven bellowed, and they quietened down again.

'That's better. We all know why you took this stance, don't we? You are frightened of losing all that money and wealth. If no one believes in you anymore, you will all have to get proper jobs. Aliens don't believe in God. In fact, I have seen them laugh with great gusto at even the mention of God. They consider us primitive. There was a time, long ago, when they did believe. They tried every conceivable test there was, with technology a lot more advanced than ours, and found nothing. No proof of anything. They put it all down to luck and coincidence.

'But there are young men and women out there right now who believe. They believe in God. They are the ones who need you. You have disrespected each and every single one of those who died protecting this world. Not only them, but their wives, fathers, mothers, brothers, sisters, cousins, grandparents and children. It isn't because of alien beliefs that you are losing parishioners, it is because you are turning your back on the people. You are just too frightened of losing all that money, power and wealth. You disgust me.'

'Do you believe in God?' An anguished voice cried out.

'I didn't when I was a child, but I do now.' He lifted his arms, 'How could I not? At the age of fourteen, I took off on a friend's bike and went under a truck. I should have died, I didn't. I was supposed to be a vegetable, but I learned to walk and talk again. I was never supposed to work, but years later I was working, standing in a car park watching the stars when those two ships almost landed on my head. I touched one of the ships and felt a connection. Why did they chose that time, that day, that night to come to Earth? That facility, that carpark? Fate, coincidence, call it what you will. They repaired me, my body and mind.

'We then discovered the Black Planet, we rescued the survivors. We were able to build a fleet of ships just in time to squash an invasion. Coincidence again, luck. We saved this entire planet, not just our own species, but every species, every plant on this world. Luck, coincidence? I don't think so. Since then we have saved this planet more times than many of you realise. If we are not being guided, protected even, by some divine hand, then what is going on? You people are the only ones that can answer that question. I have never read the Bible, the Koran, I am of no religion, but I have come to believe, despite my interaction with aliens.

'Yet here you all stand, disrespecting those that have saved countless lives, all because you think your nice little lives will go away. You spout from your pulpits about how evil I am and how I tell lies. You disrespect every life that has been given to save yours. It is no wonder your parishioners are leaving you in droves. You disgust me, now get out of my sight.'

It took a moment or two, but those at the back slowly began to file out. There were more than a few with heads lowered. Steven stood there and waited until the last one was out. Reporters rushed in but Steven ignored them and left through the back with Komoru. A car was waiting, along with a few stony-faced officials. They glowered at Steven.

Buzz's voice came from inside his head, 'Hey Tonto.'

'Kemosabe!' Steven answered in the same manner.

'What was that all about? The decks up here are awash with shit.'

'Just a few flat Earthers, a small lesson on just how flat the world isn't.'

'A bit dramatic though, if it wasn't for the smell it would be quite funny.'

'Didn't you see it?'

'Sorry bud, was too busy. We were retrieving some space junk for NASA.'

'I forgot. Lucky you were still within range.'

'Left just after we nicked the bad guy's explosives. We caught the satellite as it orbited over the US. We didn't go very far. That's it dropped off now. I will watch it later. How did it go?'

'It went…'

'That bad?'

'Yup, gotta go and face the music now.'

'Good luck. Later.'

'Later.'

He caught Komoru's scowl, 'What?'

'You said you were going to be nice.'

'I was nice! I thought I was nice, didn't you? I gave free

trips around the world and everything. I thought I was nice.'

Thirty minutes later, they were driven into the White House. It was a further twenty before they were ushered in to see the President.

He clapped his hands slowly as they approached and then waved his aides out. Unexpectedly he began to laugh.

He took a deep breath, 'Oh dear! I have been wanting to do that for the last hour. Thank you, Ambassador, for doing what I couldn't. Putting them in their place. I see you threw out the speech we gave you.'

'I lost my temper Mr President.'

'I was watching them heckle you, but they were pretty quiet considering. The flat Earthers have been screaming blue murder of course. A trip around the world, wonderful! Of course, it could lead to charges of kidnapping. We have been trying to get them onboard a ship for years. I see more than one of them messed themselves. They were a joke before, now they are an even bigger joke.'

'Do you really think they will have me arrested?'

'The leader might. You shamed him in front of the world. He has brought more than one action against the government before. Fortunately for you, there are no laws about beaming people out into space against their will. You really aren't much of a diplomat though, are you Ambassador?'

'I don't suppose I am sir.'

'Yet your style seems to resonate well with the alien species you come across in your travels. Still, I am not your boss, and it isn't me you have to answer to. I want to talk to you about the stranglehold the PD Company has on everything. I am being harassed on a daily basis by lobbyists and senators alike.'

'There is absolutely nothing I can do about it, sir. This all comes down from the Grand Commander of the

Federation's forces.'

'I am the leader of the richest and most powerful country on this planet Ambassador. You are saying that I have no clout?'

'None. Comparing yourself to the Grand Commander is like comparing the mayor of a town of two hundred folk somewhere deep in Alaska to yourself.'

The President blinked, 'Seriously?'

'He is an Emperor, his empire is only surpassed by that of the Modloch Emperor. His people number in the billions, at least. He is trusted with the protection of the whole Federation. He is the most successful Grand Commander the Federation has ever had. If you are thinking of taking him on; in the words of a friend, you had better grease up, bend over, and brace yourself.'

The President burst out laughing, 'Your friend has a fair turn of phrase.'

'He certainly has sir.'

'Can you at least explain things to me?'

'I can try sir. We are still very vulnerable. Our home planet is protected, yes, but it's very common for new members to be thrown out of the Federation inside the first five years of membership.'

'I understand that Ambassador, where are the pitfalls?'

'Smuggling basically. Selling prohibited goods, that's how most fall so quickly. Trying to sell goods to races that aren't allowed to trade in them.'

'Like illegal diamonds in Africa.'

'Exactly like that sir. The PD Company have hired experts from many different races who scrutinise all applications. We grant licences. Once licenced, if a trader tries to trade anything that is illegal, then the trader themselves are held accountable. If unlicensed traders are caught, then it is their home world that is held accountable. Illegal mining and smuggling are a massive issue too. There are plenty of materials and minerals that we can produce here on Earth that are on the prohibited list. The Grand Commander has made our company responsible for checking every last detail of every last thing that goes across the barrier.'

'Are you saying that he is trying to safeguard Humanity?'

'That is exactly what he is trying to do. We control all transport, all mining. No one else on Earth has the ability to mine off world, he believes that to be a great starting point. Funnelling everything through the one company or agency is a great way of controlling what flows back and forth across the great barrier.'

'So you have no intention of selling craft to any individual company or government?'

'None at all. In fact, he reinforced that point. With so many governments on one planet, all believing that they can do what they want before they have even learned the rules, there is a disaster waiting to happen. If you or any other government tries to seize control of my company, it will be considered a hostile act by the Federation, as we alone have the power to issue legal licences.'

'So a Federation licencing body has the protection of the Federation?'

'One hundred per cent sir.'

'One last question, an Italian company applied to sell pasta, and your company rejected it. Why?'

'Weren't they told themselves?'

'They haven't received the official report yet.'

'A moment please,' Steven took out his tablet and made an inquiry. It came back quickly.

'The wheat product wasn't the problem; the problem was in the preservatives used. Three of those chemicals can cause severe health problems in alien races. As soon as we have identified those chemicals we will update our website. We have already advised food producers to avoid using any artificial sweeteners, stabilisers and preservatives in their products, but they just aren't listening.'

'So everything is tested?'

'Everything including the wrapping.'

He was nodding to himself, 'Our people need to slow down.'

'That is exactly what the Grand Commander is trying to achieve here. He isn't against Humanity.'

'He is just trying to give us the best possible start.'

'Yes sir.'

'Thank you for clearing that up Ambassador.'

Once out of the White House, Babes beamed Steven and Komoru up.

Steven crashed onto his couch.

'Please don't have a go at me Komoru.'

She sat down beside him and pulled his head onto her lap. 'You know what you did wrong?'

'Yes I do.'

'Then there is no need to say anything.'

Steven almost dozed off. Komoru activated the TV to watch the Modloch news. The Emperor was leaving to attend a conference. Steven was half watching. He suddenly sat up.

'What the hell is Charlie up to now?'

'He isn't there.'

Steven pointed, 'Right there, at the side of the Emperor, the giant Modloch.'

'That's a Modloch.'

'Look at his side arms. That's a desert eagle and one of those light sabres. There are only two people in the whole galaxy that run around like that, and only one of them can change his appearance.' He pulled out his phone and sent a message.

'The pistol and sabre are a dead giveaway Charlie, just saw you on the news.' He lay back down on her lap.

It took a while for the message to be replied to. 'Bollocks! Thanks for the heads-up Stevie.'

Komoru leaned over, 'Is it really him?'

'Sure is,' Steven looked up and decided he liked the

view. He grinned and reached up. Her squeal turned to laughter quickly.

CHAPTER 2

Gord and the guard that was with him flew through the dining room door with an almighty crash, then slid across the highly polished floor in a rather dramatic fashion.

'Fucking idiots,' growled the giant that strolled in the door after them. The whole table was shocked at the sight. Rannalld was the first to react. He leapt to his feet, lowered his head and charged. The rest of the brothers watched on in shock as the giant sidestepped him, grabbing Rannalld by the horn as he shot past, and using his momentum, spun him round and off his feet. Rannalld shot out the door in the same manner as the guards had crashed through. They got to their feet.

Darrick's wits finally returned to him, 'Sit down all of you.' They hesitated. 'Sit down!' Getting to his feet, he met Charlie halfway across the room and stopped.

'Is it really you?'

'What do you think?'

He walked round, 'You are one handsome Modloch, Charlie.'

'Seriously?'

'I am going to have to keep my daughters away from you.'

'Cool.'

He laughed, 'Amazing.'

Gord staggered to his feet in disbelief, 'Is it really Charlie, sire?'

'It is.'

'How?'

'Are you really questioning me?'

His head dropped, 'I am sorry, sire.'

Rannalld came staggering back in. Darrick laughed at him, 'Sit down Rannalld, everything is fine'

'Who is that?'

'A long lost relation to our family,' Darrick howled at his own wit. 'Sit down. Gord stay. You need to hear this.'

When they were all seated Darrick stood at his place with Charlie next to him.

'You all know Charlie, and believe it or not, this is him. Years ago Charlie was, shall we say, in an accident. The details are none of your business. His body was rebuilt by the Human Goodwill Ambassador's ship. Only his internal organs are still Human. With the help of Builder technology he can, as you can see, turn himself into any race he wants. He is going to accompany me to these latest talks, because I require the use of his talents. Why the deception? Because some of those who will be at these talks already know of his peculiar talents, and have banned me from taking him with me.

'So, over the past few days, Charlie has changed himself into a Modloch. I chose the face myself. We are going to say that he is a distant cousin. You should all know the story of Lord Barrick Marr. Charlie is obviously the bastard offspring. His title is Lord Marr, Carrick Marr. Don't forget. He joined our forces as a youngster and worked his way up through the ranks. He has been fighting pirates most of his carrier. That's all you know, all you care about, if anyone asks.

'Charlie, can you eat hay in that form?'

'Hell no, my internals are normal.'

'Then you will have to eat with me on this journey. I will make sure I have the proper meals packed.'

'I will order some army rations from the quarter master, pay for it through the company. Just make sure your suit has cooking facilities, or my room has.'

Darrick nodded, and looked over his brothers again. 'You all know who he is, now watch your tongues. You all know about him, have known about him from childhood. Some of you have met him before. Don't go into details, you never shared any adventures, he is just a distant cousin you took little notice of. Have we all got that?'

They all nodded in unison, 'Good. Charlie, how do you

feel?'

'Weird. Hungry as well.'

'Not surprised.'

'I'm going to have to practice eating and drinking.'

'Turran?'

The youngest stood, 'Yes?'

'I am putting you in charge of Charlie.'

'Why me?'

'Because you are the youngest and have nothing else to do. Unless you would like to go out and fight with Rannalld? I am sure he could find you a spot with a marine platoon.'

His brothers laughed. 'I would be honoured to fight alongside my brother. When I am a little older maybe…' the laughter increased. 'What would you like me to teach him?'

Darrick was also laughing. 'How to eat, walk, run properly. Court etiquette, uniforms, casual clothing, the lot. Anything you can think of that will help him to pass as a Modloch. If he fails, I will blame you.'

'I think I can manage that.'

Darrick turned back to Charlie and slapped him on the shoulder.

'You look amazing Charlie, or I will call you Carrick from now on, but you must address me as sire.'

'Of course, sire.'

'How strong are you in this form?'

'I have no idea yet, and my coordination is still a little off.'

'Go back to your room and get something to eat for now. Gord, go with Carrick and make sure no one else challenges him.'

'Sire.'

Gord escorted Charlie out of the dining hall. He didn't get far before Gord had to ask, 'Is it really you in there Charlie?'

Charlie grabbed him by the scruff and lifted him from his feet, giving him a friendly shake into the bargain, 'It's Lord Carrick Marr you stupid shit. Get it into your thick Modloch skull before you make an arse of everything.'

'Let me down you prick!'

A strange squeal attracted their attention. Charlie turned with Gord still clasped in a massive hand to see a young female, wide-eyed, standing in an adjacent corridor.

Charlie let Gord down gently. Gord straightened his tunic and bowed.

'Princess Parrina, so sorry to disturb you.'

Strange noises came from her mouth, but she eventually found her voice.

'Who is this?'

'None of your damn business,' Charlie snorted and walked away.

Gord bowed hastily, 'I am so sorry. Your father's order.' He hurried after Charlie.

Parrina peeked around the corner after them. Gord growled and punched the stranger on the arm. He laughed and made a friendly swing that Gord ducked. She clung to the corner for support.

When her shaking legs could finally support her, she took a moment to straighten her clothes.

'What are you up to Parrina?'

She cocked her head at the smiling Turran, her return smile almost dazzled him.

'Hi Turran, what are you up to?'

'Your father has sent me on a small errand, we… we have a distant relative visiting. He is a bit backwards in court etiquette. I have been given the task of teaching him.'

'Really, what does he look like?'

'You can't miss him, trust me. Huge.'

'What is his name?'

'Lord Carrick Marr.'

'Never heard of him.'

'You know the story of Barrack Marr?'

'Oh! That Lord Marr.'

'That one. Direct descendant seemingly,' he shrugged in a very Human way. 'He has no manners anyway. So, it's off to work I go.'

Parrina smiled, 'Good luck.'

'Thank you Parrina.' He gave a small bow and left her alone.

Her own errand forgotten, a wide-eyed Parrina went in search of her mother.

'You can't talk to a Royal princess like that Charlie!'

'Were you actually there?'

'I was right beside you.'

'Didn't you see the look on her face?'

'What about it?'

'It's trouble, that's what it is.' His blank stare was pretty much all Charlie needed to put things into perspective. He shook his head, 'You don't have all that much experience with females, do you Gord?'

'I'm married, of course I do.'

'Really, and how many females have you known?'

'I know lots of… oh! You mean like that.'

'Like that.'

'Just my wife.'

'That's what I thought.'

Charlie tried to drink a glass of water and spilled half of it.

'Shit! This isn't easy.'

'Is it that different?'

'Beyond weird.'

There was a knock at the door and Gord let Turran in. He looked the half-soaked Charlie up and down.

'It would seem I am going to have my work cut out for me.'

CHAPTER 3

Steven shook hands with Orlath Canaries.

'It is good to see you again, Orlath.'

'May I still call you Steven?'

'Of course.'

'The pleasure is all mine, Steven.'

'This is an impressive office.'

'Come, sit down, I love the view.'

Steven sat down on the comfortable couch opposite him.

'I can see why. You have done very well for yourself.'

'It has been hard work.'

'You are a Professor now.'

Orlath laughed, 'Only because there is no one else to teach. I hear that some of my students have now been taken on by the Royal Modloch Academy.'

'That's right, and all have a job waiting for them when they leave.'

'I syphoned off the best to the PD Company of Earth. Humanity is finally taking a leap.'

'Earth owes you a great debt of gratitude.'

'No it doesn't. This is my home now, I am Human. I am wealthy beyond my wildest dreams. I vacation in places that are so beautiful it defies belief. I have a job and rank I could never have attained on my home world. Earth owes me nothing, I owe it everything.'

'You have worked hard for it.'

'The least I can do.'

'So you are enjoying life?'

'Very much thank you. What about you and the guys, are you enjoying your adventure?'

'It has had its moments.'

'What about my saviour? I hear tell he is a Modloch Lord now.'

'With his own cottage and a great big field he can grow vegetables in.'

'That doesn't sound much for a Lord. Did he refuse more?'

'A lot more.'

'So typical of the breed.'

'I suppose it is.'

'I hear you have gotten yourself into a little trouble with the crazies.'

'A dozen law suits from the flat Earth society.'

'At least the rest of them have quietened down a little.'

'Haven't they asked to meet you?'

'I had to stop it, I was getting assaulted, people trying to rip off my costume.'

Steven took a deep breath, 'I see, that couldn't have been easy.'

'There are those that are simply not willing to accept Steven. There is nothing we can do about it, but I am not willing to accept any more abuse.'

'I understand completely.'

'What is your good lady up to? I thought she might visit too.'

Steven was frowning, 'I'm not too sure, she borrowed some of my top men and they have sneaked off somewhere. I have to say it worries me.'

'She doesn't seem like the kind of person that would do anything wrong, Steven.'

Steven stared at him, 'You really don't know Komoru.'

He delved into his pocket and pulled out a data disc. 'I was asked to give this to you.'

Orlath took it and turned it in his fingers. 'This is Albany.'

'It is from your parents. It came to me through our office in the Modloch city ship. There was a personal note from your father asking to pass it on to you at my own convenience. He obviously didn't have an address and there still isn't a regular mail run from the Federation to Earth. Something I am hoping to rectify soon.'

Orlath put it into his pocket, 'I will watch it later. My

father and I did not part on good terms.'

'I understand. How are things going at this end?'

'I am completely snowed under with all the work. We are months behind on everything, with official Federation business taking up most of our time. We are slowly increasing our workforce.'

'It is the training, isn't it?'

'Yes, as with everything. I have to admit, these are exciting times, leading a new world into the Federation. It is also a grave responsibility. It needs to be done right. It helps that bureaucracy is as slow on the other side of the barrier.'

Steen laughed, 'That is so true.'

'We set up the Earth Imperial Bank to accept Federation credits. They are arguing with the Federation bank on exchange rates. There are just too many different currencies on Earth for them to deal with. The Federation bank is insisting that Earth gets its act together and uses only one currency. Obviously, there is a lot of political fallout over it.'

'What is your position on it?'

'Simple: change to Federation credits. It is what every other world out there has done. It is a bit like the Euro, where you get a German Euro, and a French Euro, with the Federation you get a Modloch credit and an Albany one, but they are worth exactly the same.'

'They don't even use coinage anymore. Tourists are having a lot of difficulty. We do our best and set up temporary accounts for them through our company and exchange their money here for credits, but it is becoming a burden.'

'Of course, because you can't exchange that money for Federation credits.'

'Exactly, and the volume of people crossing the barrier is increasing. The restrictions on precious metals and minerals we can move is also causing problems.'

'Once an agreement has been reached, you will be able

to transfer a large amount of precious metals as collateral, then things should fall into place.'

'I just wish they would hurry up, or I am going to have to stop exchanging money. We have huge demands on our resources across the other side of the barrier. The money we spend there has to be made there, the money we make here, spent here.'

'There is now an imbalance.'

'Yes, very much so. Is there any light at the end of the tunnel?'

'Well Scotland has offered to change to credits, however the big three aren't amused by it. They think that will give Scotland too much clout, and of course they could set their own exchange rates as well.'

'But they aren't willing to change from their own currencies?'

'Some of those currencies have been in existence for a very long time Steven, you know that. It isn't so much the political wing that is the problem as the citizens of those countries. The United States had a referendum where over seventy per cent said no, so the President and the Senate have their hands tied.'

'It is surprising how many people do not like change.'

'I think all races are the same Steven. The nature of people the universe over.'

'It would seem we aren't too different after all.'

'Not when it comes to money and power. Where are you staying now?'

'In Japan with Komoru. I was going to purchase a home here, a ranch out west, but I can't really be bothered. I really like Komoru's home, and it is only a fifteen-minute commute in interplanetary drive.'

'I suppose you are away so often and for such long periods it makes more sense.'

'It certainly does.'

Orlath checked his watch, 'I am afraid I have to get back to work, but it has been my greatest pleasure seeing you again.'

Steven got up and they shook hands, 'Keep up the good work Orlath, and thank you for all that you have done.'

'It has been my pleasure Steven. Good luck in your endeavours and keep safe on your journeys.'

'I will try.'

Orlath saw him to the door, then returned to his desk. His heartbeat increased at the sight of the disc in his hands. With trepidation, he took his old device from the bottom drawer of his desk and slipped it in. His mother and father sat there, both looking forlorn.

'Hello Orlath. I don't know if this will ever reach you. You are so far away from home now and lost to us forever. I was so ashamed of you, for so long. When I saw you last, I had harsh words for you. I cannot expect forgiveness for what I did; I thought I was doing what was best for our whole race. I never once stopped to think about what I was doing to my own son.'

He took a deep breath, 'I was the one who introduced you to that Human. I was the one who ignored what you were trying to tell me all those years ago. I treated the Humans like animals to justify the experimentation I was conducting on them. Now they are a force to be reckoned with within the Federation. We received word just the other day that they have been accepted as full members. What was completely incomprehensible to me back then has become reality. A very harsh and bitter reality.

'The Albany Empire as we once knew it no longer exists. One day I expect the Humans to come for me to answer for the crimes I committed against their people, or from whatever government comes into existence here. Before that day comes, we just wanted to reach out to our only child. Your mother would also like to say something.'

'Orlath,' she looked up at the camera, and he could see the grief in her eyes. 'I was very angry with you once. I ignored your feelings when you were a child. I supported your father in all his endeavours, so I am just as guilty as he is. They told us that you had betrayed our people. We were so ashamed. It wasn't until years later that we received word from a friend of your father's, who showed us the official record of what happened. We now know you tried your best to advise your Commander before that big battle, and that you didn't escape the ship until after it was almost totally destroyed.

'I understand now why you applied for political asylum. We know that you took up a position that wasn't related to the military, even though many said you did, and we know that you never conspired against the empire. You took up a civilian post that you studied for at college. When we approached the Humans for information about you, we were surprised by how helpful they were, and even more surprised, even delighted, by how well you were doing.'

She let out a bellow of anguish and his father put his arm around her shoulder. She leaned against him for support for a moment.

'Orlath, you are a Professor, you teach, you are respected, you have a very important position, and on a planet that is now a part of the Federation. I am very proud of you and very ashamed for my behaviour towards you in the past.'

Orlath felt himself choke up. It was unexpected, and he stopped the recording. This wasn't the time or the place to dwell on the past or wallow in his own feelings.

CHAPTER 4

Komoru watched the figure on the monitor like a hawk. For hours they had shadowed the man, trying to get an opportunity to catch him on his own. All day he was surrounded by people. Her instincts screamed at her to simply kill him. Yet she did not consider herself a murderer. A scan of his body had revealed that he had tracking devices on his person, and some form of electronic alarm. She had asked to meet him in person, but he had steadfastly refused.

So far she had hunted down all twelve of those bringing charges against Steven. Ten had dropped the case with a massive monetary bribe. Only two had refused after speaking to this man. He had spent the day rushing around, trying to get the others to change their decision. All had more or less laughed at him.

It was as though he knew they were following him. Day turned to night, and it was late before he returned home. Even then, he had a couple of friends over. When they made to bed down in the same room, a weary Komoru had enough. A small ashtray-like object appeared under the couch, and the smell of flowers filled the room. They were soon fast asleep.

Richard Liverington's eyes snapped open. It took him a moment to gather his wits, but a glance to his right was all he needed to know where he was. He studiously swung his legs off the small cot he had been laid on, to the side away from the view.

'You can send me home now.'

An invisible door slid open and Komoru entered.

'I know you saw it.'

His scowl wasn't pretty, 'Where's your boyfriend?'

'He doesn't even know we are here.'

'Then I will have you charged with kidnapping. Yeah, and you won't be able to bribe me either.'

'Ten million, twenty?'

'It ain't about the money.'

'Then what is it about Mr Liverington? Tell me what it is all about.'

'A slant-eyed bitch like you would never understand. Now get me home or I will come over there and choke the life from that scrawny throat of yours.' He got up threateningly.

In the blink of an eye, the door behind Komoru opened, and the biggest man he had ever seen in his life strode in. In a few steps Lewis had closed the distance. He grabbed the man by the throat and hoisted him into the air.

'Like dis? Is that what you intend doing to Miss Komoru? You be dead before you got halfway across de floor, ass-wipe. You better talk to Miss Komoru nice like. She don't like swearing much either. Watch your tongue.' Lewis tossed him across the room and left.

Liverington had got a big fright, but when the woman walked over and crouched down in front of him, the coldness in her eyes petrified him. Cold sweat broke out on his forehead.

'Please answer my question Mr Liverington.'

It took him a few moments to gather his voice. He had to cough to clear his crushed airways.

'It's about freedom of choice. I choose to believe what I want.'

'To the point where you would harm others?'

'Who am I harming?'

'Steven and I. This crew, these ships.'

'I've done nothing to any of you.'

'You had your friends press charges.'

'You shouldn't have kidnapped them.'

'They were very vocal in their beliefs, Mr Liverington. To the point where they were being absolutely abusive.'

'It was only words.'

'Is that how you justify your cult? Words can be as

damaging as action. After all, isn't the pen mightier than the sword? I am sure you identify with that saying, Mr Liverington. After all, how could your nonsense have spread so far and wide without it?'

'It isn't nonsense.'

'Look to your right and see the truth.'

'No.'

'You would deny the truth?'

Liverington growled, 'I have the right to view this world any damn way I want to.'

'No one is denying your right to see the world in whatever manner you wish. I will not, however, allow you to bring us down with you.'

'No one is bringing you down.'

'Are you aware that that Goodwill Ambassadors are not allowed to have a criminal record? You would destroy our careers.'

'Not my problem.'

'Is that all the thanks we get for saving your miserable life? How many times have we saved it now? Not just your life, but the lives of every Human being on the planet. I don't care what shape you wish to believe the world is. We, however, do not expect to be abused in the manner that you and your people have subjected us to.'

'It is all…' his words trailed off as she rocked forward on to her toes.

'Be very careful what you say next. If I deem you to be a lost cause, I will beam you into the nearest volcano.'

'You would murder me?'

'We have saved your life many times, does it not then belong to us? We did not come to your press conference and throw insults at you. We did not bring lawsuits against you. We simply proved to those who were crying at us, calling us liars, the truth. We could quite easily bring suits of our own for defamation of character. We have the money to snowball you all into hell for the rest of your lives.'

She half-closed her eyes, and a tack of gold and precious gems appeared close to them. His eyes widened. Komoru reached over and picked up an egg-sized fire diamond. She handed it to him.

'Is it real enough for you Mr Liverington?'

He felt the jewel in his hands, then held it up to the light. He could see the colours deep within, they were breath-taking.

He gave a small nod and handed it back across, then his eyes flicked to the gold. Komoru smiled and reached out. She placed a small bar in his hands.

'Is it real?'

'Yes. The fire diamond is almost priceless. That gold in weight is worth a hundred thousand, three times that much because it comes from space.' She smiled coldly, 'Do you believe we can keep you in court until you die of old age?'

'Yes.'

'We have no wish to harm you or any of your people Mr Liverington. No one understands how precious life is more than we do. Feel free to call every planet you want to flat. Sit at home and think happy thoughts all you wish. However, if you bring us to court, then you are not only endangering your own life, but the lives of everyone on this planet. We are the front-line, we are the buffer between Humanity and destruction. Do you wish to remove that buffer?'

His head moved from side to side slowly, 'No. I didn't know the lawsuits would do so much harm. It still doesn't detract from the fact that you have destroyed the beliefs of a dozen people. That is unforgivable.'

'Ten of them are now millionaires. I don't think they care all that much. It is called settling out of court, and it is perfectly legal in your country.'

The line of his mouth hardened, and she could see there was still fight left in him.

'I can see you still need a little persuading.' She stood,

'Lewis.' The door opened. 'Escort Mr Liverington to the airlock please.'

Liverington howled all the way there. He was sure he was about to die. Lewis tossed him in unceremoniously.

He pointed to a space suit, 'You better put that on if you don't want to die.'

The airlock doors slid closed. Liverington hastily scrambled into the suit. It was nothing like the big suits you saw in the movies. It was sleek and conformed to his body. A strange zip closed it at the front. He stuck the helmet over his head and felt the suit drawn to it. The helmet came alive. Red lights turned to green. His breathing began to settle. He watched the seconds tick by in the display.

About five minutes later the doors began to open. He got up and stood in front of it. It occurred to him that this might be a trick - his suit was registering oxygen in the atmosphere outside his suit. The thought had just crossed his mind when Ico dropped the shields and he was sucked clean out. He hit the ground hard and tumbled to a stop. He could just see the ship take off. He scrambled to his feet and threw up a fist at them.

'You bastards just blew me out of a goddamn airlock!' He couldn't see or hear the hilarity onboard the ship.

He began to take stock of his situation. His eyes sought out the display. His oxygen was fine, his suit intact. With a deep breath he looked around. A line of boulders to his right seemed interesting. He walked over on unsteady legs. He felt different. Scrambling on top of the nearest boulder, he almost had a panic attack. He had visited the Grand Canyon, but this made that look small. He knew exactly where he was standing. His foot kicked a small rock. He bent and picked it up. It didn't feel right for some reason. He threw it.

'Holy shit!' The rock flew much further than he expected before dipping into the canyon.

'Gravity, goddamn gravity is different…' he had said it aloud and now felt like a fool. He looked up and around, then located another fist-sized rock. He wound up and threw. The rock sailed away. He howled with delight. His predicament forgotten, he jumped from boulder to boulder to locate more rocks to throw. He began to experiment to see how far he could throw them. It was while doing this that he overstretched from a run. Brittle rock crumbled underfoot and he found himself sailing out into the void. His howl of fear did not go unnoticed. He was in the middle of chastising himself for being the architect of his own downfall, when he materialised back in the airlock of the ship. Relief flooded through him. They weren't going to kill him, at least not yet.

His tour lasted a few hours. They dropped him off on more than one moon. On each he threw rocks to see how far they would travel. The moons of Jupiter he would recount later as his favourites. When they dropped him off on a moon in Saturn's orbit, he didn't even bother picking up a rock. He was exhausted and tired. The beauty of what was before him held him enthralled. He sat down and rested against a rock. Despite fighting it, he fell asleep.

The following morning he woke up in his own home. For a moment he thought it a dream, but on his kitchen counter he found a bag of rocks, one from every planet and moon he had stood on. He went to his computer and sent a message.

An hour later, Komoru appeared at his door and knocked lightly. He opened it and leaned against the post.

'I will help you stop the lawsuits. On two conditions: you compensate those in the same way you compensated the others.'

'And the other condition?'

A smile began to spread across his face.

CHAPTER 5

Steven was dumbfounded, 'Seriously?'

Komoru let out a long slow breath, 'Yes, I am afraid so.'

'No! I mean… seriously?'

'Saying that over and over isn't going to change anything.'

'You accepted his proposal?'

'I felt I had no other choice. I had considered throwing him into a volcano.'

'That wouldn't have helped. In fact his disappearance would have had the opposite effect.'

'I realised that.'

'What is he going to do?'

'He is going to vlog our adventures.'

'Vlog… seriously?'

Komoru punched him, 'Stop saying that. It is getting annoying.'

'Right, OK, but what is he going to do?'

'He is going to travel with us and document our travels.'

'Sounds like a load of crap to me.'

'I don't think so. You should meet him.'

'No thanks.'

'This isn't a request Steven. Consider it a part of your political training.'

'You mean smile and lie?'

She kissed him on the cheek, 'Pretty much. Right now he has us by the you know what's. If either of us receive a criminal record, it is over. It was your actions that put us in this position in the first place, so you will have the decency to listen to his proposal.'

'Fine!'

Steven wasn't amused at all by the proposition, but Komoru was right, he had caused this situation, and at least she hadn't scattered the man's atoms all over the universe.

The interview took place the following day in Steven's office on the moon. Mr Liverington didn't look like much at all. Maybe a bit of a redneck. Close to middle age, medium height, broad build, scraggy short beard, hair thinning and beginning to turn grey. He slumped a little in the seat. Steven was suddenly curious as to why this man had managed to get hundreds of thousands of followers worldwide. They studied each other for a full minute before Steven decided to break the ice.

'Mr Liverington I presume?'

He half smiled, 'Is it Doctor Gordon, Ambassador, or Captain?'

'This isn't an official interview. Call me Steven.'

'Ritch, Ritchie or Richard. If you call me Dick, I will be offended.' He sat up and leaned across the desk, offering his hand. Steven returned the gesture, his hand disappearing into the man's calloused hand. They sat back in their chairs.

'Why the hell do you want to come with us?'

Richard laughed, 'You really need to know my story. I didn't do all that well at school. I wasn't really interested. I had my life all mapped out long before that. I worked for my father since I was a kid. He was a builder, had his own company. I was going to leave school and join him, eventually taking over the business. Only about the time I was finishing school, he had a fatal accident. The business folded, I was left high and dry with no qualifications.

'I became a labourer for one of my father's competitors. I suppose over time I became a skilled labourer. Ten years ago, I had my own near fatal accident. I fell off scaffolding, near thirty feet high. Cracked my spine, broke lots of bones. I wasn't allowed to work and I lost my case for compensation. I had detached my safety line to clip it on to the stage above when I fell. They said it was my own fault, not the black ice I stepped on.

'Anyway, I was on welfare and feeling like I had been fucked over by the man. Which I had been. I spent a lot of time online. Discovered the flat Earth society. I liked the message. You know: stuff convention, stuff the man. So I got stuck into the man, became an activist, grew in popularity. When the originator of the society passed away, he left it all to me.'

'The baton passed.'

'Yeah, sure, you could call it that.'

'You do realise that the Earth isn't flat?'

'What the hell has that got to do with anything?'

'Everything!'

'Every man, woman and child on this planet has the goddamn right to believe what the hell they want. We don't have to take shit from doctors, scientists or governments.'

'You have a big chip on your shoulder.'

'Massive.'

'You hate the man.'

'I hate the man.'

'I suppose in your eyes I represent the man.'

'Sure do.'

'So you hate me too?'

'Not on a personal level.'

'I'm not the man.'

'You just bribed ten of my people into dropping charges against you. You are that man.'

Steven had to think about that one for a moment, 'You might have a point. But I will ask you again now I know your backstory. Why do you want to come with us?'

'Your lady gave me a nice little tour of our solar system. Our last stop was Saturn. She dumped me on a small moon. What a view. Damn what a view. I was enthralled, no shitting. It was the first time in years I had felt at peace. It was like Saturn sucked out all of my anger and pain. Hell, I even fell asleep. Sitting on my ass, leaning against a moon rock. I have trouble sleeping in my own bed Steven, the pain and discomfort wakens me a dozen times a night. When I woke up in my own bed the next morning, I thought it had all been a dream. When I found those rocks, I knew it hadn't been. I also knew what I wanted to do with the rest of my life, and it wasn't sit on my ass here on Earth. I want to see what you guys see, I want to go where you guys go, and I want to tell all of my friends about it. I want to share those experiences with the world.'

'Half the world wants to do exactly that - why should we take you? Apart from the fact you have us over a barrel.'

'We get news reports about what you guys are up to all the time. We get the Modloch news, but without a new generation TV with a translator, it just sounds like a herd of animals bawling. To me you are no more than a plastic figure on a toy shelf, and that goes for the people who watch my channel as well. What I am going to do is Humanise the lot of you. I am going to rip every last remnant of doubt from the Human race, regardless of race or religion. That is what I am offering you.'

'You mean you are going to snoop into our lives.'

'I am going to crawl up your ass with a microscope.'

Steven let out a long sigh, 'I don't like that idea at all.'

'Of course you don't. I won't get too personal though. I do have a little decorum.'

'How are you going to market this?'

'Easy, I give you the benefit of the doubt, you compensate my people, we drop all the charges. As a thank you, you invite me to join your crew on your journey. Being the great sceptic I am, I agree. I go with you to prove the lies. What I find there is astounding. We meet the aliens on a personal level, they aren't strange creatures on the tube. By the time we reach the other side of that barrier, folks are going to love you people. When they meet your alien friends, it is going to make the impact much bigger.'

'I can see were you are coming from. I still don't like it.'

'You don't have to like it; you just have to live with it. One more thing: I join your crew.'

'Why? I thought you would go with Komoru.'

'Too many foreigners for my liking.' He held up a hand, 'I ain't being racist, I just know I will find it hard to fit in there. She also scares the living shit out of me.'

It took a moment, but Steven burst out laughing, 'Komoru is a wonderful woman.'

Richard leaned forward in his seat, 'One of my gifts is that I am a very good judge of character. That ain't no soft lovey dovey chick. That woman has a core of steel and I suspect that those who cross her regret it. Last time I saw eyes like hers was on a marine sniper.'

Steven was silent for a long time contemplating the man in front of him. In the end, he realised that he just didn't have much choice in the matter. It was obvious that Komoru wanted this man on board, and Steven now understood why. She realised that he could help in an area where they weren't represented. The guy was very sharp.

'There will be times when on diplomatic missions that we will be unable to share information with you. I will make sure that, even if you do find out what is going on, no information leaks out and compromises our mission.'

'I ain't all that interested in the diplomatic stuff Steven, it's the people stuff I'll be focusing on.'

'Then I agree.'

'Then let the show begin.'

CHAPTER 6

It had been a tough week for Charlie. Turran and Gord had worked him hard. He had learned to eat, walk and run like a Modloch. They had even taught him some basic Modloch phrases. Rumours flew around the Royal residence. Females he had never seen before would suddenly appear as if from nowhere. Many tried to talk to him; he ignored them, but it seemed to have the opposite effect to the one desired.

Charlie felt relieved when Darrick decided to move to the city ship. He wanted some peace and quiet before the summit.

They hadn't even reached the city ship when Charlie received a message from Steven.

'For God's sake!'

Darrick looked over, 'What is it?'

'Steven just saw us get onto the shuttle on the Modloch news. He knew it was me straight away.'

'That's impossible!'

Charlie slapped his weapons belt, 'These.'

Darrick grunted, 'Never thought of that. Which means Ne´ will spot you right away as well.' He thought it over for a moment. 'I like that you are armed with those weapons. Nor would I want you to take a weapon that you weren't familiar with, given your circumstances. I think the easiest solution would be to arm all my guards in a similar way. Your one is personalised; swap it for a generic one. We have a week, get it done.'

'Yes sire.'

Charlie's gun belt was sent to a local manufacturer the same afternoon. Gord requested weapons from the nearest Earth armourer, while Charlie requested escape tools from the company. All of them arrived three days later. The belts were embellished with the Emperor's seal. The following morning, Charlie had them all out at the range.

He had a number of different targets set up.

He stood and looked over the guard for a moment. Gord introduced him.

'This is an old friend of mine, Lord Carrick Marr. I know you haven't had the full briefing yet, but shortly we will be going somewhere where even we cannot gain entry. Only those of the Royal bloodline may pass into the inner sanctum. That is why Lord Carrick Marr has been called in from the front line to help guard the Emperor. We are not familiar with the new weapons we are being issued with, but Lord Carrick Marr is. He will give us a short demonstration.' He nodded to Charlie.

Charlie took a step forward, 'Both weapons you have been issued with today are extremely deadly, far more so than the weapons you are normally issued with.'

Charlie drew the desert eagle, 'This is one of the most powerful handguns Humanity ever invented. It is magazine fed. It will not be affected by any electronic device. I know your normal weapons are shielded from electronic interference. However, history has shown us that the only time an enemy has ever used such measures on a Royal guard is when they know they can actually defeat the weapon. By the time you discovered your weapons were inoperable, you wouldn't have the time to do anything about it. You and the Emperor would most likely be dead. This weapon and tool are to be used as an emergency backup only. If you are caught unholstering them at any other time, you will face severe disciplinary proceedings, especially if you are in the presence of the Emperor. Follow me.'

He brought them over to a table, 'Gather round, make sure you can all see.'

He showed them how to load the weapon with an empty magazine and handle it correctly. Then he loaded up a magazine with live rounds and had them all do the same.

'Put the loaded magazines into your pouches. Until you have had extensive training with these weapons, you will never load the weapon with a full magazine.' He took out an empty one, showed them it and slapped it home. 'I will tell you once more: these are last chance weapons, emergency use only. I will now show you why. Follow me and stay behind me.'

He moved to the range. On pedestals were a number of everyday objects and a large fruit that looked like a melon.

Charlie demonstrated how to remove the empty magazine, and how to load it with a fresh one. He cocked the weapon, describing what was happening inside.

'Normally you will wear ear defenders when you practice with this weapon. It makes a lot of noise, a loud report as it is fired. You need to get used to the recoil of the weapon and the noise. So, for this demonstration, we aren't going to use them. Please observe the objects to your front and we will demonstrate the penetrative and destructive power of this weapon. Each of those objects have about the same density as a Modloch head.'

The gun roared in his hand. The objects to his front were obliterated, some jumping high into the air. He emptied the last few rounds into the standing targets. He made the weapon safe and holstered it. The guards were all making weird noises as they tried to equalise the pressure in their ears. Charlie waited patiently. When they seemed to have regained their composure, he took them forward to witness the destruction close up. There were gasps of awe and wonder at the devastation wrought by the weapon.

'Are we beginning to get the picture now? There are no pretty cauterised wounds. Anyone hit with one of these will very quickly bleed to death; there will be a lot of screaming. It will remove large chunks of your anatomy, even limbs. That includes the Emperor's if you fire the weapon in his direction by accident. Now, I will ask you once more, are we beginning to get the picture?' There was the normal Modloch grunts of appreciation.

'All right, let's move on to the emergency escape tool.'

He walked over to a row of metal girders. He pulled the tool from his holster and held it up.

'I am all sure you have heard of this thing.'

'Charlie has one,' called out one of the older guard members.

'I know Charlie, and you're right that he has. So you have seen one before. When Charlie and the Chief Engineer demonstrated this tool to the Federation Procurement Committee, they demonstrated it with airlock doors from warships. We couldn't find any, so these girders will have to do. The batteries within only have a life span of two minutes, give or take a few seconds. Now stand back.'

When everyone was safely out of range, Charlie turned to the nearest girder and activated the tool. Light flashed in front of their eyes and large white-hot pieces of molten metal splashed onto the ground. Charlie stepped back out of the way and the girder fell into a heap of pieces on the ground. The guardsmen roared their appreciation. Gord laughed with delight.

Charlie turned to face them. He held up the deactivated tool.

'This can and will kill. There is no safety switch on it. Removing it from its holster in the presence of the Emperor will most likely result in your execution. Unless, of course, it is in an emergency. Can any of you here describe such an emergency?'

One of the older guard members stepped forward, 'A deliberate attempt to assassinate the Emperor, where our normal weapons have been made inoperable, and we are maybe locked into a room. We could cut through the doors to make our escape.'

'Why cut through the doors where your enemy might be waiting? With these things you can cut through the walls into an adjoining room, and the next and the next. You can get behind your enemy and surprise them.'

He grunted his appreciation, 'Even better, Lord Marr.'

Charlie nodded, 'This is what these weapons are for: last chance, extreme emergency only. Remember that.' Charlie slid the tool away into his holster. 'Put it on charge every night, even if you don't use it. The charging unit will discharge the battery then recharge it again to keep the battery healthy. Don't forget: both of these weapons are extremely reliable, but they have to be serviced properly. The charger services the escape tool. You will have to clean the Human weapon by hand. I will show you how to do that soon. Right now you are going to practice. When we come back from this conference, a Human marine instructor will give you proper lessons in weapon handling. In the meantime, you will just have to follow my teaching.'

He took them back to the firing line, demonstrated once more how to load and unload the weapon, then let them fire it. Despite the warnings, more than one lost the weapon the first time they fired it. Few hit the targets on the first try. Their friends howled with laughter until it was their turn. Charlie had them empty all of their magazines, reload them, and discharge them again.

He made them reload the magazines and put them away. He checked each individually that they had placed an empty magazine into the weapon. He then let them at the remaining girders. There were more than a few howls of pain as they were unable to avoid pieces molten metal, yet all enjoyed the experience thoroughly.

When they were finished, he showed them how to disassemble the pistol and clean it. Again, he checked that empty magazines went back into the pistol before dismissing them. A grinning Gord declared it to be a very productive day.

CHAPTER 7

Charlie had just finished his meal when Darrick appeared from the adjoining room. They were only a day away from the conference.

'How was your meal?'

Charlie wrinkled his nose, 'It was vile.'

'What was it?'

'Some kind of ravioli. Supposedly meat in a pasta parcel, with tomato sauce. I really hate the sauce, and as for the meat…' he shrugged, 'So small you can't actually taste it.'

'Didn't you order food you liked?'

'I did, but the bastards have slung me the crap they can't get rid of. It's not like a civilian has anyone to complain to.'

'It isn't the kind of worldly problems I am bothered with.'

'I don't suppose it is. So what's up?'

'Nothing, I just wanted some company. Is that permitted?'

Charlie took a drink of coffee, 'Why wouldn't it be?'

'You haven't been very friendly lately.'

'Practicing keeping my distance and acting like a subject, not a friend. Sorry.'

'No you're right. The sooner you are back to Human the better.'

'I couldn't agree more.'

'I am talking about my daughters and the ladies of my residence…'

'So am I.'

Darrick howled with laughter, 'I had no idea you would cause that kind of impact. I did my job a little too well.'

'It is a nightmare; I never knew there were so many females in the palace.'

'They have their own quarters and generally stick to their part of the palace. What you normally see is the working half, not those in the private residency. Your room is right on the edge of that part of the palace. That is why you started running into them. Of course, none are interested in a Human, so I thought it would be safe enough.' He hesitated, 'I never foresaw this predicament.'

'You could always tell them I had my privates blown off in a fire fight when I was young. That should put them off.'

He laughed, 'Don't be stupid, they can be regrown. Everyone knows that.'

'Everyone except for the stupid Human.'

'It was a good suggestion. You still don't find Modloch females attractive?'

'I don't think you are an ugly race Darrick, just unattractive.'

'Have you met any attractive aliens?'

'There are some out there, the cat-like races we have met. Some of them are very attractive. Haven't met a single herbivore female that I would consider attractive.'

'Yet you have a reputation with the ladies.'

'I don't know who told you that, but it is a lot of bollocks. I have simply been unlucky in love, which has led to me having more partners than most. It is no more than that. When you get to my age, it becomes more the norm. It takes a special type of woman to put up with the life of a soldier. I was one of the unlucky ones who never found that type of woman, no more, no less.'

'Were you hoping to find one once you retired?'

'I considered myself still young enough to have a family. Maybe I was. A woman who maybe had children and didn't mind having another. I don't know. All of that has been blown out of the water.'

'What about your Captain girlfriend?'

'She is a career woman, she'll probably never have children. We haven't talked about it. I'm just going with the flow Darrick. She is a beautiful woman, but sooner or later she will get frightened and dump me, or we will start moving in different circles and drift apart.'

'It doesn't worry you?'

Charlie thumped his chest, 'Armour plated. It takes a lot to break my wee heart these days. If you expect it, then it doesn't hurt quite as much.'

'My marriage was arranged, but I am happy. I would arrange one for you, but there is no one suitable in my whole empire.'

'Do you love her?'

'What a horrible question Charlie. Of course I love my wife, and my children. She was the most beautiful female in the whole realm, still is.'

'She wasn't your first though.'

Darrick barked a laugh, 'How did you know that?'

'Just the wistful look on your face. As though you were remembering someone else.'

Darrick was nodding in a very Human fashion, 'You are right. We are given females to practice on. Royalty are I mean, so we don't embarrass ourselves on our wedding night. Merry widows carefully selected for me. They weren't my first though, that was a young maid at school. Pretty but not beautiful. Very shy. It was a few weeks away from the mating season. The maids were all removed from the school the week before, so there could be no mishaps. She caught me in a towel, straight from the shower and popped, right there, right in front of me. I was overwhelmed. Grabbed her and threw her onto the bed. She submitted willingly.'

Charlie held up a hand, 'Popped, what the hell is that?'

Darrick frowned, 'Does the word hymen translate?'

'It does. A woman's virginity.'

'Do Human females have two?'

'No just the one.'

'Ours have two. If a female is suddenly overcome with passion, the sudden build up of fluids inside her can cause the outer hymen to rupture. You can actually hear it pop.'

'So that's what that is.'

'You have heard it?'

'Couple of times.'

'In this form.'

'No, my normal form.'

'To a Modloch male, it is the ultimate form of flattery. It makes the female extremely desirable. She came into season four times that year. Very unusual, very flattering. I was obviously besotted. We also got caught.'

'I bet her arse was booted out of there very quickly.'

'You would win the bet. She was nothing more than a plain ordinary girl, but she rode me to heights of passion I have never felt since. I was very much in love.'

'Aye, and I will bet very, very angry as well.'

'Furious. Years later I rewarded those who ripped us apart with high positions on that damn planet you live on.'

'You exiled them?'

'Pretty much.'

'What happened to her?'

'Shipped to a different planet, married off as quickly as possible. I made discreet enquiries after I became Emperor. She has a good life, with a good Modloch, and already had children. She seemed happy.'

'You left her alone.'

'Of course. What about you Charlie?'

'My first was a girl called Linda Hay, an English girl up in my part of the country on holiday. She was nineteen years old, I was fifteen but had developed early. I told her I was the same age as her. She took my virginity on a golf course, in the rough. Of course, it didn't take her to long to find out the truth and she dumped my arse. I didn't care, I had lost my cherry. The following year I joined the army. The rest, as they say, is history.'

'Was she pure?'

'Oh hell no. She was experienced. I found out later she was actually cheating on her boyfriend. I suppose I never really had the time to fall in love. That came later, and more than once. Each time I had my wee heart ripped from my body and shredded. For me these days, it is more of a physical necessity than a desire to fall in love and have a family.'

'I think I have been luckier than you.'

'That makes two of us.'

'Are you enjoying being a Modloch?'

'No, it's kind of scary. I don't like it at all.'

'What is so scary about it?'

'As a Human, the Modloch I encounter make allowances for my lack of knowledge. They think I am quite amusing. As a Modloch, I am supposed to know all of that. Instead of being ignorant, I am now being regarded as arrogant. As a Human my ignorance was laughed off, no one took offence. As a Modloch, I am being held in an entirely different light. Not a pleasant one.'

'Turran hasn't done a very good job then.'

'You can't cram a lifetime of experience into a week. Besides, I have barely begun to imitate all those nuances you Modlochs have, with your body language, hands and facial expressions. Turran has done as much as he can. It has just been overwhelming.'

Darrick regarded Charlie for a moment, 'It really didn't occur to me just how much you were doing, or how hard it would be on you.'

'You are my friend, if it keeps you safe, it will be worth it. Are you sure this fancy ID badge will get me through security?'

'We used the DNA from your supposed grandsire. We still had it on record. It is more or less a copy of his, with the name changed. It will work fine. The only person we have to worry about is Ne´. He knows the story of Barrick Marr, and if I remember correctly, I told him that he never had children.'

'So he will be suspicious right from the start.'

'I will just tell him I was wrong. You came to my attention for acts of valour during the recent war. It was then brought to my attention that we were related through Barrick Marr, who also had an illegitimate son, the knowledge of which had been supressed by generations of Emperors. I decided I wanted to meet you, and when I was asked to this conference, brought you along as a reward. Also, as you're of Royal blood, I would be able to take you into the inner sanctum. I would have a blood relative by my side, a decorated veteran, and wouldn't have to risk the life of one of my own brothers. I bestowed your title as a reward for your acts of valour. It will appease him. He knows how much I enjoy upsetting the hay cart.'

'I hope so. Anyway, what is the plan?'

'You have your device. You stay close and buzz me every time someone lies to me.'

'Sorted.'

Darrick rose, 'Time for bed. Sleep well Lord Marr.'

'By your command, sire.'

Darrick laughed, 'I like that. A Human saying?'

'Cylon. Long story.'

'For another day. Good night.'

CHAPTER 8

Richard Liverington was squinting all the way to the doctor's office. He had his go pro on a selfie stick.

'This is the so called famous white light. I don't know what any of you can see, but I can see damn all. Just a real bright light. This could well be a problem for further filming.'

He was following the back of a young woman. He reached out and tugged at her sleeve.

'What's your name sweetheart?'

'Hailey.'

'What do you do on board?'

'I am the navigator.'

'Oh! I suppose that makes you quite smart.'

Hailey half turned with a smile on her face, 'A lot smarter than you.'

'Ow! That hurt. I presume because I am a flat Earther?'

Hailey stopped, 'You couldn't be more correct, Mr Liverington.'

'You people aren't going to make my life easy, are you?'

'Is there any particular reason we should?' She stuck her hand out, 'In here.'

He squinted, 'In where?'

A new face appeared, 'In here.'

He jumped, 'Where the hell did you come from?'

Amanda reached out and literally dragged him inside, 'I know it is a little disorientating. This is the med bay and I am Dr Amanda Freeling, the ship's doctor. Thank you Hailey.'

Hailey seemed to simply vanish in front of his eyes. Amanda grabbed him by the arm and guided him.

'This way please. Can you feel the bed beside you? Please get up onto it.'

He managed to shuffle onto it, 'Which way?'

She turned his shoulders and lay him down, 'Just relax Mr Liverington.'

'Please call me Richard, Ritchie or Rich, if you prefer.'

'Mr Liverington will be fine for now.'

He sighed and made a face at the camera, 'Please yourself.'

Amanda went quiet for a bit. She studied the information coming up on her screen.

'You seem to have had a bit of a hard life Mr Liverington. You are not in good health. You have rods in your body. Your system is full of prescription drugs: pain killers, muscle relaxants, sleep medication. Those rods will have to come out.'

'Those rods are keeping me alive doctor.'

'They are also causing you problems. You are overweight, nor do you eat a healthy diet.'

'I am always on the go. I have a very busy life.'

'Were you in a bad accident?'

'A heavy fall.'

'Alright, I will sort all of this out for you. You will be out for about two days. We will rebuild your bones, remove the rods, clean out your system. Start to reduce all of this excess fat and tune up your muscles.'

'Wait, are you qualified for all that?'

'I am a world class surgeon Mr Liverington. I won't be operating on you in the normal way. It will be done with nanites.'

'I don't think I like that idea.'

'Then you are free to leave at any time. You have about two minutes to make up your mind.'

'Is that all?'

'I happen to very busy, that is all the time I have to spare.'

'Why knock me out for two days?'

'I won't only knock you out, I will paralyze your entire body. Some of the work your body requires is very delicate. If you move so much as a millimetre, the results could be disastrous.'

'What will the results be?'

'You will be as you were before you had your fall.'
'Seriously!'
'Of course.'
'I will be completely cured?'
'Yes of course.'
'Then why haven't I been cured before?'
'The medical facilities aboard this ship are unique. We cannot as yet replicate the technology on Earth. I spend most of my time researching ways to do just that.'
'It would seem I have a lot to learn doctor.'
'You have no idea Mr Liverington, and we are going to take great delight in teaching you.'
'I don't know about all of this…'
'Good.'
Two seconds later he was unconscious. Amanda picked up the GoPro, 'The next time you see this gentleman will be two days from now.' She switched it off and tossed it onto a tray.

CHAPTER 9

Liverington woke to a new world. His head rocked from side to side as he took in his surroundings. A figure turned from a computer screen.

'You are finally awake.'

He worked some saliva into his mouth, 'Doctor. Looks like it.'

'How are you feeling?'

'Not sure yet. Like shit I suppose. Where am I?'

'The med bay.'

His interest sharpened, 'The same one? What happened to the bright light?'

'Just as you were told: a special filter was attached to your eyes so you can see everything.'

'I forgot.'

'You will feel a little disorientated for a while. Just rest for now.'

He noticed his GoPro sitting on a strange-looking lamp.

'What's this thing?'

Amanda looked round, 'That's a charging station and lamp for your little camera. The chief engineer made it for you from the rods I took out of your body. A little welcome aboard gift from the crew.'

He was able to reach it and switched the camera on.

'Hey guys, I just woke up and guess what I found,' he turned the camera, 'It is a lamp and docking station made up from the rods that were in my body. A gift from the crew.'

'They won't be able to see it, the bright light still affects your camera. However, you can just look at it and talk and ask Babcs to record it for you. She can then download the recording to any device you wish.'

'You mean I can record stuff through my eyes?'

'That's exactly what I mean.'

'Can't I get a filter for my camera?'

'No, it is a bio filter that won't work on the camera. If you want to show people anything inside the ship, you will have to record it through your own eyes. If you want to talk to Babes use the device on your left hand. The button nearest your body will connect you to the ship, the other is for talking to other crew members. You press the button and think their name or say it aloud. The ship's voice will sound only in your head, no one else will be able to hear it. It is very disorientating at first, but you will get used to it. Please wait until you get to your quarters before trying it.'

'I feel very thirsty and hungry.'

'Not surprising. You have been fed by a drip for the past two days. Your stomach is empty. The canteen is open, your clothes are on a chair over there. They have been cleaned. When you are ready, you can get dressed and go find something to eat. Just ask Babes to guide you.'

'Babes…'

'That's what we call the ship.'

'Alright.'

Liverington closed his eyes for a moment and fell asleep almost instantly. When he woke, the doctor was gone and the med bay was in semi-darkness. He struggled to sit up.

'Are you alright?'

He jumped a foot off the bed and collapsed onto the floor.

'Who… what the hell!'

'I am sorry, did I startle you?'

'Who are you, where are you?'

'I am the ship. The crew address me as Babes.'

'Right… I thought I had to push a button or something.'

'I can talk to any member of the crew at any time.'

'Makes sense.' He struggled to his knees, 'I really need the toilet.'

A door slid open. He struggled to his feet and half

staggered to the toilet. He was in there for almost twenty minutes. When he came out, he was as white as a sheet and sweating.

'How are you feeling now?'

He almost jumped again. 'Awful. What have you people done to me?'

'That was the result of the work the nanites in your system are doing. They have activated your lymphatic system and are turning the excess fat in your body to waste products. You will feel like this for the next few days.'

'Is that necessary?'

'It is if you wish to remain healthy.'

'Look, I am hungry and thirsty. What time is it?'

'It is one o'clock in the morning now.'

'Was I knocked out again?'

'No you simply fell asleep. I can guide you to your room. You will be able to drink water there and you can use the dispenser for a sandwich.'

'You got any tuna-mayo?'

'I do.'

'Let me get my clothes.'

He dressed as quickly as he was able, and even grabbed the lamp before he left. Babes guided him to his room but it was slow going. She gave him water and the sandwich. No sooner had he finished eating than he had to run to the toilet again. Afterwards he undressed and took a shower. With a groan he slumped face down on the bed. He managed a quick two minutes on his GoPro.

'I feel like total shit. Been here for days now I think. My clothes all seem too big. I have no idea where I am or what is happening. I can see everything now, but I don't know if I am still on the ship or in some facility. I can talk to the ship as well; it's weird. It's like the voice is coming from inside my head. Sorry guys, but I am going to have to close my eyes for a minute.' Seconds later he was fast asleep again.

Over the next few days he struggled to stay awake. He only got up to go to the toilet and eat. On the fourth day his eyes snapped open and he could feel the energy flow through him. His ablutions seemed to be back to normal, so he took a shower and went to get dressed. His clothes hung from his frame. His realised his cabin wasn't very big, it had a workstation, a bed, wardrobe, toilet and little else.

'Where are the damn mirrors?' He thought to himself, before of the wardrobe doors began to change and he found himself standing in front of a full-length mirror. 'Oh! There you are.' His head cocked to the side, 'Who the hell are you?'

He rubbed his short beard but couldn't really see the skin beneath. The skin around his eyes looked healthier and younger. He stripped off his top clothes and jumped back.

'Holy shit!'

He pressed the button on the back of his hand.

'Yes Mr Liverington, how can I help you today?'

'Babes isn't it?'

'Yes.'

'What the hell happened to me? I haven't been this buffed since I was a kid. Where did it all go?'

'The nanites in your bloodstream have spent the last week removing the toxins from your body, repairing all of the damage to it and, and I think the favoured word is, "tweaking" it.'

'Is this really me?'

'Yes of course it is.'

He looked to his GoPro, 'Will that work in here?'

'I have reconfigured your cabin and taken out the security lights, so you will be able to use your device in there, but nowhere else on the ship.'

'Thank you very much. When can I upload a video?'

'As soon as you wish. Just let me know.'

'Sure, thanks Babes.'

The Black of Space

He paced around his small cabin for fifteen minutes before grabbing his camera and switching it on

'Hey guys! How's it hanging? I've been down for the better part of the week, I'm sorry about that, but I have been in a bit of a mess. You ain't going to believe this shit. I got some video of the day I got here. I got taken to the medical bay. The doctor there, a real cute chick, told me that she was going to operate on me. I don't know how or what, but I wasn't given much of a choice. It was kinda her way or the highway. Anyway, I was out for a couple of days solid. I woke up about four days ago feeling like shit. I have made the odd video. I will add them here.'

He paused for a few seconds, 'Right, you will have seen all of that footage by now. Time to move on. I was warned I was going to be ill for a few days afterwards, and as you saw, I sure was. I woke up today feeling just great. Took a shower and slung my cloths on. Only they didn't fit no more. When I came on board, I was in bad health, overweight, had trouble sleeping and was in constant pain. Those who have been following me for years know about my bad accident, that the insurance company screwed me over on. Now look at this. This was waiting for me when I woke up.'

He turned the camera towards the lamp. He went in close.

'When I woke up, I first saw this. The doctor told me that it was made from all of the rods that I was pinned together with.' He picked it up and turned it round, 'It sure looks like the rods the surgeons showed me before my operations. Of course, I couldn't tell you for sure, I only have their word for it. However, it feels like they are gone. I am in no pain and I can't even remember the last time I took pain meds. But if you think that is good, I am going to show you something that is going to blow you away. I am going to inset a picture of myself as I was a few weeks ago.'

He paused for a few seconds. 'Did you get that? That

shot was taken at home, in a t-shirt. You can see how out of shape I am right? Now check this out.'

He turned the camera slowly, 'Can you see this? Can you? I have a fucking six-pack. I haven't been this buffed since I was twenty-one. Holy shit, I can see all of my muscles again.' He took a deep breath, 'Look, I am sorry for swearing guys, I don't normally do that on video. This has all happened in a week. It has taken me by surprise. I woke up and my clothes didn't fit. That's why I am holding onto my pants with one hand, to stop them falling down. This is just so, just so…' an emotional wave slammed into him. He choked up, and tears began to stream down his face.

'Holy shit! I'm sorry guys. It has just kinda hit me. I'm pain free for the first time in years. I can sleep.' He was suddenly overwhelmed, 'Oh God, thank you, thank you…' He broke down completely. The GoPro was placed back on its new stand, still switched on, while Liverington sobbed uncontrollably on his bed.

Later that night the video took the world by storm. Steven sat back and watched the whole thing. He had never been a fan of the reality TV thing, but he was certainly impressed by the response the video was getting. Maybe he had made the right decision after all.

CHAPTER 10

Darrick and his entourage were shown to their quarters. They quickly settled in. Gord saw to the guard and their posts, quickly devising a rota. For the next couple of hours nameless officials came to and fro. The first meeting was scheduled for the following morning. In the early evening, Ne´ showed up. He chatted with Darrick for about half an hour before his curiosity got the better of him.

'Who is that hulking beast?'

'Lord Carrick Marr. He will be my personal escort throughout these talks.'

'You should have brought one of your brothers, he won't be allowed into the inner sanctum.'

'He will, he is of the Royal line.'

Ne´ frowned, 'I have met all of your family Darrick, and all of your cousins. I have never seen him before.'

'Do you remember the story of Barrick Marr?'

It took him a moment, then his eyes opened wider, 'I remember, but I thought he died childless.'

'It would seem he didn't. Born out of wedlock to a merry widow. He came to my attention for acts of valour during the past war. I was going to give him a title as a reward, no more. Of course, we gave him a blood test to see if he had any noble blood and to our surprise, he turned out to be a direct descended of Barrick Marr.'

Ne´ wasn't looking very happy, 'You sure you haven't just brought the biggest thug you know along?' He looked down and felt the short hairs on the back of his neck prickle, 'Since when did your personal guard start wearing those weapons?'

'They all wear them now.'

Ne´ relaxed a little then pointed at Charlie, 'You had better behave while you are here.'

Charlie moved right up to Ne´ and looked down on him.

'Who are you?' The menace in his voice was

unmistakable.

'I am an Emperor, and the Grand Commander of the Federation forces.'

'I am not a Federation Officer, and neither are you my Emperor. Don't dictate to me.'

Darrick quickly intervened, 'Lord Marr, Emperor Ne´ Langus is a personal friend of mine, please treat him with respect.'

Charlie took a step back, 'I understand sire. If I have to kill him, I will try and make it as painless as possible as a mark of respect.'

'Not quite what I meant, Lord Marr.'

'My old grandfather used to say that the higher the social ladder you climb, the less friends you can afford to have. The loneliest person in the world is the one at the top. He may have been wrong, but he was the wisest person I have ever known. If I learn different, I will teach my grandchildren different. Until then, I will consider everyone as your enemy sire, regardless of how you personally view your relationship with them.'

Ne´ held up a hand to stop Darrick saying more, 'Your grandfather was indeed very smart. There is truth in your words Lord Marr, it's something that most people in our position understand from birth but never wish to acknowledge. We all know that our friendships can end in a heartbeat. You are right to be on your guard. Look after my friend well, even from me.'

'I will for the short time I will be serving him,' he nodded and backed off.

Ne´ took a deep breath, 'Where is your pet Human? Did he return to Earth with the rest of his crew?'

'No, he is home waiting for the arrival of your Human friend.'

'The fair Captain. I miss her. Valachean couldn't be happier, it was a good match.'

'Have they seen action yet?'

'Yes, I moved them onto the Turaken sector, with the

Ambatta scouts. They cleared it out of pirates in just a few months. There were half a dozen bases in it. The biggest was the size of a small city, with many civilians living there. Slaves as well, it was a mess. We had to send in ground forces. Once we took out the leaders though, the resistance fell.'

'Casualties?'

'Not too bad. Only a dozen dead, all of them Ortea who walked into an ambush. Thirty injured with varying severity of wounds. Most of them were Ortea and Human. I sent in Federation marines and some administrators to sort out the mess.'

'A small city. I am impressed.'

'A small city founded by criminals, for the purpose of criminality. There are innocents there too though.'

'So you have no idea what to do with them?'

'Not really. There are a mixture of races, very few Federation citizens though. Most were born there, on these outposts. Yet they belong to races that are Federation members.'

'Where do they come from?'

'Most seem to be the descendants of miners who were abandoned by the companies they worked for. Others were miners who went bust.'

'Those fields were mined out centuries ago!'

'They have quite an intricate trade going on. I am sure they have been involved in many insurance scams. A lot of data was destroyed before we could get to it.'

Darrick thought it over, 'You could be opening up a huge can of worms. You have a choice: destroy the place in its entirety, along with its people, or you could first remove the people then destroy the place and the evidence. Or, of course, you could send in investigators.'

'That would be the proper thing to do.'

Darrick agreed, 'It would, but would it be the wisest?'

'I am going to have to put it to the committee. It is far too big a decision to make on my own.'

'If even one of them have their finger in the pie they will vote against it. Right now they will be shitting themselves. They could strike out in fear of getting caught.'

'Yes, and my people will get caught in the middle.'

'Maybe you simply got too smart for your own good Ne´.'

'Isn't it funny? When I took up the job, no one before me had ever been able to take out those pirates. I wasn't expected to either. I didn't expect to get close. Now here we are, the pirates have been taken care of but I am faced with a situation that could blow up in my face. Your Human pet is good at solving problems, I wonder what he would say.'

Darrick smiled, 'Please don't call him my pet, he is my friend.'

'My apologies Darrick, I simply don't like the man.'

'Lord Marr, you know Charlie quite well. What do you think he would say?'

'You know him?' Ne´ snapped.

'We worked together during the latest war. I have a good idea of what he would say. Remove the people, jail the pirates, repatriate all those others to their home planets and let them deal with it. Then blow the place to bits, evidence and all,' Charlie grunted in a Modloch manner.

Ne´ smiled, 'Do you really think he would say that?'

'Most likely. You are frightened that it could affect people from your own world, important people. The kind of people you turn a blind eye to because they get the job done. It may even affect your own forces. What if some of those you rely on most were making a wee bit on the side by turning a blind eye? Operations that large don't survive by themselves. I may not be an Emperor, but even I can see that. So don't ask anyone. Clear those places out. Blow them to pieces. Your fellow Emperors may shout and bawl, but I bet underneath they may well be grateful.'

'So you do have a brain in that massive skull of yours. You aren't just parroting your Emperor.'

'What is parroting?'

'Ask your Human friend the next time you see him,' he turned his attention back to Darrick. 'You haven't had any dealings with these pirates, have you?'

Charlie decided to piss Ne´ off even more. 'Neither of you would have had any direct dealings with them. You are both too high up the social ladder, so that was a stupid question. However, it doesn't mean those directly under you didn't. I will lay a bet that both of you tasted and ate blue grass before the Emperor was able to get seeds from the Humans.'

Ne´ wanted to shout the Modloch down but also felt compelled to answer.

'Of course we did, but it was from captured sources.'

'Really? Are you sure about that? Did you see the manifest of the captured pirate freighter?'

'I did actually.'

'Can you account for every bale of it? Did you send some to your Emperor friends? Did you ever wonder at how well it was lasting and how fresh it was every time you ate it? I wonder when it actually ran out, and how long your servants were able to procure it for you after that.'

'Ne´ went very still, 'Are you doubting my integrity?'

'I would never do that. You at the top live in a bubble of your own making. Your requests, wishes, and demands are met by those below you. So far below that you never see how those requests are met. Have you ever said, "I don't care how rare it is, I want it, it's your job to get it"?'

Ne´ stood slowly, he looked angry and Darrick decided to intervene.

'Lord Marr, you go too far.'

Ne´ raised a hand, 'No Darrick. He may be rude, a common trait of those who have spent a lifetime fighting, but he isn't wrong. I have used those words, and similar, many times, as I guess you have. When was the last time you asked how one of your servants met an unreasonable demand?'

Darrick smiled, 'Never.'

'Do we not most cherish those servants who are able to meet our unreasonable demands?'

'Yes, and feed them little gifts of appreciation.'

'Lord Marr has opened my eyes to the possibility that we could actually hurt those that are closest and most precious to us, that our requests could well lead to their demise. Thank you, Lord Marr.'

Charlie bowed, 'I apologise for appearing rude Grand Commander. It was not my intention to insult.'

'I accept that,' he nodded. 'It is getting late Darrick, there are still things I need to do before I retire.'

Darrick saw him to the door. They chatted for a few minutes before Ne´ left.

'Will you make me some tea Charlie?'

'Aye.'

'You might have pushed Ne´ a little too far there. You are supposed to be keeping a low profile.'

'He gets under my skin at times. I don't like being referred to as a pet.'

Darrick began to laugh so hard he almost fell off his seat. There was something that stuck in his mind.

'What is this parroting?'

'A parrot is a bird from my home world that can talk. They mimic their owners, often mindlessly repeating what they have said, over and over again. We most often teach them to swear because we consider it funny.'

'Seriously? An animal, a bird, that can actually talk?'

'Some of them are really good at it. It's just potluck if you get a bird that talks.'

'I want to see that.'

'You're going to have to wait until we get home and I can get a signal for my pad.'

Darrick shook his head, 'The more I learn about your world the more it takes me by surprise.'

When Ne´ reached his quarters, he called for the master of ceremonies.

He bowed low, 'How can I be of service sire?'

'The Modloch Emperor's personal guard, what do you know of him?'

'Nothing sire. Other than that his credentials were handed to us by the Modloch Emperor. Is there a problem?'

'Darrick claims he is of Royal lineage, but I am not so sure. He gave me grave insult tonight. I want to have him checked. He seems more of a thug. Have his DNA checked against the Royal database.'

'I doubt if he will submit.'

'I don't care, get it done before we go into session tomorrow.'

'If he isn't a Royal…'

'Have him disposed of quietly.'

'If he is?'

'I want to know first.'

'I can only give you a yes or no answer to that sire. I will not compromise myself any further.'

'I understand. I am putting you in a bad position.'

'Not if the Modloch Emperor has lied sire. You have a right to check.'

'DNA is colour coded. The Emperor did say he was a distant cousin.'

'Then he will still register sire, just quite far down the colour spectrum.'

'I would be interested in the colour.'

'I will take it into consideration. The quickest way to get a sample is to offer him a glass of water. I can have the results in less than half an hour for you.'

Ne´ smiled, 'Thank you for your service.'

CHAPTER 11

'Hi Hailey! May I sit down?'
'Uh… sure. Do I know you?'
'Richard.'
'Sorry?'
'Richard Liverington, you helped me when I arrived.'

Hailey blinked a few times then her hands flew to her mouth, 'Oh my God! I am so sorry, I never recognised you.'

'I never recognised myself either.'

Liverington was clean shaven and in a ship's uniform, supplied to him by Babes. A haircut overnight by Babes helped complete the transformation. It was his second time in the canteen, but Hailey was the first person he recognised.

'Honestly Richard, it is a total shock.'

'The doctor said they had never had anyone on board that was as obese as myself. I am already completely blown away.'

'Maybe you will start looking after yourself now.'

He laughed, 'My obesity was caused by a serious injury when I was quite young, a lot of medication, and an inability to exercise.'

'I am sorry, I didn't know that.'

'Well, I wouldn't expect you to. This looks really good.'

'A salad! You really are looking after yourself.'

'I have always loved a good salad. My father grew his own, and I had started my own garden. Again, my injuries prevented me from continuing with it. The food here is really great.'

'It is better when Mya and Cookie are here.'

'Who are they?'

'Cookie is the head chef and Mya is his girlfriend.' Hailey took a deep breath, 'They are at her home on the Modloch home world right now.'

'Seriously?'

'Yes, I know you are sceptical about aliens and all that jazz, but Mya is now a Modloch noble woman, a member of the Royal Modloch household, and the Emperor just went to war with our enemies because they kidnapped her for a second time.'

He swallowed, 'A second time!'

'She was on the Black Planet, we rescued her and the others.'

'Right, OK, heard about that. Along with that GI Sergeant.'

'Kelly. Yes, now he isn't a person I would call a liar if I was you. So when you meet him be extra polite. He is very old school.'

'You mean he is liable to punch me out?'

'Most certainly.'

'I will remember that, thank you for the warning.'

They ate in silence for a few minutes. Liverington's mind was churning the whole the time.

'So did Mya buy a home on this supposed home world of this supposed alien race?'

Hailey got up with a smile on her face, 'No, it is her official residence. A large estate gifted to her by the Modloch Emperor. If you are ever unlucky enough to meet him, then I would start running the other way. If you say the wrong thing to him, even look at him the wrong way, he will have you eradicated. I shit you not Richard, and there isn't a damn thing anyone on this planet could do about it.'

He cringed a little inside, 'I will take note of that. Thanks.'

When she had left, he finished his meal and returned to his room. He lay on his bed and switched on his camera.

'We are returning to Earth today. We should be landing any minute. They are letting me off. Today I am going to meet one of my oldest friends and supporters. I received an email from her. She thinks I have been killed and replaced by a robot or something. I have a couple of days before we have to return to the moon.

'I look in the mirror and see the young man I once was. The pain in my body has gone. Is this a miracle, is it a hallucination? I don't really know, but I know someone who does. Today I am going to meet up with Abby Jones. She knows me like no one else does. You all know Abby; we've done many videos together. I have been accused of being an imposter. I have received a lot of hate mail. Abby will know, trust in her. Right now, I don't know what or who I am.'

He followed the flashing light until he came to a small open room.

'Please stand still Richard.'

'Okay Babes. What happens next?'

His vison began to blur. He could smell the sea before his eyes focused. He snapped around. The ocean broke gently against the shore. Fresh air filled his lungs.

'Richard!'

He swung the other way, 'Abby!'

She took a step back, 'Who are you?'

'It's me, who else would it be?'

She stood there, thin, lank blond hair dripping over her shoulders. Her bandaged hands clasped in front of her holding a GoPro.

'It doesn't look like you Richard.'

They were only a few metres from her mobile home. Outside it sat her picnic table where they had spent many hours planning their campaigns.

'Let's go sit down Abby. You can ask me any question you want.'

She flicked away a limp strand of hair, 'Alright, let's talk.' She was dressed in full flower power mode and the green woollen hat she wore on her head had seen better days. She sat down in her normal spot and he sat in his. She put the GoPro on a small stand.

She flicked away the irritating strand again, 'For the record, I don't recognise you at all.'

'Don't you remember the pictures I showed you of me when I worked with my father?'

A small jolt went through her, 'I remember.' Her head dipped low, then came up again, 'Alright you do look a lot like that guy. Right now though, I am going to ask you a lot of questions.'

'Please do.'

Miles away in orbit, Steven and Komoru were watching the interview live.

Komoru took a sip of her tea, 'She really doesn't believe that it is him.'

'Can you blame her? The transformation has been radical.'

'Why are her hands all bandaged up?'

'Warts.'

'Uck! Seriously?'

'Yes, our new friend asked the doctor if she had any advanced remedies for warts, Abby suffers from them badly. It is in her bio. Amanda gave him some nanites programmed to hunt down the virus and kill it, also to repair her skin. But I asked for Amanda to upgrade them a little.'

'Steven!'

'Oh nothing spectacular or astounding. When she wakes up tomorrow morning though, she is in for a bit of a shock.'

'What have you done?'

He grinned, 'Nothing much.'

Abby was exhausted. After two hours of constant questioning she hadn't been able to trip up the stranger. She turned the camera towards herself.

'I am going to take a short break now. During it I will ask him personal questions about his family that only he knows, but I don't want to discuss in public.'

She switched off the camera and checked the link was broken.

'I need a cup of tea. Coffee?'
'Yes please.'
'Stay here Richard.'

She came back five minutes later with two cups. She sat down and they both took a sip.

'What happened the last time we made love?'

'Well, it was better than the first time. I came off my meds for a few days. I was able to perform, but it was quick, messy and agonising. You also lied about having an orgasm.'

She flushed red, 'I did have an orgasm. It was a little later on, and you were asleep.'

'Oh! I must have been out of it.'
'Zonked.'
'Sorry about that.'

She smiled, 'I loved you for trying so hard. For the pain you put yourself through.'

'So you finally believe it is me?'

'I have no choice. I don't know what to do Richard.'

He reached out, 'Hold my hand.'

She shook her head, 'No, my hands are bad just now.'

'Then touch the tip of my finger. I just want to touch you Abby. Please,' His smile disarmed her. She reached out.

She snatched her finger away almost instantly, 'Oh!'
'What is it?'

'A static shock I think,' she smiled and reached out again. A strange warmth began to infuse her. A single tear ran down her face.

'I am going to lose you now, aren't I?'
'Not if you marry me.'

His words took her breath away, 'No, never.'

'Why not Abby? We have both been in love with each

other for years.'

'Because you are now beautiful Richard, and I am a hag.'

'I'm not on medication anymore,' he raised an eyebrow.

'Absolutely not.'

'I woke up this morning with a you know what.'

'Seriously?'

'Oh yeah!'

Her look of surprise turned to a scowl, 'Definitely not.' The colour of her cheeks told a different story.

She reached over and switched on the camera again. Her unhealthy pallor quickly returned.

'Abby Jones here.' She looked at Richard, 'I cannot say the man before me is not Richard Liverington. He knows everything Richard does. If you consider that no one would know what I was going to ask, then it would be impossible for a doppelganger to answer all of my questions correctly.'

She lifted her hand in supplication, 'I have to give him the benefit of the doubt. So tell me Richard, when I last saw you, just over a week ago, you were very ill, in constant pain, and much heavier. So what happened?'

He smiled, 'Thank you Abby, for at least giving me the benefit of the doubt. As you can imagine, my reception has not been really all that welcoming. I am being treated nicely, but no one has any respect for my views.'

'Did you expect any?'

'I suppose I expected more hostility, maybe a little fear that they are about to be found out. I think I am being treated more like a country cousin that has arrived in the big city for the first time.'

'What did they do to you when you got there?'

'When I got there, I couldn't see a thing. Snow blindness is the nearest I can come to a description of what it was like. They told me I needed nanites in my bloodstream, that they would attach some kind of filter to my optic nerve. I protested, but I was given a choice. Accept or leave. I felt duty bound to accept. The doctor gave me an examination. Within a few minutes she had made a complete assessment of everything that was wrong with me. Before I knew what was happening, I was waking up. I have no idea how long I was out for. The rods that have been my constant companion and bane of my life were sitting on the bedside table in the shape of a lamp.

'I was told to go and rest and that I would feel quite ill for the next few days. They weren't kidding. I spent most of it sleeping. I took little notice of myself; there was no obvious mirror. Eventually I began to feel better, had a shower, tried to put my clothes on. They didn't fit. The only clothes I have that fit now are these uniforms.'

'How are you actually feeling Richard?'
'How do I look?'
'You look amazing.'
'That is how I feel Abby.'
'This is a lot to take in Richard. Where did all this happen?'
'I have no idea. I was taken on board here but was told we journeyed from the moon this morning.'
'Did you see the moon?'
'No. I don't have a window, or at least I don't think I do. That might sound a little funny, but I didn't have a mirror either, until I asked aloud for one.'
'You mean one just appeared?'
'Exactly. Full length on my wardrobe.'
'How did you get here today?'
'I don't know. One moment I was on the ship, the next I was here.'
'They claim to have beam technology.'
'Did you see me appear?'
'Yes. Out of nowhere.'
'Did you record it? Can I see it?'
'I missed it; I am sorry.'
'That's a pity.'

'Richard, are we setting ourselves up for a fall?'

'I don't know Abby. I feel not. We are here, I am here to prove things one way or another. If all of this has been one elaborate hoax after another, perpetuated by the governments on Earth, I will refuse to be embarrassed by our beliefs. I will campaign endlessly for the truth.'

'What if their truth is the real truth?'

'Does it matter? It will simply become our truth. A truth we discovered for ourselves. Not a truth pushed on us by others.'

'Our time is up for today Richard.'

She turned the camera towards her, 'This has been the strangest day of my life. I don't know what else to say. I am going to spend some more time with this Richard. Is he my Richard? I really don't know. I will find out the truth.'

She switched the camera off.

CHAPTER 12

Ne´ looked at the report in front of him. He read it three times before he was satisfied.

'You are absolutely sure about this?'

'Yes sire. The database is never wrong.'

'How can this be possible?'

'He could be a genetic throwback?'

Ne´ slid the tablet back across, 'That is as much information as you can give me? You got the right Modloch?'

'Yes of course. I oversaw it myself. To get more information I would have to get permission from the Modloch Emperor to take the investigation further.'

'There is no need to take it further. My question has been answered. You are dismissed.'

'Yes sir.'

Charlie was surprised by the opulence of the inner sanctum. They were shown around by an usher. The rooms the meetings would take place in were more functional, but still very opulent. Darrick wandered over to a table and picked at some titbits. He was joined by others and soon was deep in conversation.

Their conversation was interrupted by the wailing of a child coming from behind a wall of plants. Darrick turned to Charlie, 'I am going somewhere a little quieter. I won't be long. Stay here.'

'You sure?'

'This has nothing to do with the conference. It is also private. I will be fine. We have our devices. I will be in this side room here.'

'Alright. Buzz me if you need me.'

'I won't hesitate.'

The crying began to feel like it was coming from inside Charlie's head.

'Shut up!' He commanded silently.

The child's cries ended abruptly. The crying was replaced by a strange burbling nonsense in his head. A chill ran down Charlie's spine. The child began to cry again.

'Stop. Do not cry. Listen to my voice and only my voice. Listen to my mind, no others. Concentrate on my words and my mind alone. Always concentrate on one mind, one person. If you do that the others will go away. Listen to the one.' Charlie tried to form pictures in his mind of how he did it.

A single word shot into his mind as clear as day, 'Dada.'

Charlie's eyes closed and he took a deep breath.

'I am Dada. Listen to me, hear only my voice. Once you hear only one, then block it.' He pictured a wall in his mind and the voice vanished. The crying had stopped.

On the other side of the plant screen, Wiola had been regretting taking the child. The amount of people had ensured a restless night for him and today he had been very upset. She and her ladies were getting a little frazzled. She had taken a turn. When he stopped crying suddenly she had felt a moment's relief. Then the child opened his eyes and pointed.

'Dada.'

A chill ran the length of her body. The boy was trying to look for something or someone. When she came out from behind the screen with the child in her hands, recognition slammed into her. She shook her head. The largest Modloch she had ever seen in her life stood across the room, but she would recognise that stance anywhere. The weapons on his hip confirmed her suspicions. She was about to take a step towards him when he moved towards her.

Her heart began to beat faster than it ever had in her life. A flick of his wrist told her he didn't want to be seen and she stepped back behind the wall of foliage. Her heart was racing.

One of her ladies stepped towards her, 'Are you alright, Your Majesty?'

Wiola's mouth opened and closed but no words came out. Charlie appeared a moment later. The lady stepped forward.

'Who are you?'

'Lord Carrick Marr.'

'Lord Marr…' Wiola spoke his name in almost a whisper. The lady stepped back in shock as Wiola sank to her knees. She held up the child in her hands, her head bowing.

'Dada,' the child reached up for him.

'Lord Marr, may I present your son. Your son Charval.'

Charlie was swept up in the moment. He bent down and took the child in his massive hands. It was a moment he had been dreading.

'Get up,' Charlie commanded.

She did so, her eyes glowing, 'It has been a while.'

'Hello Wiola. I had no idea you would be here.'

She turned to her ladies and waved them away, 'Leave us, quickly.'

The shocked ladies in waiting hurried away.

'Hello Charlie.'

'How the hell did you recognise me?'

'I would recognise the man I love from a million miles away.'

'Seriously?'

'I knew it was you the moment I looked at you.'

He could see it in her eyes, there was no point in denying it.

'You really are stuck aren't you?'

'Yes.'

He shook his head, 'You know you are in a position of your own making.'

She touched his arm, 'I know. I thought it would be easy. I had no idea.'

'Where did you get his name?'

'A great grandfather. It sounded so much like yours. He knows who you are.'

'I know, our minds touched. I showed him how to cancel out the voices.'

'He understood.'

'I think so.' The boy was reaching up and playing with Charlie's face. 'You know you are going to have bigger problems soon.'

'How so?'

'He may well have a desire to eat meat.'

'We eat a lot of fruit and vegetables.'

'It may not be enough. He may well need proteins. You can get substitutes.'

'So you actually did it. You changed your whole body. It is amazing, you are so handsome as a Modloch. Why?'

'Darrick needed my talents. I was banned, I think it was by Ne´. So I changed. I am supposed to be a Royal from a bastard line. Some great-great-grandfather of theirs whelped a son to a commoner on the planet I live on. The boy became Lord Barrick Marr. I am the bastard, bastard grandson or something.'

'What is the back story?'

'I came to his attention for feats of valour in the recent war. He wanted to give me a title. They checked my DNA to see which Lord, if any, I was related to.'

'I understand.'

'They had to make me a Royal to get me in here.'

Wiola burst out laughing, 'Really?'

'Aye. What's so funny?' He felt his device buzz against the back of his wrist. 'Darrick is looking for me I have to go.'

The child wailed as he handed him back. Charlie shushed him with sounds straight to the child's mind and he quietened. Wiola reached up and touched his face.

'It feels so real Charlie.'

'I'm not Charlie, I'm Lord Carrick Marr, don't forget or I will end up being executed in some back alley.'

'Sorry, of course,' she dipped her head and Charlie hurried to where the Emperor was looking for him.

Wiola sat down. Her ladies rushed over and sat with her; she let out a long sigh.

'Well, now you know.'

Both reached out to her, 'Your Majesty, he is, he is… I'm not sure how to put this without hurting your feelings.'

'Perfect,' her friend offered.

Wiola laughed, 'That's how I feel, thank you Bealla.'

She squeezed her arm, 'You said he was a noble Lord, I didn't realise he was of Royal lineage. I apologise for ever doubting you.'

'His lineage is from the wrong side of the bedsheets,' Wiola noticed something, 'Faran, are you drooling?'

'My Queen, forgive me, there is more male in that Modloch than any other I have ever met. I am fighting my own body here. I am so sorry. Why are we so attracted to them? Compatibility is also hard. You must have had to do a lot of genetic restructuring.'

'I had to take out most of what made him Modloch, but I think it was worth it.'

Faran leaned over for a peek at the now sleeping child, 'Charval recognised him. I know that seems impossible, but I am sure he sensed his father's presence before he saw him.'

'I think so too. Look how settled he is now.'

'Have you asked him to reign with you?'

Wiola sighed again, 'I have offered him everything, the whole kingdom. He refuses.'

'He isn't married is he?' Bealla asked, scandalised.

Wiola laughed, 'No, of course not. I will confess, I threw myself at him. He warned me he had no interest. I was foolish in believing I could just do it and walk away.'

'I want to throw myself at him too,' Bealla confessed.

Wiola scowled at her, 'You will do no such thing. I forbid it. If I can't have him, no other woman of our race will.'

'Bealla may have a point majesty. Maybe if you offered all three of us. What male could resist that?'

'You too,' she snapped.

'Yes Majesty.'

Wiola opened her mouth to scold, however her train of thoughts changed. It would be a big pull for any male. Three willing females to mate with. Three willing females to fulfil his every wish and desire. Would it be enough for Charlie? Her spirits sank. Most likely not.

'I doubt if he would be interested, but I could put the proposition to him. In the meantime, stay calm and keep away from him. This is a serious manner we are dealing with. It would totally ruin it if any of us came into season early.'

CHAPTER 13

Charlie took up a stance just a few feet behind the Emperor. His eyes, ears and mind searched for any brewing trouble. It had taken a lot of effort for him to get his mind off Wiola and the child. Having a life in his hands that he had helped to create had shaken him to his very core.

Darrick was blissfully unaware of what had transpired, but it occurred to Charlie that there were others in that room that may have noticed what was going on. He was sure that none saw her on her knees, but more than a few walked past while the child was in his arms.

It took him a moment to read her mind when she sat down. She even licked her lips in a provocative manner. Charlie shook his head and looked away, she was disappointed, but not surprised.

The top half dozen members of the council became seated. The Albany Emperor was there as a special guest.

Darrick was scowling at him, 'What is he doing here? My terms were met, and I have complied with the wishes of the council. My forces are now only acting as escorts to legitimate trade through the regions.'

Ne´ was the spokesman for the council, 'It is at the Albany Emperor's request that we are all here.'

'What is his problem now?'

The new Albany Emperor interrupted, 'Billions of citizens starving. Chaos in the region. Pirates, you know about that. Hundreds of thousands murdered as they try to find a new home. Refugees moving back and forth across dozens of star systems trying to find a new home, work, food. We need help.'

'Why turn to me? It is the loser of a battle that make reparations to the winner, not the other way around.'

'Because we are desperate. Every other Federation member is doing what they can to help. You have the biggest empire in the whole of the Federation. You are doing nothing.'

'I just told you we are protecting the shipping lanes. That isn't nothing.'

'What we desperately need is food. We need the people to go home and plant grass, to tend the fields. We need supplies to keep them going until that grass grows again.'

'So you are Blang's whelp?'

'You knew my father?'

'Quite well, but I didn't like him.'

'I am not my father.'

'How did he die?'

He hesitated for a moment, 'He died of a stroke.'

'A simple thing to cure.'

'It happened in his sleep.'

A slow smile spread across Darrick's face. He had been aware of Charlie's signals. The buzzing against the inside of his wrist changed. The new Emperor had lied. Not about the stoke, but in the manner it happened.

'Tell me the truth. I know you are lying.'

'Darrick!' Ne´ snapped.

Darrick turned on him, 'Did you think I would never learn anything from my absent friend? If he answers my question truthfully, I will consider listening to him further. If he lies, I will walk away.'

Ne´ reached out and grasped the young Emperor's hand.

'He knows you have lied, if you lie again, he will know and will walk away. If you want help, you need to tell the truth. We are all Emperors here. We know how things are done. Tell the truth.'

There was a lot of handwringing. There was no judgment in the eyes of the other council members.

'Alright. He did die of a stroke. That was true, it was just the timing of it I lied about. He took the stroke while I and most of his top aides were trying to get him to surrender. We had lost, it was obvious. I was trying to get him to face up to the fact. He was screaming at us, refusing to surrender. He took a stroke. Instead of getting him to hospital, I ordered him put to bed where he died during the night.'

Darrick smiled, 'Alright, I will listen further, but as you have already said, I have the largest empire and the most mouths to feed. I have very little left to spare anyone.'

'Even a tiny amount will help. We are desperate.'

'Fuska, isn't it?'

'Yes.'

'At least you have a pair of balls boy. I admire that. I will look into it. I am sure I can release some foodstuffs, but it won't be anywhere near what you require. You will have to think up something else.'

'Which is why we are here, to brainstorm,' added Grand Chancellor Serrivelli. 'Between us we should be able to come up with something. Within this room sit the greatest minds of our time.'

Darrick agreed. A few hours later he began to realise they were going round and round but getting nowhere. Refreshments were brought and they talked about domestic matters for a while, before getting back to the problem at hand. An hour later all were almost exhausted.

Ne´ was rubbing the back of his neck to work out some of the stress, when his eyes fixed on the immobile Charlie

'Lord Marr, you are of Royal blood, do you have any insights into our problem?'

'I am a simple soldier Grand Commander. Not a bureaucrat or a leader of empires.'

Grand Chancellor Serrivelli snorted, 'Leave him be Grand Commander. Royal blood or not, this is far above his head.'

Fuska agreed with the chancellor, 'He may be of Royal descent Grand Commander, but his Royal blood is very thin, far removed from the true Royal line. No insult intended Lord Marr.'

'None taken.'

The Black of Space

'I can assure you Lord Marr's bloodline is as true as anyone's here. His grandsire was one of the best strategists the Modloch Empire ever had. I am curious to see if any of it has rubbed off on him.'

Charlie grunted Modloch style, 'My great grandsire was brought up in the Royal household and trained by the brightest minds of his time. As far removed from my upbringing as you can imagine, Grand Commander.'

A few sniggered. Ne´ didn't. Wiola didn't like the sniggers.

'I would also like to hear what Lord Marr has to say.'

Charlie's mind was wide open. Darrick was still frowning at an earlier remark that Ne´ had made, but he had missed nothing that was going on. Three voices sang clear in Charlie's head. Wiola was pleading for him to step forward and show them what he was made of. Ne´ wanted him to put the academic in his place, as did Darrick.

Charlie gave off a very irritated Modloch grunt, 'With your permission sire?'

Darrick lifted a hand, 'They are all yours Lord Marr.'

Charlie took a step forward, 'The Modloch Empire has one more resource that hasn't been considered yet.'

Darrick's head snapped round, 'What resource?'

'Biscuits sire, your emergency biscuits. Every ship in the fleet has them now, and I heard you had enough stockpiled to supply the whole fleet again.'

Darrick thought it over, 'We have indeed Lord Marr, but those supplies are a drop in the ocean to this crisis. One biscuit is one day's supply of food for an adult.'

'I wasn't thinking about the adults sire. The biscuits are not fulfilling, but they are life sustaining. One day's food for an adult, but how many days for a young child?'

'Depends on the child's age, the younger the longer. The youngest maybe two weeks, older children maybe a week to four days. Well done Lord Marr, that never occurred to me.'

'There is another resource that all are ignoring,' he

received a lot of blank stares. 'The Humans.' They all passed puzzled looks.

'Explain please,' encouraged Grand Chancellor Serrivelli. 'How can a race of meat eaters help?'

'They have domestic stock that eat exactly the same food as we do. I spent a lot of time with a few Humans on that last campaign. I am sure they will have some surplus that could be bought. They also have an untapped resource that none of you even know about. One that is discarded.'

'Now you have my attention Lord Marr,' Grand Chancellor Serrivelli admitted.

'Every great house has a garden, or so I believe. The commoners on our worlds don't. On the planet Earth though, billions of commoners have gardens and things they call lawns. Every week the Humans cut their lawns and throw away the cut grass.'

'Sacrilege,' murmured one of the Chancellors. 'How do you know of this?'

'When soldiers are stuck in a hole between battles and their bellies are grumbling, talk often turns to food. It was where I learned of this, and something the Humans call humanitarian aid. One of them told me it was common in the aftermath of a war for the victor to help the vanquished rebuild. It would seem they discovered that it was the easiest way to prevent another war, to have the vanquished beholden to the victor. It may well be worth an ask.'

The young Albany Emperor shook his head, 'I cannot imagine why they would even consider helping.'

Darrick stepped in, 'You underestimate the heart of the Humans, as you have underestimated everything else about them.'

Ne´ held up a hand, 'I spoke to their President a few weeks ago. They are a bit stretched at the moment.'

Darrick shook his head, 'You are talking to the wrong people Ne´. Earth's politicians will never agree to something like this, you have to go around them.'

'How?'

'Exactly the same way I go around them when I need something, the same damn way you went around them to secure your new warships.'

'Ah!' Ne´ sat back. 'The Gordons and the PD Company of Earth. They also control all the fast freighters.' He nodded, 'Well done Lord Marr. Even if nothing comes of it, it has been the most productive suggestion of the day. You do your Emperor proud, and your grandsire.'

Charlie snorted in the normal Modloch way. Wiola sighed.

'Darrick, could you assign Lord Marr to my planet?'

'Don't be stupid.'

'I have a few spare planets and an old asteroid field that isn't completely mined out yet.' There was no mistaking the look in her eye.

Darrick hesitated, 'The answer is no Wiola. What's got into you?'

'Spoil sport.' She sat back, 'I have some Human contacts as well. I could implore them to help. They are all female, so they should be more open to helping starving children, regardless of the race.'

Ne´ was shaking his head at her. His mind snapped back to the present.

'The son isn't here, is he?'

Darrick shook his head, 'The Goodwill Ambassador is home resting at the moment.'

'How do we get in touch?'

'I know someone who can get in touch, he has a direct line straight to the Doctors Gordon,' Darrick smirked.

'Ach! I presume he is on his estate on that damn planet.'

'He is doing something for me at the moment. I imagine he will be at home in a few days.'

'I suppose I'll have to pay him a visit then.'

'There may be some good news for you - his girlfriend

may well be there by the time you arrive.'

'Captain Wilson! Then it may well be worth the time. I will get there as soon as I can.'

Grand Chancellor Serrivelli interrupted, 'Won't circumnavigating the political body piss them off?'

'That's true,' agreed Ne´. 'We will have to offer them something to placate them.'

Fuska had a suggestion, 'I could offer the Humans an apology for what my father tried to do to their race and their planet. We could also offer to form a team that would operate under Federation supervision and that would dismantle all the centres of research and destroy the research materials. Maybe throw in a few heads as well.'

The other leaders admired him for a moment. Darrick put their thoughts into words, 'I think you are going to make a better Emperor than your father. I will be watching you. That was a good suggestion.'

Over the next couple of hours, they thrashed out a cohesive plan. The meeting broke up. Darrick pulled Ne´ to the side.

'What were you getting at when you were talking about Lord Marr's bloodlines?'

'I owe you an apology old friend. I had his DNA checked by the master of ceremonies. I doubted your word. I saw the results. He must be the direct descendant of Barrick Marr. His colour is as deep as you or I.'

Darrick was in shock, but did not show it, 'I did tell you. I suppose your plan was to have him disposed of if I was lying.'

'You know me so well Darrick. I will have to go. I hope I haven't hurt your feelings.'

'You have, but I will get over it.'

'I need to leave.'

He walked away as Grand Chancellor Serrivelli approached.

'Your new Lord is quite impressive.' He glanced round,

'Popular with the females as well.'

Darrick spotted Charlie surrounded by the Queen and her female attendants. He didn't look very happy.

'You know I think she was serious about that offer. Have they met before?'

'Not that I am aware of.'

'That's strange, I saw him holding her child earlier on, and more impressively the child was actually quiet.'

'Does it cry a lot?'

'I hear she keeps it at a country estate, it never stops. If Lord Marr can shut it up, it's no wonder she wants him so badly. I was stuck with them earlier; a very unpleasant hour. That aside, I wish to thank you for your understanding. With the discovery of the new Empire, we are all feeling a little vulnerable. A strong united Federation is the face that we wish to portray to this new Empire. Not one gutted by war and weak.'

'I don't think we have anything to worry about there Grand Chancellor. I have read quite a bit about them. Their ships I think are more advanced than ours, in their field harmonics and weapons, but I think the new ships the Grand Commander is bringing into service will be up to the task. This Empire is much smaller than the Federation. We could swamp them with numbers. Yet I understand your thinking. Fuska is shaping up to be a far more responsible leader than his father was.

'The Albany more or less ruled their part of space. With their military might broken, the others around there will be far less willing to fight in needless battles. We also have the Humans. Ne´ is integrating them and their tactics into the Federation.'

'Isn't it strange how things have changed in such a short time? A short while ago we were in mortal fear of all meat eaters. Now, because of them, we have avoided getting into a conflict with this new Empire. Eventually we would have lashed out, thinking them all meat eaters. Or they would have lashed out. Races would have blundered in believing there to be easy pickings. They only reached out to us because of the Humans.'

'I am not confident that there will be everlasting peace.'

'Neither am I. For now though we have a chance to learn about them, to discover their strengths and weaknesses. What has prevented us from clashing badly so far is pure logistics. Six month's travel for most ships is a long way to haul food with no hope of replenishment at the end of your journey.'

'A new era dawns Grand Chancellor. There will be good, there will be bad.'

'Yes, exciting times. Let us go forward in a position of strength Emperor.'

They parted ways. Darrick strolled over to Charlie. 'If you have finished playing with your admirers, we have to go.'

Charlie bowed, 'Duty calls. If you will excuse me.'

The women cried out in disappointment, but neither paid them any heed.

'Thanks for the rescue. What took you so long?'

'Emperor stuff. Charlie, do you keep secrets from me?'

'I keep secrets from everyone. As for you, just the ones you would have me killed for.'

Darrick half smiled, 'Of course. We all have secrets.'

CHAPTER 14

Charlie was having a late meal when the Emperor barged in.

'Do they no have manners in the Modloch Empire? Or is barging into someone's room the prerogative of every Emperor?'

'Why, what would you expect me to do?'

'Knock.'

'I'm the Emperor, I don't knock.'

'That answers that then.'

'Why would I knock?'

'I could have been having a private moment.'

Darrick laughed, 'It isn't the mating season.'

'I am not Modloch.'

'You're eating,' Darrick sat down with a sigh and a strange expression on his face.

Charlie put his spoon down, 'What's wrong with you? You look like your brother just stole your favourite lollipop.'

Darrick barked a laugh, 'I do feel like someone has taken something precious from me.' He showed Charlie the tablet he had in his hands, 'Do you know what this is?'

'Two dark lines and a shit load of Modloch writing. Rather than waiting for me to fire up my translation program, why don't you just tell me?'

'There is a way of judging how closely related a person is to a Royal family, based on current Emperors and their sires. The deeper the colour, the closer you are to the Royal line. The line on the left is mine, the one on the right is yours.'

'Yeah so? You gave me Barrick Marr's DNA, he was the son of an Emperor. They should be about the same.'

'That is true. However, this isn't Barrick Marr's DNA it is your DNA. Ne´ had you tested.'

Charlie was puzzled, 'I don't quite get it.'

'They got your DNA from a glass of water you were

drinking.'

'The sneaky bastards. Alright, I got that, but why am I still alive? He must know I'm not Carrick Marr.'

'The test doesn't include your race. It only compares it to the DNA of every Royal in the Federation. According to this, you are an Emperor.'

'I am still a little lost,' he scowled. 'You are obviously at it, so piss or get off the pot.'

'Have you ever met Queen Wiola Maleck before?'

'Ah!' Now it began to dawn on Charlie, 'Been doing a little checking up on me have you?'

'There is very little information outside my reach Charlie. Only that which lies within someone's heart, and I have professional interrogators to get that.'

Charlie kicked back and slung his legs up. 'So, what is your conclusion?'

'You tell me.'

'No. You tell me.'

'I am your Emperor.'

'Only because you gave me no other bloody choice.'

Darrick barked a laugh, 'That was very clever of me.'

'Spit out what you think you know; I will fill in the blanks.'

'You were the one who fathered her child. Don't deny it. I know the dates don't quite match up, but we both know that is nothing. She left my residence and came to your planet. The following year she had a child.'

'You're right. She came to me. I am the father of her child. She also has another eleven eggs in stasis and is planning on having more children.'

'I don't understand Charlie. Why, why wouldn't you tell me?'

'Why do you think?'

'A secret Charlie. She must know something about you.'

'What makes you think that?'

'I saw your face when she was speaking to you. I saw

your dislike. It has to be some form of blackmail. There is no other way I can see you having sex with her. I know your dislike of females from other races. I could see the distaste written all over your face.'

'You are getting very warm Darrick, impress me ever further. If you can find the key, I will unlock the door to one of the biggest secrets in this galaxy.'

Darrick wasn't sure why his heart was hammering so fast. Yet the thrill of the chase was on him, he was sure he was now going to lose his friend, but he was compelled to strive forward to gain the truth.

'The key has to lie with the visit of the Human females to her world. I am quite sure she wasn't even aware of your presence until then. It has to be through your Captain lady friend, or the female Ambassador. Knowing the lady Ambassadors dislike of you, I would guess it to be her. Soon after that visit, and just before our mating season, Wiola arrived for a protracted stay. I remember she got Ne´ and I drunk one night. I can vaguely remember her asking questions about you. I thought nothing of it at the time. Now it makes more sense. She wasn't there for a state visit, she was hunting for information. She then used that information to blackmail you into impregnating her.'

Darrick felt a chill run through him as Charlie reached for the weapon hanging from his chair. He took it from its holster and cocked it. He turned it sideways.

'This is the safety catch. You need to depress it before it will fire.'

He offered it to Darrick, and he accepted it, 'You are placing your life in my hands once more.'

'I am.'

'You are going to tell me.'

'I am, and you are going to want to kill me.'

'I am?'

'I only ask that you do it yourself. Quick and clean, as a friend.'

'I was right.'

'Bang on. The question that remains in my mind is, do you even have the slightest clue as to what the information is?'

'No.'

Charlie leaned forward and took a drink of water from his glass.

'For deductive reasoning, I am going to give you ten out of ten. It was Komoru that let the cat out of the bag. She was trying to piss off Captain Wilson by having a dig, or putting the boot-in, to try and split us up.'

'Why?'

'Because she hated my guts. Nothing more nothing less.'

'Females…'

'Right.'

'Wiola obviously had them observed constantly.'

'Exactly.'

'So you posses a genetic trait that she wanted for her offspring.'

'Oh! Twelve out of ten. But no sweetie for guessing what it is.'

'What is it Charlie? What is it I am going to want to kill you for?'

Charlie took a second to compose himself, 'After my accident, as you like to call it, when I first came to, I could hear voices. Dozens of them. The thing was Darrick, they weren't people's voices, they were people's thoughts.'

Darrick went very still. His grip on the pistol tightened, 'Are you telling me you can read people's minds?'

'No, I can hear their thoughts.'

'Is there a difference?'

'Of course. I can't go into your mind and search for information. I can only hear what you are thinking about.'

'You mean you can hear what I am thinking right now?'

'I could if I wanted to.'

It took Darrick a moment to digest the information. 'So you can switch it off, is that what you are telling me?'

'It is always off. I have to keep it off. I can hear minds from miles away. Can you imagine the thousands of thoughts that are bouncing around this ship right now? I can switch it off, I can concentrate on a single individual, or a group. It took a bit of time to master, but there it is.'

The pistol came up unwavering, 'You have been spying on me.'

'Nope.'

'You must have.'

'Nope.'

'Your Ambassador friend knows.'

'Of course he does! Who the hell do you think has been keeping him alive for this long?'

'He orders you to use it?'

'He asks me, the choice is mine to make.'

'Has he asked you what I am thinking?'

'Many times.'

'So you have been spying on me.'

'No, I refused to tell him anything. I told you the choice is always mine.'

'Why would you refuse?'

'Because I like you, because you are my friend.'

'I can't trust you Charlie.'

'I know. You can't afford to trust me now. Can I just say one thing?'

'One.'

'Thank you for all the fun and laughter you have given me these past few years.'

Darrick shook his head, 'It explains so much. All that body language stuff was just shit.'

'No, it is a real thing. To perpetuate the myth, I have studied just about every book on body language that has ever been written. I am truly an expert in it.'

'What is my body telling you now?'

'That you are about to pull that trigger. Remember the safety catch.'

'You are not frightened?'

'I should have been dead a long time ago. I live here now on borrowed time. I have always known that if any of you found out I would be dead. I'm just happy it was you who found out first. When Wiola found out, it was no more than a matter of time.'

Strange emotions welled up inside Darrick as he clicked off the safety catch.

'If there was only a way of knowing if you were telling the truth.'

Charlie laughed, 'You just lost five points.'

'What?'

'What is the one thing you really dislike about me Darrick? The only thing really. One you have told me to go and get checked out more than once.'

It hit Darrick like a lightening bolt, he tipped the muzzle of the weapon upwards.

'Your nose. It bleeds.'

'When I am concentrating hard.'

'It didn't bleed today.'

'In that bin over there, there are two wads of cotton wool I had stuffed up this massive nose. Ne´ has seen my nose bleed before. I couldn't afford him to see that. He is far too smart.'

It was on shaking legs that Darrick got up to check the bin. He gave it a shake. They were at the bottom. He sat back down again.

'You have read Ne´s thoughts.'

'Heard them. Many times, but it isn't easy.'

'Why not?'

'Because of the speed his mind works at.'

'What about mine?'

'I have no idea Darrick, I have never needed to. You hide nothing that I am interested in. When we talk, you tell me straight. I have no interest in the other things you do.'

'My cousin. You bled very badly that day.'

'Of course I did, but you asked me to help.'

'Is that bleeding bad?'

'It is the rupturing of blood vessels in my brain, of course it is bad. If it wasn't for the nanites in my blood, I would have died a very long time ago.'

'So you risk your life every time you do it?'

'It depends on how hard I have to concentrate, but yes.'

'It was bleeding the day you saved my son.'

'I was reading your guests when I picked up the thoughts of the gardener.'

'I see. It still doesn't make much sense.'

'It isn't so much the hearing of people's thoughts that is hard. That is easy, it is cutting out the ones you don't need to hear that is hard.'

'You mean you are inundated.'

'Totally.'

'The gardener?'

'He was a new voice, if you will. I had cut off those from your wife and the others. He came in from nowhere. His thoughts were very strong, loud even.'

'You have helped me out many times Charlie.'

'You are my friend, as is Steven.'

'Did you hear any of my thoughts today?'

'Of course. It was too large a group for me to cut you out as an individual, but I concentrated on those that you were talking to. You weren't really thinking anything that wasn't coming out of your mouth. The only time you really thought anything that stuck out was when you wanted me to get them. "Get them Charlie", that was what I heard. Ne´ wanted me to put the academic in his place and Wiola was also rooting for me to say something particularly bright. The rest were sniggering.

Darrick barked a laugh, 'That's right, that's what I was thinking. What else was Wiola thinking?'

'She spent most of the meeting trying to persuade me to go live with her. She was trying to fill my mind with dirty thoughts of herself and her two ladies in waiting, in bed, howling for my huge Modloch dick.'

Darrick suddenly lost it. He howled in delight. Charlie waited until he was finished laughing. At least Darrick wasn't waving the pistol around anymore.

Darrick caught his breath, 'How did she know you were there, did you tell her?'

'Nope, she just knew. I think it was when the child stopped crying. She felt something strange had just happened.'

'Had it?'

'Aye. Our minds touched.'

'She was after that particular gene.'

'That's exactly what she was after. My ability occurred an accident, but now it is written into my DNA. I spoke to the child, communicated to him how to cut out the voices. She realised something strange had happened. When she saw me, it just clicked. She said she would always recognise the man she loves, regardless of how I look.'

'Does she love you?'

Charlie sighed, 'I am afraid so.'

'She wants you?'

'Badly. She wants me to marry her, to rule alongside her.'

'You said no.'

'I can't stand her. She blackmailed me into giving her a whole damn family.'

'You don't think ruling an empire of your own is worth that?'

'That kind of shit is for people like you Darrick. I am not interested in the slightest. My excuse, of course, is that her people would never accept a Human as a ruler, a meat eater.'

'Now she has seen you as a Modloch.'

'Aye. Now her ladies in waiting think the father of her son is a Modloch Lord of Royal standing.'

'She could try blackmailing you again.'

'No she can't, because now I know her son can also hear minds.'

'Of course, if she told anyone about you, you could then tell about her son. Which means I can't kill you.'

'Why not?'

'Because then she will know that I knew about you. Which means there is a good chance I would know about her son. She would have to kill me before I killed him.'

'Is that the best excuse you can come up with?'

Darrick roared with laughter and handed the gun back, 'Isn't it good enough.'

'It works for me.'

Darrick sat back with a huge smile on his face. 'You know this could be a lot of fun. Is there anything else you are keeping secret?'

'I can see through walls and stuff.'

'Just walls?'

'Anything.'

'Do you perv females?'

'Only Human ones.'

Darrick howled with delight.

CHAPTER 15

Jean was caught by surprise as the huge Modloch advanced on her. She glanced round for her weapon, remembering it was in the bedroom.

'Relax Jean, mating season is a couple of days away yet,' Charlie threw himself down into the oversized chair he reserved for the Emperor. He got up as quickly and took off his gun belt, then sat back down, 'Better.'

Jean took a hesitant step forward, 'Charlie!'

'Aye it's me.'

'What the hell is going on?'

'Long story short: Darrick wanted my talents at a meeting, but I was banned from going. So I turned myself into a Modloch so I could accompany him. I am now Lord Carrick Marr, bastard offspring of Lord Barrick Marr. Kissy?'

'Oh hell no!'

Charlie howled with laughter, 'I'm afraid you are going to have to wait a couple of days then. Your friend the Grand Commander is going to appear soon. He needs to get in touch with Mary Gordon. I need to have changed back by then. I will lock myself in my bedroom. I can't be disturbed.'

'Can you do that in the spare bedroom?'

'Will do. I had better get to it.'

'So fast?'

'I just put every young Modloch female I passed on the way here into early season. The quicker the better.'

Jean laughed, 'Yeah right!'

'Oh I ain't kidding. Their fathers will be knocking at the door soon. You need to say that the Modloch who was here only stopped to pass on a message and left straight away,' Charlie got back to his feet. 'You didn't find a black box of any kind did you?'

'There was a package waiting by the door. I put it through into that cupboard at the back.'

The Black of Space

Charlie quickly located it and took it through to the spare room. He stripped off and put on a towel. His clothes went into the machine. It would clean and dry them.

Jean came through, 'Would you like something to eat?'

'No thanks. Once I am in there, do not disturb me.'

'Was it what you were looking for?'

'Aye, it's a special box full of extra nanites. I'm just going to have a shower.' Charlie stood up straight and turned, 'Really?'

'What?'

'I heard that.'

'Oh you did not, I never. I mean…'

Charlie swept her onto his shoulder, 'Your wish is my command. You can scrub my back.'

'You are not supposed to be listening!' She squealed in protest.

'I was listening for anyone approaching.'

'Aye right.'

'Honest.'

In the bedroom he tossed her onto the bed and whipped off his towel. Her jaw dropped.

'What the hell is that?'

Charlie laughed aloud, 'It's what I got bitch!'

CHAPTER 16

Ne´ was panting by the time he reached the small cottage, even though he considered himself fairly fit. His aide banged on the door. He was faring no better.

Ne´ felt instantly irritated the moment the door was open.

'Grand Commander, how can I be of service?'

'Noch Man Drich. A pleasure to see you again'

Charlie shook his head, 'Really?'

Ne´ felt he had the right to smirk in a very smug manner.

'Just call me Charlie for God's sake, it is so much easier.' Charlie glanced at his guards, 'Have your men stand close to the walls, the gravity extends out for about a metre. Come inside.'

The guard nodded his acknowledgement and Ne´ stepped inside.

'Do you know why I am here?'

'I have been informed.'

Charlie turned down the gravity. Ne´ sighed with relief.

'Thank you. It was even more intense here.'

'That is our own natural gravity. This way.'

Ne´ followed him through. His eyes lit up when he saw Jean.

'Captain Wilson. It is a pleasure to see you again.'

'Grand Commander, the pleasure is all mine.' Her eyes glanced down, 'I see you are wearing your pistol.'

'I go nowhere without it now. I also practice three times a week.'

'Then I am looking forward to the next time we compete.'

'I will definitely give you a run for it Captain.'

'Wonderful. Can I offer some refreshments?'

'I haven't long eaten, but the walk from the front of the main house has caused me to become hungry.'

'I have a nice salad waiting.'

'Have you any of those small round green balls?'
'Peas?'
'That's them.'
'Yes we do. Lots and lots.'
'I love those.'
'Then you have something in common with Charlie.'
Ne´ grunted, 'Are you all set up?'

'Take a seat,' Charlie indicated with a hand. When Ne´ sat down, Charlie moved a small table in front of him with a tablet on it. He pressed the connect button. It rang on the other end for almost thirty seconds.

'Grand Commander.'

'Doctor Gordon. Is your husband with you?'

'No, I am afraid he is indisposed at this time. My son will be returning with your new ships soon. They are undergoing trials as stipulated by your engineers. They will be delivered on time. I thought I made that clear in my last communique?'

'Ah! This isn't about that at all. It is an entirely different matter.' He quickly explained the problem. He knew enough about Human facial expressions to realise she didn't seem amused at all.

'Why me Grand Commander? Why not the politicians?'

'You have the resources, they don't.'

'It wasn't all that long ago these same people went to a lot of trouble to kidnap my son and turn him into paste. If it wasn't for Charlie there, he would have been lost. It wasn't the Federation that saved him, it wasn't the Federation that brought us into the fold, it was the Modloch Emperor. I really don't see why we should help out. The costs would be astronomical, and we still have no way of converting Federation credits into our own money.'

'You have a good point Doctor Gordon. I myself have no fondness for the Albany, or any sympathy for what they have brought upon themselves. However, those most responsible for this are either dead or unseated in power. The new Albany Emperor is willing to make an official apology to the people of Earth. He is going to allow your people to come and destroy the facilities used for their research and give an assurance of that research's destruction. Completely.'

'That will not help the mothers of the thousands of people who have already perished.'

'I realise that.'

Charlie gripped his shoulder and Ne´ sat back.

'Mary…'

'Charlie, no!'

'I'm sorry, but I am responsible for a part of this request. I mentioned something in a shell-hole on one of the Albany home worlds, just before I destroyed it.'

Mary shook her head, 'Is it one of your ideas?'

'Sort of.'

'Most of our food stuffs are banned because the Modloch Emperor has the rights to distribution. Any surplus we have, we send to him.'

'He buys it at a reasonable price.'

'That's true, but it means we have no real surplus.'

'We do, it isn't banned either.'

'Oh Charlie… is this one of your crazy ideas?'

'Afraid so.'

'I'm still not convinced.'

'We have only lost a few thousand people since that war started. We won all of our battles. It wasn't us that paid the highest price. It was the Modlochs that bore the brunt of it. The Modloch Emperor destroyed the Albany's inhabitable planets yet they never hesitated to ask him for help. Not one member of that council even considered asking us for our help.

'The rich and the powerful are still eating well Mary, it is the poor that are suffering, their children who are dying. The people who had no say in the matter at all. Is this not an opportunity for us to really show the Federation that we can play a more significant part within it? Show them the real heart of Humanity?'

'Oh Charlie! Why do I even listen to you?'

'Because I am extraordinarily handsome and sexy.'

Jean, Ne´ and Mary all joined together in laughter. Eventually Mary wiped away a tear.

'All right Charlie. Make your pitch.'

'What is the one thing Brian always bitches about the moment he arrives home? The second he walks in the gate?'

It only took Mary a second, 'The grass.'

'What does he do with it?'

'He cuts it and tosses it onto the compost heap.'

'Exactly.'

Mary got over her surprise quickly, 'You mean collect all the grass cuttings!'

'Exactly.'

'That would be an enormous undertaking Charlie.'

'Maybe, unless the kind-hearted people of Earth dropped it at specified points in every town and city. People are always bitching about the price of removing garden waste. If they donated their grass, we could remove the rest of it for them for free. We can always use it.'

'We are always on the look out for new resources. Maybe your idea has merits, but the grass won't keep Charlie.'

'Make silage out of it.'

'What is that?' Ne´ asked.

'You call it fermented grass.'

He nodded his understanding, 'Most races eat it. I am sure the Albany do. They will also take the fermented juice. They can make it into various nutritional drinks.'

'Including beer.'

'Have you tried it?'

'Most of us have, every one of us was violently sick.'

Ne´ laughed, 'I didn't know.'

'Alright Charlie, I will look into it. When do you need this to happen?'

'Couple of weeks ago. Things are desperate here.'

'I will look into it, but you must be in charge of distribution at that end.'

'All right.'

Mary turned her attention back to Ne´, 'Well Grand Commander, is there anything else I can do for you?'

'The next time you are over our side of the barrier, you could come and stay on my home planet as my personal guests. I would love for you to meet my wife and children. My youngest daughter has a passion for Human flowers.'

Mary smiled, 'Thank you Grand Commander. I think I would enjoy that.'

'I am afraid I have to go now Doctor Gordon, thank you for your time.'

'A pleasure Grand Commander.'

The screen went blank. Ne´ nodded, 'I think that went quite well.'

Jean stood, 'Let's get you something to eat.'

Ne´ feasted on new potatoes and butter. Charlie whipped up a batch of mashed potatoes to the Emperor's great delight. He and Jean chatted away like old friends. With a bag of potatoes and another full of fresh vegetables, they saw him to the door. The potatoes were handed to one of his guards. He held onto the other vegetables himself.

'Thank you for your hospitality Captain. It was a pleasure and a delight.'

He nodded to Charlie, who nodded back.

Jean beamed a smile, 'It was a pleasure Grand Commander. I hope to see you soon.'

'Where duties permit,' he half bowed to her and turned away.

They watched until he was out of sight. 'He really doesn't like you, does he Charlie?'

'Nope.'

'He never thanked you at all, for anything. He gave Carrick Marr all the praise for the idea, and me thanks for the vegetables and the meal, even though you cooked and prepared it all. For getting in touch with Mary: nothing. He never even called you by your name, or your title.'

'Don't be too hard on him Jean. He senses there is far more to me than meets the eye.'

'He is right.'

'Of course he is.'

'You have helped him many times Charlie.'

'So?'

'I still don't think it is nice.'

'Do you know the ironic thing?'

'No.'

'He really likes Lord Carrick Marr.'

'Seriously!'

Charlie laughed, 'Aye, honest.'

CHAPTER 17

Darrick's wife watched him closely as he entered their living quarters. With a nod, her personal servants swept in. In a moment he was seated with slippers by his side, a warm drink by his hand, and his feet up on a rest. With another nod the servant vanished.

When he was sufficiently relaxed, she moved in and sat on a small stool. She began to manipulate his feet. Darrick growled with pleasure.

'Thank you Calranna, I needed that today.'

'Why? You didn't have all that hard a day. No state visits. No imperial judgments. Little more than normal routine.'

'I don't know…'

'What has been eating at you Darrick? You have been like this since you returned from the council.'

'I have had something on my mind. I am not sure how to express it.'

'That isn't like you.'

'I don't know… it is something unusual.'

'Try me.' He looked down at her. 'There is no one else you can talk to it about.'

His eyes rolled upwards, 'True. What would you do if you thought someone could read your mind?'

She sat up sharply, 'Why?'

'Would you kill them?'

'Darrick, do you want to kill me?'

'Don't be foolish! Why would I want to kill you? You can't read my mind.'

She giggled, 'I read your mind all the time. We all do. Myself, the servants, the children. Darrick, you are an open book.'

'I don't understand.'

'When was the last time you asked me for a foot massage, or a stool to rest your feet on? A hot cup of droth, or frack? We can tell at a glance what mood you are in and what you want.'

'I'm an open book?'

'Oh Darrick. Think about it. When was the last time you really had to ask for anything?'

He tilted his head back and thought it over, 'I can't remember.'

'Exactly. So I hope you aren't going to kill any of us, or any of the staff. It takes so long to train good ones.'

His laughter started deep down and bellowed forth. He felt a strange sense of relief. With Darrick now in a good mood, his wife changed tack.

'There is something I would like to discuss with you.'

Darrick was immediately on alert. When he looked down at her a stray thought flew into his mind. He could tell by the tone and look in her eye exactly what she wanted to talk about.

He laughed again, 'No.'

'Huh?'

'She can't have him, they are too closely related.'

Calranna sat up straight, 'Now who is reading minds! How can they possibly be too closely related?'

Darrick reached for his tablet. He quickly found what he was looking for, 'This is the Royal colour index. I am on the right, Carrick Marr is the one on the left.'

She took it from him, 'I cannot detect any difference.'

'Correct.'

'Are you sure about this, when did you do this?'

'I didn't, Ne´ did it at the conference behind my back. He only told me later.'

'I hope he apologised,' her face had fallen.

'He did.'

'Perrina is going to be devastated. Still, there are plenty others of noble blood who are more than willing.'

'Lord Carrick Marr has more than earned himself the right to choose his own wife, if he so wishes.'

'You know warriors like him rarely get married Darrick. They become old and crusty, lost in their old battles. What a waste.'

She fell silent, obviously disappointed for their daughter. Darrick's mind took off on a tangent. What would it be like to have a grandson of his own that could read minds? He doubted if Humans and Modloch would be compatible. Wiola's race only had one stomach like Humans did, yet they were attracted to the Modloch race. There were plenty interracial marriages but he had no idea if they produced children. It would be something to check. Wiola had obviously manipulated the child's DNA to make it more Gisha. Would that be possible with a Modloch offspring?

Charlie had obviously managed with Wiola, despite his distaste. He doubted if Charlie would submit to living as a Modloch for the rest of his life, but would he submit to fathering a grandchild for him? Perrina was obviously head over heels in love with Carrick Marr. If he put them in close proximity during the mating season, he suspected that Perrina would very quickly submit. The problem would be Charlie. What would make Charlie do it? It would have to be a direct order, and then Carrick Marr would have to disappear forever. He could not allow the Modloch male who impregnated his daughter out of wedlock to survive. It would not be an easy thing to accomplish.

'I wonder how your bloodlines can be so closely related?' It was almost a murmur.

Darrick glanced down, 'The master of ceremonies thinks he is a genetic throwback.'

'Tragic.'

Darrick hid his smile. He knew exactly why Carrick Marr's colours had turned out the same as his. His DNA had matched his son's, who was a Royal Prince, which made him the equivalent of an Emperor. Charlie could have had it all. An empire of his own. Any Modloch noble worth his salt would have accepted in a heartbeat.

He remembered his grandfather's words, 'Empires are

built by the greed of the nobles and Emperors. They are won by the strong, and the honest. One will obey the other to the death but are totally distrusted by the nobles. If a commoner rises above them in station, they will do whatever they can to discredit him and have him removed. No noble wants to share a table with one who is honest, because it won't be long before his dishonesty and greed is displayed in its true colours. If you find someone who is honest and that you can trust, then you must guard them carefully. Keep them as far away from your nobles as possible. Those who follow the path of truth and honour are more often than not blind to the scheming of those around him.'

Charlie and his Chief Engineer. Both of different races, but cut from the same cloth. His noble Lords had laughed aloud when they had discovered the Emperor's generosity towards his new nobles. He had managed to keep them all apart. Neither had ever been invited to any gathering, or meeting to discuss the issues of empire. Both had slipped from the minds of the nobles. Both were assets he would continue to keep safe. Now he had an even more important reason to keep Charlie away. If any of them felt threatened by Charlie, it wouldn't take Charlie long to figure out what they were up to, and he didn't give them much of a chance against him. Better, far better, to keep them apart. He smiled to himself — unless of course he really wanted to know what they were thinking himself.

'You are doing that Emperor thing again, aren't you?'

Her question brought him back to the now, 'What do you mean?'

'Planning, scheming, Emperor things.'

'You really can read minds.'

She smiled, 'It is quite a turn on.'

His mind became alert in an instant, his nostrils flaring, 'Are you coming into heat early?'

'You know, I just may be.'

'Order the servants to retire. I am going for a bath. Join

me there.'
'Yes darling. I will be as quick as possible.'

CHAPTER 18

Abby had awoken with a thumping headache. A long cold glass of water seemed to help a little. Her arms itched badly as well. In fact her whole body seemed to itch.

It was time to change her dressings. As soon as she began to unwrap her hands, she knew something was wrong. She sat and stared at the thing that had fallen free from the bandage. She knew exactly what it was but couldn't understand why. She looked at her finger. It was gone. She looked down at the floor.

Her heart began to beat faster. For a moment she was afraid to remove any more of the bandages. She sat there for a long time wondering what to do. Eventually the itching got the better of her. As more of her skin was revealed the quicker her heart beat, and the faster she began to remove the bandages. By the time she was finished, she was crying. On the floor lay a bundle of loose dirty bandages, and within them the warts that had been a bane of her life.

She quickly gathered them up and swept up the pieces of dead skin. She felt disgust as she put them into her burning bin outside and set fire to it all. The itching had almost dissipated. She went back inside and almost leapt into the shower. She cried as she soaped her skin. She had never seen it so clear, so blemish free, not since she was a young child. It was only when her skin began to wrinkle that she finally stepped out of the shower.

In her bedroom she put on the light and sat in front of her small dresser. A complete stranger stared back at her. Her skin had a youthful sheen to it. There were no lines, no dark circles under her eyes. The mirror was small, and she had to move around a lot to see most of herself.

Liverington grasped the cell phone from his bedside table. He swiped it and stuck it to his ear.

'Hey Abby, what time is it?'

'Don't you dare "Hey Abby" me, Richard! What the hell have you done to me?'

He came fully awake, 'Oh! Did it work?'

'Did what work?'

He took a deep breath; she did not sound happy. 'Well… I asked the doctor if she had anything that could improve your condition. She gave me some of those nanite things. They would kill the warts and hunt down the virus that caused them. That's all Abby, I thought you would be pleased.'

'You gave me tiny robots!'

'Yes,' he sighed, 'I am sorry I didn't ask, but I knew you would say no. I just wanted to help.'

'Are you still in that hotel room?'

'I am.'

'Get your ass down here right now.'

'I am on my way.'

He had found it difficult getting to sleep the night before. He had been worried about her reaction. Now, even more fraught with worry, his stress levels were through the roof by the time he reached her mobile home. He tried the door handle, it was open. He stepped inside. The curtains were still closed and it was dark.

'Abby?'

A figure appeared from the bedroom. She stopped at the door.

'Are you sure that she only gave you something to make the warts disappear?'

'Yes of course.'

'Put the light on Richard,' he put the light on and squinted against the sudden brightness.

'Explain this then,' she dropped her dressing gown. Richard's jaw dropped.

'Oh my!'

'Is that it. "Oh my"?'

'Is that really you?'

His eyes were having a feast and his throat dried up.

'Funny you should ask that Richard, because I don't bloody know!' Her voice had risen to near hysterical.

'Abby, have you really seen yourself?'

'Yes, sort of.'

'Abby, you are stunning.'

'What?'

'Seriously. You are beautiful.'

'Where did these boobs come from Richard?'

He reached up and scratched the back of his head, 'I honestly don't know. I only asked for something to help your skin, not turn you into a Venus of love.'

'What?'

'Wait,' He took his phone out.

'Don't you dare?'

'It is to show you. The whole you.'

Her face was flushed with colour. She was really mad at him. 'One picture and throw the phone over.'

He took the picture and tossed it over. Her eyes boggled.

'No!'

'Oh yes.'

She scowled at his tone, then snatched up her dressing gown. 'Go get me a full-length mirror.'

'Uh, where from?'

'Anywhere!' She screamed at him.

Richard launched himself out of the door, his head still spinning. He ran to the small shop. The attendant was amused at his request but couldn't help. A grubby old man that was in at the same time confronted him as he left. He said he could sell him one. Richard followed him to a unit with a large garage behind it. The garage was full of junk and stank. At the back stood an old wardrobe. The mirror wasn't in great shape, and it cost Richard fifty bucks.

By the time he got back to her unit he was sweaty and angry.

'Where do you want it?'

'In the bedroom of course.'

She glanced at his clothes, 'You look dirty.'

'Well, the dirt and the mirror just cost me fifty bucks, so don't ask and don't complain.'

Her eyes were ice as he shuffled past. He placed the mirror against the wall and got out.

After fifteen minutes waiting, he put on the coffee maker. She always drank herbal teas; the coffee had always been for him. He had actually bought the maker and the coffee. He brushed himself down and went outside. While he drank the coffee, he concentrated hard, but couldn't hear the ship. He realised he still didn't have his phone. The coffee helped a little, but sitting back inside, she still hadn't appeared. It was almost an hour before she reappeared.

'What have they done to me?'

'I have no idea,' he just wanted to ask what the hell she had been doing.

She leaned against the wall; her body took on a rose colour hue.

'Are you going to take responsibility for this Richard?'

'Yes of course.'

The robe slipped off her shoulders onto the floor. 'Well come on then.'

He was half undressed before he reached her.

CHAPTER 19

Richard watched himself disappear for the umpteenth time. It wasn't just the fact that he vanished, it was Abby's face too: her astonishment, the way it glowed. It had been the most wonderful week of his life. They had made love like the world was about to come to an end. They got up to eat, went out to shop for food and went back to bed. He could believe the difference in her body. She couldn't stop looking at herself in the mirror, her face full of wonder. They had made love in front of it in as many positions as they could dream up. He was still in the afterglow.

They were late picking him up. Once aboard, he had asked the ship if he had a window. His wall shimmered and disappeared. He watched as they came in to land on the moon. He got up and went down into the main complex. He discovered a number of bars still open and a few of the food vendors. There were all kind of parties: birthday parties, stag parties, wedding parties; all from visitors. He had a few beers from an American style bar, then visited a British one, before buying a pizza. He was mesmerised by people jumping off a small platform in the central plaza. It was weird the way they floated towards the ground. Laughter surrounded him and his GoPro moved from group to group.

He was still admiring Abby's face when he was asked to attend the Captain. Babes guided him to his office.
'Morning Richard.'
'Do I call you Ambassador or Captain?'
'You aren't officially a member of the crew, please call me Steven. How did you enjoy your week?'
'What did you people do to Abby?'
'I added a little gift to the nanites. Did you both like it?'
Richard suddenly burst out laughing, 'Oh, we enjoyed

it.'

'Are we a convert yet?'

'I was a convert the moment I woke up a week ago. It isn't Abby and myself you have to convince now.'

'I don't have to convince anyone Richard, you do. That is your job now. Right now, I am making you an official part of this crew. You are going to be our media officer. Anything to do with the media will come straight to you. We get a lot of requests. At this moment in time we don't really do much with them. Few of us have the time. After discussing it with the senior staff, we realise that may not have been the right approach. We have to take a portion of the blame for what is happening.'

'Kidnapping people and sending them all over the place isn't quite the way to do it either. It is effective, but you are destroying someone's belief system in a very brutal way. People have a right to believe what they want, when they want. You have the right to try and persuade them differently, not brutalise them.'

Steven thought it over, 'Alright, I accept that. As I am now your boss, you may call me Captain from now on. You will be involved in most briefings. Non-military briefings that is, and only those we see fit to add you to.'

'Do I have to do this on my own?'

'Of course.'

'This isn't a one-man job Captain. It normally involves a team.'

'We really don't have the room for a new team. I can give you one person.'

'It has to be Abby.'

'I would rather you picked or hired a professional.'

'She is a professional. She has a degree in media studies. She took reporting classes, all different kind of stuff at college, and is a wonderful editor.'

Steven thought it over, 'I will need to see her relevant qualifications first. Otherwise, I will leave the recruitment to you.'

The Black of Space

'Do I salute?'

'No, we aren't soldiers. Babes is preparing a space; she will lead you to it. One more thing: as a member of the crew, you will need one of these,' he slid a card across, 'It is an employee card and credit card. It works here and across the great barrier. As you have accepted the job, you have been credited with two weeks wages,' he slid another card across, 'This is your Federation identity card. Do not lose it. There are a number of different ways of carrying it. A popular way is to wear it on your wrist. You can wear it around your neck or carry it in your wallet. When we are off the ship, most normally wear it on their wrist. There are different types, but that is the common type all citizens have. Is there anything you want to ask?'

'What about equipment?'

'Give a list to Babes. She will procure it for you or give you something much better.'

'That's everything, I think. I may have a little problem persuading Abby. I think a little trip like the one Captain Komoru gave me would help persuade her.'

'I will ask her.'

'Thank you.'

The room was completely bare and quite narrow. A tall and very elegant woman appeared at his back. Her look immediately intimidated him.

'Who are you?'

'I am Richard Liverington. I am the new PR guy.'

'I am not familiar with the term.'

'I will be dealing with the media.'

He could see her thinking it over, 'The person who believed the Earth was flat!'

'The person who chose to believe the Earth was flat. May I ask who you are?'

'Lady Montgomery Royce. I work next door.'

'What do you do?'

'We keep the Ambassadors alive.'

He waited for more, there was none forthcoming.

'Alright, not very informative.'

'I'm not sure if you have the intellect to understand.'

'I see. You could give me the benefit of the doubt.'

She thought it over, 'No, I don't think so. To believe the world is flat in the face of so much evidence to the contrary, you have to be a complete idiot.'

'I did say it was a personal choice.'

'Then you are an even bigger idiot. I could forgive someone with extreme learning difficulties, or someone who is uneducated from some obscure tribe in the Amazon. For an educated person to chose to take that stance, you must be little more than a moron. Good day. Oh! We may well be neighbours, but please don't bother us. None of us have any time for idiots, and two of our number are quite brutal when accosted by fools.'

'Jeez Jane, who the hell are you giving to this early in the day?'

'Our new neighbour who thinks the Earth is flat.'

Jeb appeared from behind her and looked over her shoulder.

'He looks quite normal too. Guess there really ain't no judging a book by its cover. Ain't you ever looked out of the window around here son?'

'As I have tried to explain to your friend, I have a right to believe what I choose to believe.'

Jeb's eyes turned cold, 'Oh yeah, like those Nazi bastards back home who choose to believe the Holocaust never happened.'

'I'm not like them, but a person has a basic right to believe what they want to.'

'People who don't believe what they see with their own eyes, what history tells them, are the kind of idiots that repeat the mistakes of history over and over again. Ya'll had better take heed of the Lady's advice. Let's go woman.'

Jane turned and walked out. Jeb's cold eyes had

The Black of Space

Liverington rooted to the spot for another few seconds, then he turned and followed her.

'That was rather profound for you Jeb.'

'You have the right to speak English,' was the last words Richard heard.

'Should I move your room? I never realised they would be so hostile.' Babes offered.

Richard slid down the wall, 'That would be nice, but it would also be cowardice. Are those two of the people who were on the Black Planet?'

'That is correct.'

'Which, if it is true, makes them both over a hundred years old.'

'That is not something I would repeat in front of Jane's face, but you are correct.'

'I have been warned.'

'What would you like done in here?'

'Nothing, I am not the expert. We still have to get Abby on board.'

'I understand. Komoru leaves tonight. Her flight path will take her over the United States. Shall I ask her if you can accompany her?'

'Yes please.'

He waited for almost a full minute. 'She would be more than happy to, and she has spoken to Steven. She will give your friend the tour.'

'Awesome.'

He knew exactly where he wanted to take her.

Seventy-two hours later, they sat together on one of Saturn's moons. It was the same place he had fallen asleep a few weeks before. He sat with Abby cradled in his arms as they watched, enthralled, by the beauty of the scene. It had taken more persuading than he thought it would, but she had reluctantly agreed. They talked in hushed whispers, pointing out things. Richard felt totally at peace. When Komoru picked them up, he could see the glow in Abby's eyes.

A week later Abby joined the crew. Her door was right next door to his, and they spent every night together. Abby took great delight in their new job. Their workroom soon filled up.

CHAPTER 20

Steven looked around the table, 'Good morning everyone. As you all know, we will be heading back very soon. We are to help provide an escort to the new Federation vessels. Their trials are complete, and a Human crew will be taking them to the great barrier, where they will be picked up by new Federation crews. Those crews, however, are not their permanent crews, and will not be expected to fight. That means we will have to escort them all the way to Federation 3937.

'It would seem that Federation 3973 is a top-secret facility. It is only a few days away from the great barrier, so the Federation is trusting us to deliver them in one piece. That will save them diverting resources. We will not be allowed onto the space station. Our mission will end the moment they dock. We are to turn around then and leave. Our escort will be two hundred ships of the home fleet. That is the minimum requirement as stipulated by the Federation.

'Once that task has been completed, we have to return to the Modloch city ship for orders. Not all of us will be partaking of this mission. As you should all know by now, there is an ongoing humanitarian crisis.' He made a face. 'Well, I am not sure if humanitarian is the right word. Right now my mother is cramming as much grass cuttings as she can into every available fast freighter. Believe it or not, she has already filled three. Whether they truly sympathise, or they just want to get rid of their garden waste for free, we will probably never know.'

There were a few chuckles. He held up a hand, 'We shouldn't laugh. I am sure there are more than a few of us who don't wish to help either, considering our personal experiences with the Albany. However, I want a few volunteers to go with the ships. Abby and Richard will both be going, to record and document the event. This is their first mission, and I want them escorted. Charlie will be waiting for you at the other end, he will be with Cookie and Mya. They are handling things there.'

'I'll go then Captain.'

Steven smiled, 'I thought you might Jeb.'

David Hammersmith held up his hand also, 'I think I would like to go too. I could do with a change of pace.'

'Excellent. There will be a company of marines on every ship. They will have plenty ammunition with them but bring your own weapons. All weapons are now 7.62, so there will be no ammunition worries. Alright ladies and gentlemen, I think that's it.'

David smiled at Jeb, 'I think we had better take a few six packs for Charlie.'

'That's a good idea.'

CHAPTER 21

Abby clung to Richard's side, a hand grasped to his sleeve. Her heart was hammering in her chest. To their right were men from the marine company who they had got to know on the trip there. Between them were their own crew members. David had been wonderful the whole trip, but Jeb had remained distant. All had one thing in common: their eyes were cold and hard, their bodies tense

'This is it, isn't it Richard?'

They tensed as they hit turbulence. A voice sounded all around the ship.

'Brace yourselves everyone, we are experiencing turbulence as we enter the atmosphere. It will pass quickly.'

Richard grasped her hand and squeezed.

'Yeah, this is it. This is where we find out if everything, we have believed in all these years has been total bullshit and the governments have been telling the truth. Are we really going to meet an alien race?'

'Oh God I hope we are right.'

They had spent the past few weeks interviewing the crew and the marines. David Goldstein had been more than happy to be interviewed; Jeb had remained stonily silent. Millions now watched their daily broadcasts. Thousands of questions were fired at them every day. Many from people that once knew them, who now doubted who they were. It had taken a lot to convince them. Many requests were from family, and they spent a lot of time tracing individual family members on the ship and interviewing them.

The vibrations got worse, then there was a smack from below than almost put them to their knees. The voice returned.

'Listen in, we are now down. The other ships are

landing now. We are going to wait until almost all are down before opening the doors. We have arrived on the Plains of Macoo. Plains is the right word; it is a huge dustbowl out there. Standby.'

After what seemed an age the large doors came down. Officers and NCOs shouted; marines dashed down the ramps to take up defensive positions around the ship. The four of them were left standing. Behind them a large group of farmers waited to be told that it was safe to go outside.

The air was full of dust. Vibrations reached them through the ground and up the landing legs of the gigantic ship as other ships continued to land. Richard sent a silent command to the small flight of drones that had been hovering over their heads; the machines shot out of the door in front of them. Jeb and David stepped off the ship first, Richard and Abby followed. At first, they could see nothing. Then the landings ceased, and the dust slowly began to settle.

It was Abby that saw it first. Her grip on his arm tightened until it was painful. A second later he saw it too and he forgot the pain. The plain was flat for as far as the eye could see, it was what was beyond the horizon that had caught her eye. A huge planet, only half of which they could see, filled the horizon. Her legs gave way and she dragged him down to their knees. Tears filled her eyes and ran down her face. In moments both were crying.

'Who are this pair?' It was a strange voice.

David answered, 'Hey Charlie, they are our new PR people.'

'We have PR people now?'

'You weren't told?'

'Nope,' the figure swam into view, looking bemused. 'Why are they crying?'

David shrugged, but Jeb had an answer, 'They are from the flat Earth society. Don't believe in aliens, that kind of shit.'

Charlie grinned, 'Seriously?'

'Yup, this is the kind of reaction you get when you confront people who believe in lies with the truth. Same shit happened when we dragged the local Germans up to Auschwitz. Tried to tell us they knew nothing about the death camps. They knew right enough; they just didn't want to believe it.'

Charlie was still grinning, 'What's your name?'

'Richard Liverington.'

'Richard. Dick it is then,' Richard's face turned to a scowl, and a grinning Charlie leaned forward, 'Don't worry, it doesn't translate into alien.'

Jeb laughed aloud, and David turned away.

There was a snort, 'You are the only aliens here.' Admiral Morach Valachean walked up with Jean at his side.

'Aye that's right Morach,' Charlie agreed.

He took a deep breath, 'Oh what a smell. Wonderful. Is it ready?'

Charlie waved to some of the farmers who had now stepped off the ship. One of them detached himself.

'Do you have a translator?' Charlie asked.

'No, sorry.'

'This is Admiral Morach Valachean, he is a Federation officer, he is asking if the silage is ready.'

'Was that what he said?'

'Aye, sure was.'

The farmer shook his head, 'Yeah, it sure is ready. It's been a four and a half week flight. Where do you want it?'

'We are going to use a matter transporter to load the wagons as they appear.'

'So we won't be needed?'

'Feel free to help supervise. I'm pretty damn sure you're the only ones that will know what you are doing.'

He laughed, 'We'll keep an eye out.'

Morach was looking down at the two Humans on their

knees with as much curiosity as they were looking up at him.

'What is wrong with these two Charlie?'

'It would seem that we have destroyed all their beliefs, and they are taking a little time to recover.'

'What beliefs?'

'That our planet was flat, and aliens didn't exist.'

It took a moment but then Morach went into a fit of laughter. He laughed so hard he almost collapsed.

Charlie berated him, 'Now, now Morach, every Human has the right to believe what they want to.' He looked down, 'Isn't that right Dick?'

'Yes it is.'

That seemed to make Morach even worse. Eventually he was able to take a few long gulps of breath.

'Captain Wilson, let the Albany know the ships are down and they can start sending in cargo haulers.'

'Yes sir.'

He took one last look at the couple and burst out laughing again. He beat a hasty retreat while holding on to his sides.

Charlie took a few steps back, 'Listen in everyone. Albany police forces are going to be arriving first. They will mark lanes in and out. Each cargo door will have its own line of haulers. These haulers are huge. Two of them will almost fill the space, but we only have the equipment to fill one at a time. So it will be one hauler loading in front of the cargo doors at a time. The same thing will be happening at the same time at every ship. There will be a one-way system in operation. That will be the Albany police's job. Do not get in their way, do not challenge them. They will not like it. If they make an arse of it, let them sort it out.

'Officer in charge of the marines, make damn sure your men aren't lying out there somewhere, where these haulers will fly over the top of them. The magnetic field created by these things will most likely kill them. Make damn sure they are out of the lanes once they are laid out. The haulers will ground themselves while loading. They will crush you to death if you are underneath, so either way, if you find yourself beneath one, you will most likely die. Your lives are in your own hands, so do not do anything stupid. Thank you and stand by.'

Charlie walked away. His orders were being relayed by others right down the line. He came to where Richard and Abby were now sitting consoling each other.

'Do you two have a job to do? If not, get back aboard and keep out of the way.'

Abby looked up, 'You are a total bastard. You destroy our beliefs, then treat us like shit.'

'Are you so stupid, so caught up in your own miserable beliefs, that you can't see when someone is trying to keep you safe?'

They hadn't really noticed Jean earlier, but now they both did. Richard was overawed, and Abby suddenly felt totally inadequate.

'Nasty people calling you names again?'

'It's okay, I am totally used to it, but if this pair don't move from the front of these cargo doors, they are going to get squashed flat.'

'Are they your responsibility?'

Charlie looked them over, 'They look like adults to me.'

'Let them get squashed then.'

Abby shook her head, 'Are you people so unsympathetic? So cruel?'

Jean cocked her head slightly, 'What do you want? Do you want someone to hold your hand? Feel sympathy for you? Look around. We are trying to do a job here. We have neither the time nor the inclination to help you.'

'Who are you?'

'I am Captain Jean Wilson, Captain of the Sir William Wallace, Post Captain to Admiral Morach Valachean.'

'The alien!'

'Take a good look around you sweetheart. You aren't in

Kansas anymore. We are the aliens here,' Jean turned to walk away.

'You are horrible,' Abby accused.

Jean stopped and went very still. The hackles on Charlie's neck went up. She turned slowly.

'When I heard we had a couple of flat Earthers coming, I looked up some of your videos. We were at the battle for the Ambatta home-world. My ship was badly damaged, we took a lot of broadsides. I lost friends that day, not just crew members. I saw the video you made about it. I saw both of you laugh and accuse the governments of collusion on a grand scale, a huge hoax. Where was your sympathy for those who lost their lives, for their families, their children, you bloody hypocrite? You must see now that it was the truth.'

Charlie's hand grasped her shoulder. For Abby it was the woman's eyes that held the truth, the pain, the anger. It shattered the last vestige of doubt.

'I am sorry Captain Wilson. That was very insensitive of us.'

Jean's head spun as she calmed down. She wasn't quite sure how to respond.

'Well at least that's a start,' her eyes swung round again. 'I will catch you later.'

Charlie watched her walk away for a while, before turning to the two on the ground.

'Get up, come with me. Now!'

The two got up and followed. They passed a couple of farmers who were drizzling soil through their hands and commenting on how fertile it was. He led them forward of the ship and then stopped and turned.

He pointed, they looked.

'Wow!' It was out of Abby's mouth before she could stop it. From this angle the line of ships looked like a huge wall, a fortress.

'You won't see this very often.'

They both got the hint. The drones started doing their job. They took their tablets out and Abby helped direct them for the best shots.

'This is incredible,' Richard agreed at last. He looked to where the farmers were making their way back to the ship. Something crossed his mind.

'Why are we here in this desert? Why is it a desert if the soil is so fertile?'

Charlie shook his head, 'Did you get a briefing? This isn't a desert, it's the breadbasket of this world. That is why we are here, this is where they have enough equipment to deal with the amount of food we are delivering.'

Richard lifted his hands, 'I see desert.'

'Only because we killed it. We sanitized the whole planet. It has received the antidote to the agent that was used now, but they have no seed to plant. That was also destroyed.'

Richard was shaking his head, 'Not we... this was a Modloch war.'

'Maybe, but I was here.'

Richard opened his mouth to speak, but Abby grasped his arm.

'I remember seeing something on the news. A really big guy. Some Lord or something.'

Charlie laughed, 'Lord Noch Man Drich.'

'Something like that yes, were you with him?'

'I am him. The big guy was my old commanding officer, he was here as more of an observer. Officially.'

'Oh!'

'Don't worry, you aren't the only one to get it wrong.'

'Alright, so why did they do this?'

'It is what they do. It was what the Albany were going to do to Earth. The only difference is, we used a weapon that only killed vegetation. On Earth, they would have used weapons that would have killed all biological life as well.'

'Is all this necessary?'

'When you have half a dozen planets with billions of souls on it, and you make them completely uninhabitable, what do you think will happen to the home planet?'

Abby thought it over, 'It would cause a huge crisis.'

'Huge is putting it mildly. It completely chokes up all of their resources. Their armed forces are compelled to turn on their own. More Albany citizens were killed by their own people than killed by the Modloch. It's still going on now. Many others have been killed by forces from other planets when landing illegally there out of sheer desperation. It is probably the biggest crisis of its kind ever created deliberately.'

'So it is a tactic?'

'Of course it is. A very effective one.'

Richard was looking around, 'Where are they all?'

'Waiting for orders. Come with me.'

He walked them under the ships then up a small ridge. Once they got to the top they realised the plain wasn't as flat as they first thought. Behind the ridge, a few hundred metres away, stood a line of huge vehicles. Beyond them buildings of a large complex. Charlie pointed to a small dust cloud moving behind the vehicles.

'That will be the Albany police making their way to the landing site. They will come out in front of the convoy and swing round.'

Richard was kicking at a stone. As it rolled away it broke open. He squatted to look closer.

'This looks like rebar.' His head came up, 'What is this ridge?'

Charlie shrugged, 'How would I know? Looks like rubble to me. Probably the remnants of the civilisation that went before.'

'What civilisation?'

Charlie audibly sighed, 'How the hell would I know? Ask one of the Albany when you see them, although I doubt very much if they will know. It was probably a meat-eating race.'

Richard picked up the rock, there were still slithers of metal.

'This is very old, but it looks like twenty-first century technology.'

'Your point being?'

'If they killed whoever was on this planet before, it wasn't a pre-industrial planet. They must have been quite advanced.'

'Again, your point being what?'

The penny finally dropped. He dropped the rock as if it were a hot potato.

'That is genocide.'

'It goes far beyond genocide.'

'Why?'

'Oh for God's sake!' Charlie pinched the bridge of his nose, 'Alright, I am forgetting you have completely ignored all of this stuff deliberately. What a pain in the arse.' He took a deep breath, 'Many of these herbivore races never knew war before they took to space. That doesn't mean they were nonviolent. The biggest threat to their existence was starvation and over population. A severe drought would kill millions. They took to space far quicker than Humans did. If you compare their history to ours, by the year 2001, most of these races had achieved faster than light travel. At the pace we were going, we might have gotten close about the year 3001. We are about a thousand years behind in technological terms, maybe more.

'When they came across planets like this that were far behind them in technology, they wiped out the planet and all its inhabitants, right down to the bacteria. They then terraformed it. Flattened everything, made great plains like this. Grew grass. There are a few planets that have been terraformed from scratch, but they are normally mining planets. It's all out there. Go read up on it.'

'It is all new to me.'

'That is so irritating.'

'Hey, I have a right to my own beliefs.'

'No one says you haven't. I think Jean put our feelings into perspective nicely. I don't care if you want to stick your head in the sand, but if people are dying to keep you safe, what gives you the right to sit and gob off about it? Most of us have lost friends, so at least try to take that into consideration before you start calling people liars.'

Strange vibrations reached Richard beneath his feet, 'I am sorry about the loss of your friends. Truly I am. I would also like to apologise to the families of those who have died. We are free spirits, and we will not compromise on the truth.'

Charlie shook his head, 'That statement has no meaning to me at all, I don't give a damn what you do. I will accept your apology though, you both seem sincere enough.'

'We are going to make a fresh start in life. Right here, right now.' He reached for Abby's hand, 'There is nothing like this anywhere on Earth.' He looked around. 'There is no company, no government, who could ever reproduce this. I was wrong and freely admit it. From now on Abby and I will dedicate ourselves to the truth. We will only report what we see. We will not speculate, nor make assumptions. I simply did not understand just how far this went beyond myself, our people and our own planet.'

Charlie looked from one to the other, 'Well happy, happy, joy, joy day. Have fun kids, I have a job to do here and need to get going.' With a little wave, he left them alone.

Richard waited until he was out of sight.

'I don't think that guy takes us seriously.'

'How did he become an alien Lord?'

Richard turned to the nearest drone, 'If anyone wants to find out, then give us a like and leave a comment.'

Abby laughed, 'Seriously?'

He shrugged, 'Why the hell not, this is what we do.

Hell, it's all I know how to do these days.' He sat down and picked up a rock, 'This is concrete. I wonder what happened here.'

'No one seems to really care.'

'Someone should.'

'I don't think we are going to be here long enough Richard. It might be kind of dangerous trying to find out.'

'Let's walk along this ridge for a little way. See if we can find anything more than concrete and rebar.'

They hunted the rubble for the next hour. It was Abby that spotted the pale splash of colour. It was the corner of a metal box. Richard pulled it from the rubble; it was a little larger than a shoe box.

'I think it is aluminium. It could be from Earth.'

'It can't be!'

'A box is a box Abby. There are only so many ways of constructing one. The clasps are quite unusual. I am going to take this home with us.'

'Is there anything in it?'

'I don't know.' He fiddled with it for a while and managed to get the clasps open. 'It is sealed quite well.' His head arced back, 'That smells!'

'Bad?'

'Not too bad. Musty cloth smell.'

They began to pull out an assortment of objects. Abby pointed, 'Is that a photograph?'

'It is, but it is made of metal. Oh wow!'

'What is it?'

'Look.'

'A family, they look weird. Oh shit! They have four arms.'

'And they look kinda bug like.'

'They do.'

'I know what this is.'

'What?'

'The one in the middle, look at his chest, look at these.'

It took her a few seconds, 'Are they medals?'

'I think so,' he took out a carefully folded piece of cloth from the bottom of the box.

'What does this look like?'

'A folded flag.'

'Right.'

Abby's hand came to her mouth. 'I see. So this creature must have been a soldier or a policeman. Someone who died in the line of duty. That is very Earth-like isn't it?'

'Help me.' They unfurled it. It had strange patterns and colours on it.

'It is very pretty, and the colours are still good. Let's fold it back up.' They did so carefully. 'Is there anything else?'

'Yes. One thing,' he plucked it out. 'It looks like a knife. A ceremonial one.' He pulled it from the sheath. A silver blade sparkled in the sunlight for the first time in thousands of years. 'It is engraved. It is a thing of beauty. This green handle also has beautiful engraving on it and some strange face-like figure on the end. It seems to be made from some green stone like jade.'

'It is beautiful.'

'This stone feels warm.'

'What are we going to do with it?'

'I'm not leaving it here.' He looked up at the nearest drone, 'This is Richard Liverington, I am sitting on a pile of rubble. From it we have just pulled a box that seems to contain the memories and medals of some military hero, from a race long dead. I am wondering if any museum on Earth would like this. I wonder if you would be interested in other things like this. I don't know.'

Richard ran his fingers through his hair, then gave it a bit of a frustrated scratch.

'I think things have just taken a very peculiar turn Abby. We are here to disprove the government's actions, to show that they were lying and that the Earth is flat. To prove that we have a right to believe what the hell we want. It has gone far beyond that point. They have forced their beliefs on us, taken us from our lives to ram their versions of things down our throats. Alright, we agreed to go.

'What we have uncovered here goes far beyond any of that. We will live with the decisions we made. This is bigger than us. They said that the aliens were going to wipe us out. I never realised that the aliens had already done this before. This is probably the biggest crime ever to have been uncovered in the history of the universe. Look at this place. A whole race, with the technology of our age, wiped out. Not just this planet either, not just this race. If what that Charlie guy said was true, every race on this side of the great barrier has wiped out trillions of innocent souls. What the hell are we doing making an alliance with these creatures?'

He stood and picked up the box, 'I am really going to have to think about this. Let's get back to the ship and see what is happening.'

CHAPTER 22

One of the farmers helped them climb up the stairs and into the ship. The first haulers were slowly approaching. Charlie was talking to two Albany policemen, they were on bended knee, with their heads lowered. They looked up when he pointed to something.

The farmer was shaking his head wistfully, 'Have you ever seen anything like this before?'

Richard realised he was talking to him, 'No, we just joined the crew.'

'Do you know that guy?'

'Nope, just met him the same time you did.'

'Seems to know how to deal with these Albany guys.'

Richard decided to test a theory that was building, 'Did you know this planet once belonged to a race of meat eaters a bit like us?'

'Nope, what happened to them?'

'The Albany wiped them out. They had the same level of technology as we have.'

'So where are they now?'

'Extinct.'

It took a moment to sink in. The expression on his face darkened.

'You're serious?'

'There's a ridge out the back made of rubble from an old civilisation. We found this.' Richard pointed to Charlie, 'He told us they wiped out the previous people. All of them. Domestic animals, pets, bugs, everything. Flattened it then grew grass.'

'Just for grass?'

'Yup, I guess.'

'Then why the hell are we helping them?'

'Hey, I just got here, same as you. This was what they were going to do to Earth.'

'Bastards! Well I ain't helping them no more, that's for sure.'

The Black of Space

He burst past and headed for Charlie. The policemen had just left when the farmer made a grab for Charlie's shoulder. He missed and stumbled. Charlie caught him in a vice-like grip and pushed. The farmer went down and Charlie followed.

'Got something on your mind?'

A chill went through the farmer, he was used to strong men, but no one had ever handled him like a child before.

'Just heard we are helping a bunch of murdering bastards.'

'Have you been hiding under a rock?' Charlie made himself comfortable, 'I presume you are talking about this planet.'

'Sure am.'

'You're a farmer, you know the weak die, and there is sometimes very little you can do about it.'

'This isn't a calf in the middle of winter.'

'Have you ever heard of omnicide?'

'Nope.'

'It refers to the complete destruction of the Human race, either by ourselves or other factors.'

'Like an extinction level event?'

'Aye, exactly like that. These people take it further. They wipe out almost every living thing on a planet. About the only thing they don't kill is the creatures in the sea, because they catch them and use them as fertiliser.'

'Right.'

'It almost happened to us, but we prevailed. We aren't the only race to prevail. Sometimes they have lost and been wiped out themselves. Right now, we are hanging on by our fingertips. Federation status gives us the right to survive. If anyone does mess with us, every other race within the Federation will turn on them and wipe them out completely. Right now, we are doing the right thing. The same thing we did for the German people in 1945.'

'What about the people who lived on this planet?'

'They are gone. It is the same with every other planet

on this side of the barrier that was taken by force. I have seen the destruction wrought first-hand. It is shocking, but if we lose Federation status, it could well be us next. As I said, we are hanging on by our fingertips. Lots of Federation members have been expelled in the past and been totally destroyed. Ignorance is our biggest enemy. We need to do things right. We need to burrow deeper and deeper into the Federation. Make ourselves invaluable, worth something in their eyes. This is a start. What I don't need is some dickhead running around screaming in self-righteous indignation about how the Albany, and all the herbivores on this side of the barrier, shouldn't receive our help because they are the baddies.'

'Still…'

'No, don't go there. The Albany are the only race that have found a way of surviving on our side of the barrier. They have offered up all of that research for total destruction, which will help us considerably. It took them damn near a hundred years to crack that, we need that shit destroyed. That research is probably worth billions, more even, because our whole solar system is completely untapped and richer in mineral wealth than anything the people on this side of the barrier have came across in thousands of years. We need to play it straight and we need to do it right. Am I making myself understood?'

'You are, but it doesn't sit right.'

'This all happened thousands of years ago.'

'Maybe, but they were going to do that to us.'

'You knew that before you came here.'

The farmer relaxed a bit, 'I suppose you are right. It just sort-of hit me, you know.'

'Aye. We have all had that moment. Trust me.'

'Humanity has practiced genocide on itself many times.'

Charlie could only agree, 'Aye, and on a grand scale. Right now, all I need is for you and your guys to get this job done. Make it worth the Albany's time to hand over that damn research.'

The Black of Space

He grasped Charlie's shoulder in a massive hand, 'We will do our bit.'

'It is all I need.'

Ten minutes later Richard found himself sliding up a wall with a pistol rammed up his nose.

'If I catch you spreading dissension among these farmers again while we are here, you will never leave this planet alive. I am being serious. Don't fuck with me Dick, or this operation. Am I making myself understood?'

'Perfectly.'

Charlie dropped him and turned on Abby, 'That goes for you too. Don't turn your twisted little minds to making trouble here. I mean it.'

He walked away and left them alone. Richard flattened himself against the wall.

'Wow, I didn't expect to get caught that fast. We will edit this little incident out.'

'We need to tread very carefully around that guy. Let's just play it straight until we get back to the protection of the ship. Please.'

'You got bad vibes?'

'Very bad.'

'Then we play it straight, like we are normal reporters. We take the footage we made today, turn it into a special.'

'I agree. We will need to change the tone of it a little, so we aren't considered to be too judgemental. Some of these guys are dangerous.'

For the next five hours they went everywhere. Everyone did their bit. When the last of the silage was loaded up, the large haulers were replaced by tankers that took away the silage bree. It was a long day. Richard and Abby spent the last half hour on the mound, filming the activity in the complex. Different aircraft had began to arrive and leave. Smaller haulers were also leaving by road. They had even been able to do some short interviews with some of the Albany policemen.

Finally they were herded to a Federation shuttle. Richard asked if they could wait until the fast freighters had taken off. Charlie discussed it with Jean. She agreed. They got themselves to a safe distance and waited. It was, all agreed, a phenomenal sight. By the time the third had began to take off, a huge dust cloud had enveloped them. A dusty but laughing group boarded the shuttle. Twenty minutes later they were being shown to quarters on board the Sir William Wallace.

CHAPTER 23

Steven was lying down on his couch staring at a blank wall when Komoru found him. He made no effort to sit up, so she simply sat down across his legs.

'I hear the first mission has been a success.'

'So I heard.'

'They are on their way back.'

'So I heard.'

She sighed, 'What is up with you today?'

'Bored.'

'Is that it?'

'Jealous.'

'Of what?'

'Charlie, Cookie, Jeb, Mya.'

'Why?'

'They get all the fun while I am stuck here.'

'You are jealous of them delivering silage?'

'It's something isn't it? A new planet, doing something exciting. Living in the moment. They get all the fun.'

'We have fun too.'

'No we don't. We get politics. I hate politics, it is so damn boring. Everyone lies, no one tells the truth. They run round and round and round the bush squawking puerile rubbish at one another until they choke.'

'Oh, you have it bad.'

'Charlie got to change himself into a Modloch and took part in some secret talks, and was almost found out as a Human.'

'Steven!'

'What?'

'That was a political meeting.'

'Eh?'

'It was all about politics. He spent it standing against a wall.'

'Well, I suppose... but he can still see through walls with his x-ray vision and hear people's thoughts.'

'Yes, and run and jump faster and higher than any Human ever has. Maybe we should all make ourselves into cyborgs.'

'The thought had occurred to me. He has utilised the computer part of his brain in some very interesting ways.'

'Yeah, we could turn our hormones up to a level where we almost explode.'

He lifted his head slightly and glanced round at her, 'That would be interesting.'

'We could actually do that.'

'I suppose.'

'If all of the guys were cyborgs, Himari would stop bugging Charlie.'

'Is that a good thing?'

'Maybe not. She would have so many men to choose from, she might explode!'

'I don't know about explode, but I imagine after a few weeks there wouldn't be much left of her but a soggy puddle.'

'Oh really!'

He shrugged, 'Well you know. He also gets to run around finding really cool stuff.'

'Oh!' Komoru threw herself down on his back and wracked her arms around him. 'Only because everyone tells him to. He doesn't have me. Never will. You always have that.'

'Good point.'

'Saying that he does have a room in a palace, and a residence. Two titles.'

'When we get home next time, do you want to buy our own island and build our own palace on it?'

'I like that idea, but I love my home. Maybe we could buy one on a planet here.'

'That's an idea. I like that better. Which one?'

'We wouldn't be able to buy one on the Modloch home world, but maybe on the planet Charlie lives on, that would be most comfortable.'

'The Modloch Emperor hates the place; I wonder if he would let us buy the whole planet.'

'Even we couldn't afford that. Isn't it also illegal for us to have a planet on this side of the barrier?'

'I don't know if that stretches to a private planet.'

Komoru thought it over, 'What about our own asteroid?'

'No, I want to see the stars at night.'

'Good point, an island on a planet it is,' she smiled.

Steven cocked an eyebrow, 'Are you playing with my man boobs?'

'Mmm.'

'Really?'

'Mmm.'

He sighed, 'A man's work is never done.'

'Mmm.'

CHAPTER 24

Charlie had just received the weirdest request from Steven. He went into his room and dumped his gear. When he came out he almost bumped into Perrina.

She gave a small nod of her head, 'Lord Noch Man Drich.'

'Princess Perrina.'

'I have heard that you are a personal friend of Lord Carrick Marr.'

'I wouldn't go as far as to say that. We shared a few muddy holes in the ground a couple of times.'

'I was just wondering if you knew where he had gone to?'

Charlie felt sorry for the lovelorn young Princess. He smiled.

'I am sorry, I have no idea where he is. I have no doubt that he has re-joined his regiment and is off on his next tour of duty.'

She gasped with exasperation, 'No one knows!'

'Do not set your sights on him, Princess.'

'Why not?' She snapped back.

'Because he is like me. We are not comfortable in polite society. We don't mix well with the kind of people you know. We are old soldiers. We find it hard to form relationships, especially with lovely young ladies like yourself. We are far more comfortable with experienced females who don't want to talk to much. If you know what I mean…'

Her skin tone changed colour a little, 'How do you know until you have tried it?'

'Because we were young once. We were innocent once. We remember the innocent beauties of our youth,' Charlie paused while he sought the right words. 'War is a brutal mistress, and a very jealous one too. Your mind and body become corrupt with the horrors you have seen and experienced. The more you experience, the further we get from those we serve and protect. We also realise that our mistress will one day call us to her bosom. Every battle, every wound, takes us closer to her final embrace. That is where we will all end up one day. So please, find a handsome young Modloch, fall in love, get married and have lots of children, and pray that none of them are ever called to her embrace in the same way that we were.'

Parrina tilted her head to the side as though seeing him for the first time.

'Are you saying that even if I did get him, I probably wouldn't be happy?'

'This palace is full of old warriors. They are like the shadows that surround you. You know they are there, but you never look too deeply into them. They are often alone, unmarried, and only really talk to others like themselves. Have you ever imagined yourself living, loving, one of those?'

She thought it over, she knew the people he was talking about.

'No.'

'You are chasing a shadow Princess. To you he may be the nicest looking Modloch you have ever met, but he is still a shadow.'

She turned away and took a couple of steps.

'Will you walk with me Lord Noch Man Drich? My father is looking for you. I will guide you to him.'

'It would be my honour, Princess.'

'We are family, please call me Parrina.'

'Charlie.'

She smiled up at him, 'It nice to finally meet you Charlie. My father holds you in high regard. Today I have had a glimpse into why.'

'Ach, he just likes me to pour his tea. I am rather good at it.'

She giggled, 'If that is how you wish to look at it, then I will accept that.'

'Where is he?'

'The throne room.'
Charlie frowned, 'That's unusual.'
'He has guests.'
'Right.'

Charlie was in for a big surprise when he reached the throne room.

Parrina bowed before her father, 'I managed to find him, Father.'

'Thank you.'

She turned and left. Charlie was left gawping. Before him stood the Première of the Behema race, Merro Macdoe, and his girlfriend Taylana. His sister Florina was also there with her lady-in-waiting Aurora Malinci.

'Wow! This is a surprise.'

Darrick laughed, 'Then you are acquainted?'

'Oh hell aye,' Charlie stepped forward. Merro met Charlie hallway across the floor and stuck his hand out.

'A pleasure to meet you again Charlie.'

'Aye, and you Merro. I had no idea you were coming.'

'My father and the council sent us.'

'Fact finding mission huh?'

He laughed, 'Of course.'

Charlie looked around, 'This seems quite unofficial.'

'Low key, not unofficial.'

'Alright. I believe I was summoned,' they walked back together.

'What's up Darrick?'

'I want you to look after them while they are here. We have no meat. Can you procure the kind of rations they require and a chef?'

Charlie scratched his head, 'I think we are here for another week. How long are they staying?'

'A month. I could talk to your President, delay your ship's next mission. There is an old kitchen in the left wing. I could house them there; your people could move in to look after them.'

'Sounds reasonable.'

He grinned, 'The Première has also suggested a possible alliance through marriage.'

'You gonna tell Jean or am I?' Charlie sniffed.

The smile slid from his face, 'Ah! I never really thought of that.'

Merro smiled, 'Is she of Royal blood?'

'No,' Charlie admitted.

'Then where is the problem?'

Charlie looked to Darrick, 'Are you going to tell him or am I?'

His grin came back, 'Maybe he should meet her.'

'You have to be shitting me!'

Darrick laughed, 'Maybe that isn't such a good idea.' He turned to Merro. 'Captain Wilson is a legend amongst her people, and the Federation. She is the first female to ever Captain a Federation ship, she was a fighter ace in her own world, a hero, and wears a cannon at her hip that she could hit a pimple on the end of your nose with.' He turned to Charlie, 'That's right isn't it?'

'Pretty much. She holds more trophies for her marksmanship than anyone I have ever met in my life. Add to that the fact that she commands a bloody big battleship, as well as a crew that would give their lives for her, and you have a woman you really don't want to get on the wrong side of.'

Darrick was smiling to himself, 'Still, it would be interesting.'

'You are just an evil shit.'

He roared with laughter, 'I am sure the good Captain is probably sick of the sight of you by now anyway.'

A guard appeared and spoke into the Emperor's ear. Darrick roared with laughter and nodded his ascent to something.

The smile never slipped from his face, 'We are about to find out. It would seem your lady friend has come to spend the night.'

Surprise was evident on Charlie's face, 'Thought she wasn't coming until later.'

Darrick's laughter filled the throne room.

Jean appeared like a Valkyrie ascending to the heavens. Her long blond hair spilled out behind her like a golden veil. She was as stunned by the sight of the Emperor's guests as they were by the sight of her.

She bowed low, 'Your Royal Highness.' She turned to Merro, 'If I am not mistaken,' she bowed again, 'Your Royal Highness.' Then she turned to Florina and gave a smaller bow, 'Your Royal Highness.' Her whole demeanour changed when her eyes latched onto Aurora, 'Oh my God you are so cute. You must be Aurora,' she bent over, 'How would you like to visit my ship. My crew would just love to meet you.'

'You know me?'

'Charlie showed me your pictures. I never expected to meet you in person.'

'You are so beautiful,' was as much as Aurora could think of to say.

Jean smiled, 'Why thank you so much.'

'I would love to see your ship. Are you really a Captain, and a hero?'

She turned and fixated Charlie with a look, 'Have you been telling tales?'

He shook his head, 'Never opened my big gob.' He pointed to Darrick. 'All his own work.'

Her whole demeanour changed again, and she gave another small bow, 'You do me great honour.'

Darrick acknowledged with a small nod. Merro was looking at her closely.

'I don't see the cannon you are infamous for.'

Jean was a little surprised, 'In the case the guard is carrying. We are not allowed to wear weapons within the palace. It is locked.'

'I am curious.'

'It is very like the weapon I carry,' Charlie informed him.

'It is quite different actually. Bring me the case.' Darrick ordered. 'If you would Captain? Make sure it is unloaded and show it to the Première.'

'Yes sir.'

He opened the case and she checked it was unloaded before presenting it to the Première for his inspection, along with the holster and belt.

'It is very heavy. The workmanship is exquisite. May I see the belt?' She handed it over, and he seemed to inspect it in minute detail. 'We also have tooled leather on my home-world, but I would rank this as some of the best I have ever seen. Did you buy this yourself?'

'It was a gift from Charlie.'

'Ah! I see.' He turned around, 'My curiosity is now boundless.'

Charlie looked skywards for a moment. 'She and her crew saved my life after a mission. I was badly incapacitated and days away from the medical attention I needed. The Captain came and sat with me for a short while every day. I was deeply impressed by her sincerity. It was a gift to show my appreciation.'

He looked Jean over, 'Are you sure it wasn't just her beauty you appreciated?'

Charlie opened his mouth to answer, but Jean beat him to it, 'He was struck blind at the time. He couldn't see me. It wasn't about my looks. We became friends. The gift not only honours me, it also honours my crew. The belt has my ship and its name on it. We all love it; I just have the pleasure of wearing it.'

He looked from one to the other, 'This certainly paints both of you in a different light.' He handed the belt back, 'Thank you.'

Darrick waggled a finger and the belt and pistol was returned to its case. He offered it to Charlie who took it from him.

'How long are you in port for Captain?' He asked her.

'About three days I believe.'

'Are you heading back out to the edge of Federation territory?'

'I don't believe the Admiral has received orders yet.'

'Then could you ask the Admiral to avail himself to our guests?'

'I certainly can.'

He turned to Merro, 'Have you ever seen a bee?'

'No, is it big?'

'Not at all.'

CHAPTER 25

Darrick looked over the people gathered in his war room. Earth's Ambassadors were there, along with Charlie, Admiral Valachean and Jean. There were also members of his guard present at the briefing.

'You all know by know that our guests are of the Behema race, and that they represent their great Empire. By order of the great Council of the Federation, you are all tasked with their safety. After a five-month journey, their food stocks have been completely depleted. Ambassador Gordon, that will come under your responsibility. Make sure that they receive the finest food available. Make damn sure that everything you feed them is tested first. If they get so much as a dose of the shits, it will be your head on the line.'

'Yes sir, I understand.'

'Admiral, their protection is your duty. You will have a small fleet. Federation vessels will make up the bulk of it and I will assemble some scouts made up from both my forces and the Humans. They will turn any approaching vessels out of your path. If anyone is stupid enough to refuse, you will destroy them. Understood?'

'Of course sire.'

'Charlie, you are to stick close to the Première at all times. You will provide personal protection.' Charlie nodded.

'Ambassadors. We, the Federation, require you to show these people a wonderful time. We know they are on a fact-finding mission. They may well want to see things that we don't want to show them. They want to meet some of the different races. There is little doubt in my mind that they will want to meet the meat-eating races that have recently joined the Federation. Step lightly Ambassadors.

'Keep them away from the races that have a dislike for meat eaters. You must keep them away from the Evolka, and big foot.' There was a spontaneous outburst of laughter. 'Try and show them nice things, but we cannot hide the history between the Federation and meat-eating races. They aren't stupid, particularly this Première. If he says something derogatory, you will point out the nice things and the progress we have made. Your political senses are diabolical. Both of you. It is a common consensus that as Ambassadors you are both so naive that you are practically useless. It is most likely reason they have asked for you.'

Steven opened his mouth to say something, but Darrick brushed him aside.

'It is this naivety that has led to your success in bringing peace with the Ambatta, the Ortea and of course the Behema. Your sincerity has shone through and won you great accolades. Unfortunately, that isn't what is required at this moment. We need someone who can bullshit the hell out of them and make them believe that if they try it on with us, we will wipe them out. Your greatest asset is now our greatest liability. Do you understand?'

Steven sniffed, 'I hate politics.'

'Why are you still alive?' He held up a hand, 'No don't answer that. You are still alive because of the quality of the people that surround you.'

'I was actually going to agree with you.'

Darrick shook his head. 'See what I mean? Any politician worth his salt would be standing up in self-righteous indignation screaming out his qualities. Please keep your wits about you.'

'I will, we both will.' All could see that Darrick had grave doubts about that.

He growled at Steven, 'They came straight to me because you and members of your crew told them how understanding I was towards the meat-eating races. Because of that the responsibility now falls on me. Do not make me look bad. I have ways of dealing with people who make me look bad, and don't think that because you aren't Modloch you will get away with it.

'I believe that you will all receive more detailed instructions from the Federation council. I am sure they are still thinking them up. Admiral, will you stay behind with your Captain?'

They got up and left. Darrick waved out his guards. Once the room was empty, he indicated a door to his left.

'Admiral, could you wait there until I have a word with the Captain?'

He looked surprised, 'Yes of course.'

'It is a private matter.'

Valachean nodded, 'Of course sire.'

'Captain, if you will,' he indicated a seat next to him.

She made herself comfortable and he waited until the door closed.

'Are you aware of the other reason the Behema are here?'

She shook her head, 'No sir.'

'So he never told you.' He sighed, 'They want me to marry off the pretty little princess to one of my brothers.' Jean felt the hair on the back of her neck stand up. 'You must realise exactly which one I am talking about.'

'You mean Charlie.'

'Of course I mean Charlie. How serious are you about him?'

'I don't see how it is of any business of yours.'

'Of course it is my damn business,' he snapped at her. 'He may be Human, but he is still my brother. He is a member of my family and I am still his Emperor. More to the point he is stuck with that, whether he or you like it or not. Now answer my question.'

'We have never really talked about it.'

'That does not comfort me Captain. You see I am sure you will be tested in the coming weeks. If you cannot fight for him, then my arm may well be forced, and I am damn sure I don't want to lose him. I want him to serve me, my sons, and maybe even my grandsons. He cannot do that if he is married into Royalty on the far side of the bloody galaxy.'

It dawned on Jean what he was after, 'You don't want to lose him.'

'I just said that.'

'I am sorry. This has taken me by surprise. I am not used to people questioning me about my private life, especially someone like you.'

'With you here, I have a good chance of deflecting their advances. They have met you, and they are impressed by you. Without you I lose him but gain new territory in unknown planets.'

'They can't force you.'

'You don't understand the position I am in or the pressure I will be put under if they announce their intention to the Federation council. Is it worth my while resisting?'

Jean took a deep breath, 'I don't know sire. We are a couple. I am not head over heels in love with Charlie, nor he me. However, that is probably more due to our life experiences and expectations than anything else. If I could describe my feelings accurately, I feel comfortable when we are together and when we are apart. I don't fret, nor do I believe does he. We have both been taking it very slowly, and I look forward to our time together. I enjoy it.'

'You know my own daughter wants to marry him.' Jean looked shocked. 'Not as Charlie, but as Lord Carrick Marr.'

She felt immediate relief, 'He was impressive.'

Darrick laughed aloud, 'Thank you for answering that question.'

Jean went bright red, 'I answered nothing.'

Her face colour turned even deeper, and Darrick laughed even harder.

'No need to lie Captain. We are both adults. I will not embarrass you by asking you directly. I simply wondered if you would take the opportunity. You have answered my question to my satisfaction.'

Jean crossed her arms, 'I will forever deny it.'

'You must realise that Charlie has been teaching me body language, but feel free to deny it. It also demonstrates the level of trust you have in him.'

Her colour began to return to normal, 'He can be a little bit of a pain with that. I just wish he wouldn't teach it to everybody.'

'So he hasn't told you about that either?'

'About what?'

'I know his secret, I know he can hear other people's thoughts.' Jean went very still. 'I know that you know, because he informed me that the female Ambassador told you on the Gisha planet.'

'He always thought that you would kill him if you found out.'

'I had to think very hard for an excuse not to. In the end it came down to trust.'

'That is a biggie.'

'A biggie. Yes, I like that. So now you know another reason why I don't want to lose him.'

'Of course, it puts you at an advantage if you know what everyone around you is thinking.'

'That makes him worth a thousand soldiers. It is why you must make sure that the Behema get the message that you two are something special. That you are not to be trifled with.'

'You really don't mind him being able to read your thoughts?'

'It would seem that what goes through my mind is also what comes out of my mouth.'

Jean burst out laughing, 'I can see that.' She nodded. 'I understand. I will endeavour to do my best.'

'Then go collect your Admiral and get back to your ship.'

She stood and saluted. He gave her a small nod.

CHAPTER 26

Aurora's eyes boggled. Jean had taken her into the wardroom, where she had gathered some of the women from the ship's crew. It was their hair, the length and the different colours, that fascinated her most. There was also a variety of skin tones that she found captivating. Jean introduced her around. The women were as interested in her as she was in them.

Jean showed her around the ship, then they ate in the wardroom with the officers. They were very careful with the food and tested everything for her. She wasn't so fond of some of the vegetables but loved the meat and the pudding.

She then sat beside Jean on the bridge as Jean conducted the daily business of the ship. Despite being in port there was plenty to do. In the afternoon, Jean took her on a shuttle to one of the domes, just the two of them.

Aurora sat in the navigator's seat, her eyes gleaming.

'Have you enjoyed your day?'

'It was wonderful. You are a wonderful pilot too.'

Jean smiled, 'I would rather have taken you over on my personal fighter but going anywhere near the Emperor's precious domes in that is a sure way of getting shot down.'

'He is quite handsome, but quite ugly too.'

'You mean the Emperor?'

'Yes.'

'The Modloch do take some getting used to. For us it is their size that took us by surprise. Many of the herbivores are very tall.'

'We are more like you Humans.'

'Only you look like wild cats from our planet. We think you are a very handsome race.'

'You must be considered a beauty amongst your own people.'

'Maybe some consider me so. It has been more of a

hinderance than an asset as far as I am concerned.'

'You mean senior officers currying sexual favours?'

'That is a little forward for such a young person.'

'I am a member of the nobility; I was taught from a young age that sex is a tool that that every noble woman should know how to use to her advantage.'

'That is very different to the way I was brought up, but there are many women on my own planet who think the same way.'

'I imagine you would have said no.'

'I did, and it did hamper my promotion to some extent, especially in the early and later years.'

'You mean you didn't put out.'

Jean laughed, 'Of course I didn't. I would receive little gifts, which I would promptly send to their wives.'

'Oh! So you were not popular then.'

'I most certainly wasn't, but I don't regret it.'

Aurora smiled, 'You didn't return Charlie's gift.'

'No, because his intentions were not romantically inclined.'

'Was he really blind?'

'As a bat.'

'A what?'

'Sorry, a creature from my world. He was only a sergeant at the time. He got up off his sick bed and saluted the wall.'

Aurora laughed, 'That must have been funny.'

'It was, and impressive, he was nearer death than life at the time. What impressed me more was that he knew who I was.'

'So he was an admirer of yours?'

'From afar. He had no amorous intentions.'

'So you pursued him.'

'I suppose I did.'

'I am so jealous.'

'You could join your armed forces.'

Aurora gave her a sideways stare, 'I have no intention

of joining our armed forces. I was talking about Charlie.'

'Oh! I didn't see that coming. Isn't he a bit old for you?'

'Love recognises no boundaries,' she sighed.

Jean thought it was kinda cute, but not for long.

'So, is he good in bed?'

Jean snapped her a disapproving look, 'That is none of your business young lady.'

Aurora watched her reaction closely, 'Ah… you didn't like that.'

'My private life is none of your business.'

'So you do have a weakness. That isn't good. Florina will suck you up and spit you out.'

'Excuse me?'

'Florina, she will exploit that weakness of yours. Has no one told you that her father wants an alliance with the Modloch Empire through marriage with Charlie?'

'I am aware of that.'

'Then you need to be far more careful with your response and tone. Florina will bait you, and if you snap at her, she will consider it a challenge and bring all that she has to bear, to force the Modloch Emperor to consent to it.'

'But why isn't she doing so already?'

'Because she is stuck in a box of her own making. She has declared loudly that she dislikes Charlie intensely and has no wish to marry him. The exact opposite is the truth. The closer we got to here the more nervous she got; the more excited. She tried to hide it, saying it was disgust at what might befall her, but she was latterly trembling with excitement when she realised he was actually here.

'Last night after she met you, she was devastated. She cried for hours. You are a rare beauty, even to our race. Today she was putting on a brave face, saying she was happy that he was taken. What she needs now is an excuse to pursue him. If you make one slip, one bad remark that she can class as offensive, then she will take that as a direct challenge. She can then pursue him with everything she has to try and steal him from you, without losing face. She is a Royal Princess. Her father wishes an alliance with the Modloch.'

'Why!?'

Aurora shook her head, 'Can't you work it out for yourself?'

Jean scowled, 'From what we know, the Federation out gun your Empire by at least three to one. If all the races add their home fleets to Federation forces, that could turn out to be closer to thirty to one. The largest force within the Federation is the Modloch and Human forces combined. An alliance would severely hamper the Federation's ability to field an overwhelming force against your Empire.'

Aurora clapped excitedly, 'That's exactly what they are trying to do. That is why we came to the Modloch home world. A Royal Princess is a very valuable commodity. At this moment in time the Federation isn't in good order. We are aware of the recent wars that have reduced the Federation's ability to field a massive and overwhelming force. They must be wary of us. They really don't know much about us at all, so stabilising the relationship we have at the moment must be high on their priority list. They would not want anything untoward to happen in the short term. An alliance at this moment would help stabilise that relationship.'

'So you are saying that your Empire also requires a stabilising period?'

'Of course it does.'

'So a marriage of convenience would help both.'

Aurora leaned closer to Jean, 'It would not be a marriage of convenience for Florina. She wants him and wants him badly. She would give him her everything and more.'

Jean was getting annoyed again, 'What the hell is it she sees in him?'

'Your composure is slipping again Captain. You must be aware that he is extraordinarily strong.'

'Yes of course.'

'That's a huge turn on for the females of our race. Florina finally met a man that wasn't even slightly in awe of her. She is a holy terror. Does that translate?'

'Yes it does, I understand. He has a really bad attitude when it comes to authority.'

'Yes, but he also has the strength to back it up. Very rare. We need to keep her in her box, trapped by her own words, her own vanity. We can't give her even one excuse.'

'Why am I getting the impression that you are on my side?'

'I am on my own side Captain, no one else's.'

'I am lost now. I don't understand how this helps you.'

Aurora clasped her hands to her breast, 'When I am twenty years old, I will be at the height of my beauty and desirability. I am going to seduce him. I will waylay him with my beauty, I will wear the most provocative nightwear, give my innocence to him, cry with my desire for him,' she squealed and drummed her feet against the decking.

'Wow…' was about as much as Jean could find to say.

Aurora breathed deeply and came out of her fantasy world. She looked directly at Jean.

'It is important for me that you win this battle. If I steal him from you, no one will care. If I try and steal him from Florina, it would cost me my life.'

Jean flushed as she came into the landing pattern, 'You are not quite the innocent young lady I thought you were.'

'I am a noble woman of the blood. You are obviously a commoner. There is little comparison between us. That will be another thing that will annoy Florina. You have to be able to conduct yourself like a Lady.'

'That's not what we would call it.'

'Never mind that, how is he in bed?' Aurora smirked at her.

Jean thought it over, 'Okay I suppose.'

Aurora hid her hand in her face and drummed her feet on the deck plates.

'No, no, no. You are demeaning him now. You cannot demean someone in the Royal line of ascension.'

'He is not.'

Aurora was becoming exasperated, 'Of course he is! He has been declared as one of the Emperor's brothers. Even if he is the last in line, he is still in line to the throne. If some disaster happened and he was the only one left, he would serve as regent until the Emperor's son was of age. If he wiped out his line, then he and his sons would rule. You cannot, must not, demean him in any way. That will get her Royal back right up.'

'Then what the hell am I supposed to say?'

'You have one advantage over her.'

'What?'

'Your sexual experience.'

'I don't think so.'

Aurora skewered her with a look, 'You did not go to Charlie's bed a virgin.'

Jean flushed a little, 'No, of course not.'

'Then you have sexual experience. Something she does not have. Even I get flustered and embarrassed when some of the older women talk about sex.'

'Ah! I see where you are coming from.'

Aurora sighed heavily, 'You are going to be hard work.'

They came into land. She had one last thing to say to Jean.

'Remember that we have to keep her shut up in that little box she has made for herself. You have to come across as wonderfully suited to one another, so in love that you make him happier than any other woman out there could.'

'So that in four years from now you can seduce him and steal him from me.'

'Yes, exactly.'

Jean was still shaking her head as they alighted from the shuttle. A Royal Modloch guard was in attendance. He waved them over and another guided them through.

CHAPTER 27

Jean had never been in any of the domes before, she was as stunned as Aurora by the beauty.

She took a deep breath, 'Oh, it smells like home.'

A large group was sitting in the pavilion. Aurora and Jean were escorted over to meet them. The more they saw, the more they were astounded. The trees beyond weren't set out in lines, or a pattern. Instead there were meadows of wildflowers, with patches of green for picnics, winding paths and streams of clear water. Jean noticed Florina's eyes fix on her. Charlie was standing looking out over the meadow with his arms folded. She walked over and pulled his arm down, slipping her hand into his. Surprise showed on his face.

'Just run with it,' she thought as loudly as she could. He smiled and nodded.

'It is beautiful.'

Charlie nodded, 'It is something else.'

A bee flew towards her then seemed to bounce off something.

'What was that?'

'A sonic field of some kind. It protects the paths, pavilions and picnic areas.'

Merro smiled at Aurora, 'Did you have a good time?'

'Wonderful. The food was good for a military vessel.'

'Are you full? Try one of these pancakes.'

She wrinkled her nose but tried a small bite. Her eyes suddenly shone.

'Oh that is wonderful.'

'Isn't it? Walnut pancakes with honey. The ingredients were all grown here. This came from the Human's home planet. A gift to the Modloch Emperor.'

She looked around, 'The planet Earth must be extremely wealthy.'

A gardener approached with a basket. Darrick took it

from him.

'You came just before the harvest. They are ready. Charlie, leave your woman alone, come and crack some nuts for us.'

Charlie dropped her hand, 'So am I the Royal nutcracker now?'

'Of course. They neglected to give us some nut crackers.'

'Typical.'

Charlie delved into the bowl and cracked open a dozen with his hands. He laid them on the table. Merro delved into the basket and tried to crack one in his hands. The look of surprise on his face made Darrick laugh.

'Leave it to Charlie.'

He handed it up and Charlie cracked it and handed it back. Merro stared at it for a moment before trying it.

'It has a very subtle flavour.'

'They can produce a wonderful oil, but what we are after is the protein. It's highly concentrated and digestible by my people.'

'I have heard you make biscuits.'

'I am sure you are aware that most races here eat grass and hay. It takes a lot to feed us all. One biscuit can provide the same protein and energy as a bale of hay; actually, that isn't quite right, they provide more.'

'Is there a disadvantage to them?'

'They aren't filling. My race has three stomachs.'

Merro laughed, 'I hear you use those biscuits for your soldiers. I bet they aren't very happy.'

'They love the taste and hate the emptiness. However, they give me a tactical advantage over many other races.'

'Of course, your biggest tactical weakness must be the large amounts of hay you have to transport.'

'I am sure you also have races in your Empire with the same tactical weakness.'

'We have, that is why it is so obvious. Do you store these biscuits on your ships?'

'A six week supply one each.'

'So you can send out a fleet immediately at top speed without having to wait for your freighters.'

'You know your stuff Merro.'

'We have to, don't we? How did you come up with this idea?'

'It was Charlie really.'

'No it wasn't. This is all your doing. I just introduced you to a few breakfast cereal bars. You got the idea to make biscuits with them.'

'Only after you told me how you Humans often carry your own food into battle, up to five days of rations at a time.'

'That's nothing, common knowledge. All this was your idea and it was Stevie who made all this possible. He built them and even stole the engines to have them transported here.'

Steven smiled, 'It was your idea to steal the engines.'

Charlie had forgotten about that. He rolled his eyes, 'So, I get the blame for everything around here. That's it, isn't it?'

They all laughed.

Merro raised his hands, 'It is still a wonderful idea and concept. Moreover, the implementation of that idea is wonderful.'

Darrick was pleased with the praise, 'This is my show piece. The others are more straight-forward orchards. This is my little piece of the planet Earth.'

'Is this stone also from Earth? I can't help but notice the beauty of it.'

'No, the stone is from the Ortea home-world. They were the first non-Human meat eaters to be brought into the Federation. The stone is their greatest export, it's very popular now in many Royal households.' Darrick smirked, 'It was Charlie's idea.'

'For God's sake!' He grabbed Jean's hand, 'Let's go for a walk and let the kids blether.'

Their laughter followed them down the path for a short while.

Jean took a deep breath, 'Thank goodness.'

'It will be short lived; I need to get back there.'

'Do we have to?'

'No, we don't, I do. I want you to go back to your ship.'

'Why?'

'Because my mind is wide open, and all I can hear is your mind screaming, "I don't want to do this, I can't deal with this shit. Why am I getting dragged into this shit?"'

She tried to pull her hand away but he held on, 'Just try and relax, switch off. The reason I am listening is because Darrick has ordered me to. He wants as much information as he can on these people.'

She relaxed a little, 'Am I really shouting that loud?'

He smiled, 'You are. I realise you are having a hard time dealing with this, I can't blame you, but try and stay strong until these people have left. The last thing I want is to end up halfway across the universe hitched to a chick who is furry from head to toe.'

Jean suddenly burst out laughing, 'I can see why you wouldn't like that.'

'It is also because all of my friends and family are here.'

She squeezed his hand, 'Yes, I am sorry.'

'You won't have to deal with it after they have departed, not if you don't want to.'

She flushed, 'I didn't expect this.'

'It wasn't a part of the deal, was it?'

'No I don't suppose it was.' She stopped and took his other hand, 'I promise I won't abandon you in your time of need.' She shrugged, 'I don't know about what comes after.'

'What will be, will be, but thanks for your support.'

'I will put on my feminine armour and sharpen my swords.'

'Awesome.'

'I will get back to my ship.'
'I will walk you back.'

On the way past, she waved to Aurora. Charlie passed her to one of the guards and returned to his vigil.

CHAPTER 28

Steven was winding up the meeting, 'Our first port of call will be the Ortea home-world, then they want to visit the Ambatta. Obviously they want to see how the Federation is treating its newest citizens. Their first few days will be taken up with the Modloch Emperor. He is going to give them a guided tour of his home planet, then the city ship. They will be staying one evening at Mya's home, the mountain one, then moving on to the world Charlie lives on. They will stay at the Chief Engineer's mansion. There isn't too much of a difference between their world's gravities, so they should be all right. Cookie, you have their itinerary?'

'Aye. We are directly responsible for their food while they are on the Modloch home-world and the city ship. However, when they are going up to the mountains, they will be responsible for their own food. We are only supplying the ingredients. It will be a weekend off for them. When they are at Charlie's we will be trying lots of different vegetables and greens on them. As for the Ortea and Ambatta home-worlds, they are going to take responsibility for feeding them. The rest is Buzz's domain.'

Steven turned to Buzz, 'How is that going?'

'Right now their ship is on fresh rations. Tomorrow I am meeting the Captain and we are going to go through the army ration packs. We will give them enough fresh meat for about half of their journey. Most will be frozen. What we are looking for is freeze-dried or tinned goods that they can eat for the second half of their journey home.'

'That's good. Colonel Howe, how are your preparations coming?'

'Very well for their visit to our President on the city ship. I have liaised with his staff. They are going to have a two-hour informal meeting with a small buffet and various teas from Earth. As they are not part of the Federation, we can trade directly with them, and they us. The President is hoping to lay the groundwork for future relations. The President has his own staff for their protection. He also has a couple of scientists with him so they can swap periodic tables and such things, working out what we might have that they need, and vice versa. The Modloch Emperor is supplying an escort, so Beaver and a couple of our guys will be providing an escort for yourself and Komoru.'

'Thank you.' Steven looked over his notes, 'That's it from me, anything else?' There was nothing, 'Alright, let's all get some rest. It has been a long day.'

The meeting broke up. On the way to his quarters, he discovered Charlie on watch with the girls. They had all kicked back and were listening to soothing music while watching a replay of something.

Charlie made to get up when he noticed him, but Steven put a hand on his shoulder.

'Don't move, I'll sit next to you.' He took Buzz's chair and kicked back. 'What are we watching?'

'Footage from the other side.'

'Ah! When we were orbiting the Behema home world.'

'Aye, you recognise it.'

Steven pointed, 'I want to go visit that star cluster.'

'You're not the only one. Every lady here is howling to get there too.'

'Glad you're back onboard.'

'I'm just glad I have somewhere to hide and an excuse to get away.'

'Bad is it?'

'Bedlam. Not to worry though. From here on in it is my job to fade into the background and yours to step forward and guide our noble guests on their quest for information about the naughty Federation.'

'Do you think that's what it is all about?'

'What else is it ever all about? Power and greed.

Regardless of how it all goes, or how hard we all work to make things seem rosy, if their intentions are bad, they will glean what they will from this visit.'

Steven thought it over, 'I get you. Any advice?'

'No.'

'Ouch!'

'Sorry, getting pissed off with being blamed for everything.'

'Even if it's good?'

'I am just a very small part of the cog Stevie. There's too much song and dance made about the things I have done. You tell me to help people out. I find something, I pass it on. I'm just doing my job. There's no need for praise, I am not going above and beyond the call.'

'Everything all right between you and Jean?'

'Nope.'

'Problems?'

'Yup.'

'Want to talk about it?'

'Nope.'

'Did you know my guard arrives tomorrow? Your buddies will be back.'

'Sounds like fun. Now shut up and kick back.'

With a grin Steven obeyed. The music began to seep into his soul. His mind began to wander amongst the stars. A few minutes later he was fast asleep.

CHAPTER 29

Richard and Abby couldn't believe their eyes. The trip underground had been quite tedious. They had been ordered to put away their drones and switch them off for the journey. Now they had arrived at the city, they received permission to release them. The whole city was blue, a light blue that shimmered across the underground sea.

Richard guided the drones to focus on Abby as tears streamed down her face.

'Richard, this place is beautiful,' she wiped away a tear. 'I want to get married here.'

He was momentarily stunned, 'Really?'

She nodded vigorously, 'You asked me weeks ago and I said yes. This is where I want to be married. It is incredible.'

'I wonder if they have churches.'

Abby laughed, 'I doubt it, but they will no doubt have somewhere for a ceremony. Instead of returning to Earth when we get leave, I want to return here.'

Richard nodded, 'It looks like we aren't the only ones to be taken by surprise.'

The looks on the faces of the Behema were novel. Richard turned to the camera.

'Ladies and gentlemen of Earth. We are standing on a platform overlooking the most beautiful city I have ever seen in my life. The story of the Ortea surviving persecution is barely known at home. When I first heard the story, I doubted its authenticity. I imagined a race dwelling in caves, this is anything but a cave. This is a large domed underground city with its own sea. I can't wait to get down to street level. What do you think Abby?'

Abby laughed and wiped away a tear, 'I am crying again. It is overwhelming. I was very frightened when I saw my first Ortea. They looked a bit like what I imagined a werewolf would look like. Now I see their cities, their homes, I will never be frightened again. How could anyone be frightened of a people that created such wonders? I feel shame towards those races that began the two-thousand-year war. A war it took we Humans to put an end to, thanks to the endeavours of our two Goodwill Ambassadors. My admiration for them has just increased tenfold.'

Steven was surveying the scene with a smile on his face, 'I never tire of this view.'

Merro regained his wits, and his mouth closed, 'I have never seen anything like it.'

'Few have.'

'Why?'

Darrick barked a laugh, 'Because everyone is shit scared of the Ortea. It wasn't all that long ago that the curious used to end up on their dinner plate.'

'I was told that you were the first Emperor to visit?'

Darrick nodded, 'My race has never really had much of a problem with meat eaters. The Ortea found our people to be unpalatable. They kept any they caught and gave them jobs. In fact some of my people, the moment they were released from captivity, returned home, collected their families and returned to their life here.'

'Your race is an astoundingly courageous one. What about the other meat-eating race we are going to visit? Have you been to their planet?'

'Of course. We have never had any problems with the Ambatta either. My father actually had a secret alliance with them. Their situation was totally different to the Ortea though.'

Merro turned to their guide, 'Commander Oralia?'

'Please just call me Morval sir. My rank is now only honorary. We have long since abandoned what you would call a civilian title. We simply just don't know what to call the official guide.'

Merro laughed, 'It is so ingrained into your people now.'

The Black of Space

'Every member of my race was a member of our armed forces with a role to play. There were no civilians as there are now.'

'What do you think of the peace?'

'That is not my place to say. However, I will tell you that my wife and I have just had our second litter of kids. That was previously unheard of.' The smile on his face was evident. He looked around, 'Excuse me a moment.'

They watched Morval walk over to where Charlie and the Chief were standing. He had obviously passed on the news by the way they laughed and back-slapped him.

'They are acquainted?'

Darrick nodded, 'Thick as thieves. I have no doubt that three will be roaring drunk later on tonight. I first sent the pair of them here on a mission.'

'Who is the Modloch?'

'My Chief Engineer. The only Modloch to ever survive a trip to Earth.'

'I thought there were laws concerning that?'

'He survived where all of his crew mates had perished. I felt he deserved the chance to live. He became the first Ambassador to Earth. On that mission Charlie saved his life when he fell down a hole. When he returned across the barrier, he did come down with the plague that had all races banned from crossing back over. It was the Humans who treated him initially. They had him in an isolation chamber, so there was no danger to anyone else; they are immune to it. He survived and we collected a lot of data on the disease that struck him down. I eventually made him a Lord. He hates it as much as Charlie does, but those two have done more for the Modloch Empire than all of the rest of my Lords put together.'

'You made an Engineer a Lord? Well, I suppose he was an Ambassador. Do you keep them apart from your other Lords?'

'Of course I do. They would eat them alive, or Charlie would end up killing all of them. He has a great intolerance for fools and liars.'

'I have had a demonstration of his strength. It is quite frightening.'

Their attention was diverted to the approach of an Ortea. White hair cascaded behind her as she walked. She was obviously a female, but very different to any other they had met so far.

'Who is that?'

Darrick grunted, 'General Barum Lee, or at least that is who she was. She is in charge of off world accounts. No doubt after Charlie.' They watched her walk straight up to him. Charlie took a step back and offered his hand. She seemed to reluctantly take it.

Merro was shaking his head, 'Does he have that effect on all females?'

Darrick laughed, 'Mostly those not of his own race.'

Merro burst out laughing, 'Are all Ortea females that good looking?'

'No, most have very short fur like Morval. She is descended from the surface dwelling Ortea.'

'That makes sense, more fur to protect them from the sun. It is quite harsh. I am impressed by your knowledge of these people.'

'I have been here a few times. I have even taken my wife and children here.'

'Wonderful idea. But I don't think the other members of my family would like the five-month journey.'

'Didn't they put you in stasis?'

'Yes of course, but you know Royalty, most have an abhorrent fear of it. I feel I am too far down the line to warrant assassination.'

Morval noticed them watching and obviously felt guilty. He marched back over.

'Please excuse my absence. Would you like to go down to the city now? I would suggest the airway.'

'Lead on,' Merro smiled.

They split into groups and travelled down to the city. All were mesmerised by the sight. At the bottom waited an official welcome. A small ceremony was held.

When it was over, Merro leaned into Darrick, 'They aren't very good at this, are they?'

'The Ambatta are worse.'

'Seriously?'

'Easily.'

Merro laughed, 'It is quite entertaining. How were you greeted by the Ambatta?'

'A cup of very old, very bad tea, and a small bowl of hay. It was just as bad as the tea.'

Merro laughed but kept it restrained in case their hosts thought they were laughing at them.

That night they rested, but the following day they set off early. As Darrick had predicted, the three friends looked a little the worse for wear. General Barum Lee put in another appearance but was side-tracked by the females in the party. They were fascinated by her. At some stage in the day, the Chief disappeared. An official had requested his aid. He re-joined the party just shy of the end of the day's tour, looking quite dirty and embarrassed. The moment the guards were changed for the Royal parties, he and Charlie disappeared. That night there was a special surprise for the Royals.

The lion brothers roared their challenge into the night, and it electrified the audience. All of the animals were restless. The keepers put it down to there being a high percentage of meat eaters in the audience. The tiger leapt right up in front of Merro, his tail swishing angrily as his keeper pulled him away.

Merro was breathless, 'My God he was magnificent.'

'I think he wanted to eat you,' Darrick grumped.

'He was challenging me, getting my scent. We are descended from animals similar to these. What wonderful creatures. The lions too.'

'Have you any like that on your home-world?'

'No, nothing like that at all.'

Even Jambo was a bit skittery surrounded by the scent of so many strange meat eaters. He trumpeted his warning. The audience was spell bound.

Merro felt a tear at the corner of his eye, 'My appraisal of the Human race has just gone up. Now I understand why they fight so hard.'

'I have seen these creatures half a dozen times now, but it never fails to entertain me. The Humans are a very unusual race. Some of my favourites come next.'

The horses were ridden into the arena. They had notched up the entertainment factor. They had dressage, and cowboys. Last came the Clydesdale and the Shetland pony.

'My brother rode one of those before he passed away. I have a fondness for that footage.'

'How did he die?'

'He was on Earth. A guest of the Humans. He is still there. I will tell you about it later if you wish.'

'I think I would like to hear that story.'

Lastly came the domestic cats. An old friend quickly found Darrick. After undergoing the normal painful trial, it settled down for a nap. Darrick sighed with relief and petted it.

'An old friend perhaps?'

'Every time he finds me. I have offered to buy him so many times, but they won't part with him.'

There was a squeal from the females. Taylana held up a kitten.

'Oh Merro, can we take it home?'

'Good luck with that,' grunted Darrick.

'I will ask my dear.'

'She is so beautiful.'

The kitten seemed to find her as attractive. Merro had

rarely seen her so moved by any creature.

He sighed, 'Are you sure they won't part with them?'

'You are a meat eater; you might have a better chance than me. One of the reasons they won't sell them to us is our laws on the transportation of meat.'

'I think I understand. It must have been difficult changing those laws.'

'Federation legislation often binds us with chains of our own making, with no regard to the future.'

Merro smiled, 'Is the show over? What next?'

'How big are your balls?'

'Excuse me?'

'If you want, we can go pet them.'

'Ah! I find myself strangely humbled by the thought.'

Darrick smirked to himself.

CHAPTER 30

Darrick eyed the two in front of him. They were both filthy. According to his time piece, the sun would just be rising at home. He had woken an hour earlier, showered and breakfasted on a large bowl of muesli. A report of this pair's return had prompted him to grab them.

His eyes settled on Charlie first, 'I thought you were told to stay close to the Première. What have you been doing?'

Charlie made strange noises through his nose, which he eventually wiped on his dirty arm.

'Stuff.'

He sighed and latched his eyes onto the Chief, 'You tell me.'

'The Ortea uncovered a very large digging machine, one that had been abandoned in a collapsed tunnel. They required help to figure out how to get it working again. It must be over two thousand years old. Remarkable piece of machinery.'

'I see, and you needed him for a little muscle.'

The Chief rolled his eyes towards Charlie, 'Yes, he also made a recording of the schematics of the machine that we can download later.'

'Yeah!' Charlie snorted, 'Stuff.'

Darrick tapped the table with his fingertips. He was aware of just how more advanced the Ortea were at one time.

'Get out and stick to your normal duties. Next time you get a request from the Ortea, ask me first.'

They both nodded and left.

'Why is it every time we get together Charlie, I get into trouble?'

Charlie looked up, 'You dragged me into it.'

'I was just starting to enjoy myself,' he ignored the accusation.

'Emperors; bloody kill joys.'

'Yeah, they sure are.'

They almost walked right into Princess Florina as she walked out the door. She squealed in fright before quickly recovering her composure. She looked them up and down in disgust.

'What have you two been doing?'

Charlie snorted. 'Stuff!' They replied in unison and walked around her. At the end of the corridor they burst out laughing.

Ten minutes later Charlie was on board the ship. He was starving so only washed his hands before going for breakfast.

'Hey Murison, you're supposed to have a bloody wash first.'

He flashed his hands, 'Piss off!' A minute later he sat down with Eddie, his plate piled high with bacon, sausage and egg.

'What the hell have you been up to?'

'Civi stuff.'

'Jeez. You in a mood?'

'Nah!'

'Something's bothering you.'

'No the place for it.'

'Right. So what have you been doing?'

Charlie sighed, 'Digging out an excavator and getting it working.'

'Manage?'

'Aye, we got there in the end. Way over my paygrade though.'

'Been the Chief's idea was it?'

'Aye. They asked him for help.'

'I'll bet he jumped at the chance. Get bollocked by anybody for it yet?'

'Darrick.'

'You gonna join back up and give us a hand?'

'Nope. You're a big laddie now. Did you get some time at home?'

'Aye, a couple of months training sprogs.'

'Get laid?'

'Heaps of times. You still banging her with the big tits?'

'Aye, but maybe no for long.'

'She getting itchy feet?'

'Later.'

'Right.'

Charlie cast a professional eye over him. Eddie was half dressed in ceremonials.

'You got a parade on today?'

'Aye, a wee one.'

'Is everybody back?'

'Aye they are.'

'Who were you teaching?'

'Wooden tops.'

'Guards eh! Won't just have been sprogs then.'

'Everyone is a sprog to me.'

Buzz pushed his plate onto the table and sat down, 'What the hell are you guys talking about? What is a sprog?'

'New guy, a greenhorn,' Eddie explained.

He grinned at Charlie, 'You been pulling an all-nighter?'

'Aye, was with the Chief, we got a wee bit carried away.'

'Helping the Ortea?'

'Some underground drill; thousands of years old. Still in good nick. Some parts were crushed and had to be replaced, they couldn't get it working.'

'Did you?'

'Aye, the Chief and a few Dent engineers went at it. We got it working. The thing is brutal, the Chief says he has never seen anything as efficient. Saying that, it isn't his field of expertise. It spits out those damn blocks like there is no tomorrow. We ran it for almost an hour and had thousands of them piled up. Almost walled ourselves in.

They now have to work out how to move them away.'

'They have lost all of that knowledge?'

'All of it.'

Eddie grabbed Charlie's mug and went for more coffee.

'How are you Charlie? You seem a bit off.'

'I want to go home to Scotland, visit my parents, my family. Eat my mum's soup and macaroni cheese. Get soaked in the rain or snowed in for a week. I'm fed up of all the shit that's flying around me.'

'You haven't been home for a long time have you?'

'A very long time Buzz.'

When they had finished their meal, Buzz went to see Stevie.

'I think your bud has a problem,' Buzz started.

'You mean Charlie?'

'Sure do.'

'I know. He is in a bit of a pickle right now.'

'What's happening?'

'You know about him and Komoru? The reason behind all…'

'Yup, sure do.'

'Get this, Charlie managed to change himself into the form of a Modloch and followed the Emperor to a big meeting of the council. They claimed he was of Royal blood to get him into the meeting. Thing was, they tested his DNA secretly, and of course discovered he really was of Royal blood.'

'Because of his kid?'

'Spot on Buzz. It was checked against a data bank of Royal bloodlines, not individual races or species.'

'Right.'

'He was exposed to some of the other Royals before he left. Guess what? The Emperor's daughter falls head over heels in love, wants to marry him. He had the Gisha Queen on his back at the meeting too. She saw right through the disguise in an instant, thrust his kid right into his arms, offered him a kingdom. To her, the prospect of being married to a Modloch is far more attractive than being married to a Human. Of course now that Behema Première wants to strike an alliance through marriage with the Modloch Emperor, who only has one brother who is compatible.'

'Oh God, Charlie!'

'You got it. Thrown into the middle of all this is the good Captain Wilson. Charlie really likes her, she likes him. Now she is being forced to up her game as it were, because the Modloch Emperor doesn't want to lose Charlie. She doesn't like being thrust into the limelight, and Charlie thinks she is going to dump him after this is all over. Charlie also found out that the Princess's maid is scheming for Jean to win, but only so she can steal Charlie off her in a few year's time.'

'Eh?'

'Women think Buzz, she can't steal him off her own Princess, but she can steal him off Jean without causing a scandal at home.'

'No wonder the poor guy wants to go home. But he can't do that either.'

'Nope.'

'What are we gonna do?'

'I have no idea Buzz. I am well out of my depth. Right now, the Modloch Emperor is successfully deflecting attempts at a union. They don't really seem to be trying all that hard either. The thing is that the Princess is deeply in love with Charlie but is denying it. If she suddenly decides she ain't leaving here without him, the balance will tip. It will be harder for the Emperor to say no if the Behema petition members of the council for help.'

'Why would they?'

'The Federation and Empire are scared shitless of one another. Right now, each side is measuring up the other. Each will be wanting to build up their forces just in case.

Neither are ready. It's a cold war scenario. An official alliance would be a great start for both sides. Better for the Empire, because an alliance could keep the Modloch out of any future war. The Federation, however, want time. The war with the Albany has seriously affected what forces the Federation can throw into a conflict right now. So much of their resources are being taken up policing that situation, they are on the backfoot.'

'Wow! Who thought so much shit could be stirred up by just one guy.'

'I think Charlie is just as bewildered. All we can do is be there for him Buzz.'

'Try and deflect some of the shit?'

'I am out of my depth in that department.'

'Well, it's nice to know what is going on behind the scenes. Thanks bud.'

'Any time.'

CHAPTER 31

Komoru had never seen this particular city before, the stones seemed to radiate a rainbow of colours. She inspected one of the walls in the main square.

Florina came to her side, 'Beautiful, isn't it?'

'Spectacular. I wonder how it would look in daylight.'

'Probably even nicer.'

Komoru looked around, 'Charlie!'

He came over, 'Aye?'

'Do they have stocks of this stone?'

'Ask the Afghan chick. She will know.'

Komoru slapped his arm, 'Don't say that.'

'Why no? It isna like she would know what the hell we are talking about anyway.'

'She might well find out.'

Charlie shrugged and walked off. Komoru sighed, 'That man is impossible.'

'What is an Afghan?'

Komoru shook her head, 'It isn't important.'

'Please. I have the feeling he was being bad. I want to know how bad.'

'He was,' Komoru pulled out her tablet. It didn't take her long. She showed Florina some pictures of an Afghan hound. Her hands flew to her mouth.

'What is that thing?'

'It is a dog, I have never been particularly fond of dogs or pets.'

'Please pinch me Komoru.'

'Why?'

'I want to laugh so hard.'

'Florina!'

'I am so sorry. It is just so…' she made a face.

'That would be lowering ourselves to Charlie's level of black and horrid humour. Please don't.'

'I am sorry, it just caught me by surprise.' Their eyes followed his back for a minute. 'You don't like him, do you?'

'No.'

'Why not?'

'Do you have a spare day?'

'Honestly?'

'We are just too different. We are from an entirely different culture. Mine is steeped in formality, respect, politeness. Charlie simply has none of those virtues. Some of his people are very nice. Wonderful in fact. Charlie, however, is the extreme opposite.'

'He seems to have very little respect for anyone. He referred to my brother by his first name on their very first meeting. Simply unheard of.'

'Yet he accepted that?'

'He did. I think part of my brother would have liked him to be lying about his connections and status in life. He would have killed him if he had been.'

'Then your brother would be dead and our people at war. Charlie can take retribution to a whole different level.'

'You hate him!'

'I did, but not now. I don't like him, but I respect him.'

'I get the feeling that respect was hard won.'

Komoru sighed, 'So hard. We have come to some sort of impasse. We have learned to respect each other, to partly understand each other and what the other is capable of, what they are prepared to do. There will never be any form of friendship though.'

'Steven is friends with him.'

'They shared a childhood together. Until they reached school age that is. Steven's brilliance soon separated them.'

'I didn't realise that.'

'His parents took him to a different country where he could receive the very best education. By the age of fourteen, Steven was almost finished his doctorate. Charlie was struggling in a normal school.'

'Is that good?'

'Sorry! Most don't receive their doctorate until they are

in their late twenties, or thirties.'

'I see. So Steven was brilliant. What about you?'

'I received my doctorate when I was sixteen.'

'Ah! I see, a meeting of minds.'

Komoru smiled, 'I fell in love with Steven long before I met him. I fell in love with his work, his theories. His thinking was so clear and sharp, his insights wonderous.'

'Ah!'

Komoru suddenly saw she was on the point of losing her. 'What about you, is there no dashing handsome guards officer waiting for you?'

Florina was pulled back into the conversation. She laughed aloud.

'Oh there was one. He was dashing, handsome, all the young ladies were in love with him. As a Princess, I thought I was in with a much better chance than the rest. We were all wrong.'

'How so?'

'He was in love with another guards officer.'

Komoru frowned, 'I don't remember seeing any female guards officers.'

'That's because there aren't any.'

The penny dropped, 'Oh!'

'Do you have that particular peculiarity on Earth?'

'We do. It is quite a big thing.'

'You mean people are open about it?'

'Yes, and there are laws to protect them from persecution.'

'We have the same. We were all heartbroken of course. They were both dismissed from the Royal guard though. They may have civil rights, but no Royal ones.'

'What are they doing now?'

'Who cares.'

'Good point.'

Another figure arrived on the scene and went straight to Charlie. They touched hands and he led her away out of earshot of everyone else. Their eyes followed. Florina smiled at the look on Komoru's face.

'You don't seem to like Captain Wilson either.'
'We have exchanged words in the past.'
'Over Charlie?'
Komoru sighed loudly, 'Am I so easy to read?'
'You are an open book.'
'The fault rests with myself. She did nothing wrong, however my dislike of the man made me say things that were not appropriate.'
'You alienated her.'
'Very much so.'
'Do you care?'
'Not really. I am, however, ashamed of myself for stooping so low.'
'Are those things real?'
'I do believe so.'
'How unnatural.'
'Isn't it?'
They both began to giggle then laugh.

Steven looked over at the giggling women. He could tell by the tone that they were laughing at something or someone.

Merro also noticed, 'They seem to be getting on well.'
'At someone else's expense, judging by that laugh.'

He looked round for Taylana. She was engaged with the Ortea General. They were no doubt in deep discussion over fashion. The Ortea had very little in the way of it, and Taylana had been dropped right into the middle of the drought. She had barely ceased talking about it. Merro was still trying to get a handle on Humanity.

'Your people seem to have many races Steven.'
'We do. Our planet is seventy per cent water, and there are many continents and islands. It has created a great diversity within our own species.'
'Our planet is very similar. We seem to have far more

in common with your people than most. What I don't understand is the lack of continuity, politically speaking, amongst your people.'

'We have many different nations, different languages, and different leaders.'

'Ah! Then your society is fragmented into many different factions.'

'Pretty much. They are trying hard to grasp the concept of one world, one voice.'

'It never works. I have seen other societies like yours. It eventually culminates in a huge tangled mess that ends in war. Some species have even killed themselves off, or got to a point where some other power has come in and taken over. Normally at the cost of the eradication of the native species.'

'What about yours?'

'One voice, one leader. An ancestor of mine began the conquest of our world in the time of sailing ships. By the time we had steam power, the world was ours.'

'No rebellions?'

'Many, but we crushed them. We married into our family the females of the former leaders, killed all of the males. There are some great stories and dramas about those times. When we discovered we weren't alone in space, attitudes changed. There is no longer any discord, and all are treated equally. We have a system of succession that we accept.'

'Which means you cannot have children.'

'You can never say never, Steven. If the heir apparent isn't deemed a suitable successor by the Emperor, things can change. It has happened. I think the Ortea also have many different races.'

'More than one anyway.'

'It is quite unusual for a race to live above and below ground like this, but the end result is startling. There are few places you could build like this on my planet. We have tectonic plates that shift a lot.'

'Ours too.'

'I am looking forward to the tour of the surface. I wish to see with my own eyes the devastation caused by the herbivores.'

'I hope you aren't conspiring against us?' They hadn't noticed Darrick moving up behind them.

Merro smiled, 'Of course not. I just want to get an idea of what would have happened to my own world if we had lost.'

'Survival of the fittest Merro. You should know that.'

'I am well aware of that.'

'Now where the hell has Charlie gone?'

'I saw him with Jean a few minutes ago, over that way.'

Darrick scowled, 'He had better be behaving.'

A few seconds later a group of Ortea rushed off. Darrick turned to Gord, who was listening in on a device. 'What is happening?'

'Charlie has spotted a group of people in a building a few streets away. They are going to check it out. He is directing them.'

Darrick grunted in satisfaction, 'At least he is doing his job.'

The stir caused a little consternation amongst the dignitaries. Morval eventually found them.

'I am sorry about this.'

Darrick wasn't happy, 'I thought no one was supposed to be here.'

'It is a group of teenagers. Their family was originally from this city before it was evacuated. They still have the address. They were looking for their old family home. They have been camping out here for a week, long before we declared the city as off limits for the day.'

Darrick grunted, 'Well, you can't help the young being curious. I hope no harm comes to them.'

'No of course not, they are just young and now very frightened.'

'Quite an adventure for them.'

Morval smiled, 'I suppose it is. This city was evacuated a thousand years ago. It was too close to the surface and had been detected. Part of it was destroyed too. We have spent months clearing up the debris and fixing the vaulted ceiling. Within the next few months, it will be habitable again. We are making progress.'

'The rock here is truly beautiful, do you have any stockpiled?'

'We will have yes, but we have no idea where it is yet.'

'I want to know when you find it.'

'Of course.'

A few hours later, after a light lunch, they found themselves in a totally different setting. Dust blew down a bleak highway. Many of the buildings were still standing.

Richard and Abby were on a mission. They hunted through the ruins. It didn't take them long to discover the remains of a mummified body in an obscure back alley.

Richard kicked away some lose soil, 'There lies here the remains of a surface dwelling Ortea. After two thousand years, you would have expected the body to have completely decomposed. However, this planet was sanitised. They even killed off the natural bacteria that helps bodies to decompose properly. If they had been fully able to carry out their desires, there would have been nothing left of this place. Nothing more than a pile of dust and rubble.'

'I thought they had removed all the bodies?'

'They said they had, but obviously they missed a few. I think the best thing we can do is inform the authorities.'

They left the lost soul. The alleys were quite narrow and bleak, the buildings a mixture of brick, mortar and concrete.

Abby rubbed one wall that looked like it might have had some paint on it.

'Why didn't they use the bricks from down below?'

The Black of Space

Richard paused, 'I don't know. Maybe it has something to do with the harshness of the sunlight on this planet.'

Richard felt drawn towards one particular building. It still had its natural roof on it, although it sagged badly. He went to go inside but Abby grabbed his arm.

'This place looks dangerous.'

'It looks untouched.' He went in anyway. Light filtered in through the windows, but not much. It seemed to be a shop of some type, though the shelves and goods had crumbled. He went through the back.

'Nice!'

'What is it?'

'An old workshop.' He began to look around. Work benches made from a type of wood crumbled in his hands, but there was a large metal table in the middle. He wiped it and it shone from beneath the dust. He opened metal doors and found a toolbox inside. He pulled it out.

'Remind you of anything?'

She smiled, 'It's a little bigger than the last box. What is in it?'

He opened it and sighed, 'Wow!'

'What?' She didn't seem impressed.

'Tools. Woodworking tools. They still look brand new. They aren't iron or steel, that's for sure.' He pulled out a chisel. 'The handle is synthetic too, but it is still perfectly serviceable.' He came to a decision, 'I'm taking it.'

'Should you?'

'No one is going to return for it Abby. What's the difference between taking it from here or a pile of rubble?'

'People still live here.'

'Under the surface of the planet. These are woodworking tools, have you seen any wood on your travels?'

'No.'

'Even if they knew what they were, they wouldn't know how to use them anyway. The owner of this is long dead, so are all their relations.' He concentrated hard and the box in front of him dissolved. 'Let's go.'

He would have liked to linger longer, but strange noises from the building surrounding them made him want to leave quickly. They eventually came to a broad plain on the edge of the city. There was only a tinge of green. The rubble of buildings stood out in the distance.

They were picked up there soon after. The mood of the other passengers also reflected their own mood.

CHAPTER 32

The Ambatta home-world was a complete contrast to the Ortea's. The cities on the surface had crumbled to rubble and the underground living quarters were basically bunkers, dull and depressing. However, they spent a few days in one of the new resorts. The Ambatta were in awe of their larger and brighter cousins, while the Behema were charmed by the smaller race. It started a great amount of speculation between them.

Trinnie and Lewis became their guides, with the Behema completely in awe of the couple. Their laughter often washed over the group as they walked hand in hand in front of them. None were really enjoying the experience all that much until they reached the asteroid field. The cities, small towns, picturesque asteroids with beautiful homes, cheered the visitors greatly. Taylana was actually in tears at one point; she found the asteroids idyllic and peaceful.

They were also treated to something no-one had seen before: one of the Ambatta's military bases. It was huge, the collection of ships mind boggling. Darrick had a lot of fun pointing out some very old ships. One of the colossal battleships was in docks for repairs and they were given a short tour.

Two things stuck in Merro's mind as they left the system: the beauty of the night sky on the Ambatta home-world, and the terrifying speed at which Trinnie flew her shuttle. He had wondered why Darrick had lain back in his seat with a blindfold on. Almost all that hadn't used a blindfold had been violently sick at least once during the journey.

CHAPTER 33

Cookie was splayed right across one of Charlie's large chairs, sucking on a beer. Mya cuddled into his side and occasionally took a sip. Across the other side of the room, Darrick was watching them curiously.

'Should you two be doing that in front of your Emperor? Is it part of some strange courtship ritual?'

Cookie waved the bottle at him, 'With all due respect to your title and rank, you are not my Emperor. However, I shall answer that question. No, this is not a part of some courtship ritual. It's just a bosie.'

'Uh! That did not translate.'

'A cuddle.'

'I see… it is strange that adults would want to cuddle.'

'We are both exhausted, and find it comforting.'

'As long as it doesn't turn into anything else.'

'We don't have the energy for anything else.'

'That's good then.'

Charlie appeared and handed Darrick a bottle of beer. He kicked back the chair into a more comfortable position and took a long drink. Charlie sat down and took a sip of his own.

'What are we watching then?'

Cookie lifted the remote and flicked through a menu. 'Haven't seen this in ages.'

Charlie nodded, 'Terminator. I got the whole lot of them.'

'I noticed.'

'Is it any good?' Darrick snorted.

'Lots of violence.'

'Put it on then.'

Cookie grinned at Charlie, 'Is it no a wee bit close to the bone?'

'Piss off dickhead. It doesn't bother me.'

'Why is what to close to the bone?' Darrick asked.

The Black of Space

Charlie sighed, 'Watch and see.'

It wasn't too long before Darrick burst out laughing as he finally got the joke. Cookie and Mya were both fast asleep by the time the film was finished.

Darrick eyed the couple, 'Is he a friend of yours?'

'We have been friends for years. We were in the same platoon for a while but then he joined the Special Services.'

'Cooks?'

'No, Special Services is a branch of our military that deals in particularly hard and dangerous missions. They can handle just about any weapon, any kind of explosives, fight over any kind of terrain. Experts on covert operations.'

'Assassins?'

'Not specifically, no.'

'That's a relief! Is it safe to talk?'

Charlie concentrated for a moment, 'They are both out cold.'

'How are our guests handling things?'

'Their emotions are all over the place. It is good that you haven't tried to hide anything, but Merro is finding it hard to stomach the way many Federation members fight.'

'You mean the complete destruction of an entire planet and species?'

'Exactly that. He holds unbridled admiration for you though.'

'How so?'

'He likes how you were the first Emperor to visit both the Ortea and Ambatta, how you had links with the Ambatta before and never added anything to the continued war that was waged against them. He is impressed by how you utterly destroyed the Albany but are now being gracious enough to help their citizens.'

'Have none of their races ever done something similar?'

'Not that I am aware of. They are shocked at the brutality shown towards meat-eating races.'

'I hope you pointed out that it just wasn't meat-eating

races.'

'Steven has done so on a number of occasions. Morro thought the Ortea were rather brutal for eating sentient beings but has realised that they had no real choice in the matter.'

'I see, and what about your situation?'

'Florina feels totally outclassed by Jean and is wallowing in a pool of self-pity. Merro wants to kick her arse but is also overawed by Jean. Taylana is wondering if she could persuade Jean to come home with them as a professional model.'

Darrick snorted, 'That female certainly likes her fashion.'

'It is her life and business.'

'I suppose. I was shocked that he isn't allowed to have children.'

'Different folks, different strokes.'

'Hmm. Overall?'

Charlie took a while to answer, 'I'm not sure yet. It could go either way at the moment. He isn't quite sure what course of action to recommend. Either all-out war, with a pre-emptive strike, or sit back and wait and see what happens. There is little doubt in his mind that we will eventually come to blows.'

'Do you think we should frighten him a little?'

'He is expecting that. To him it will be a sign of aggression and weakness. What he needs to see more of is co-operation between meat eaters and herbivores. When we were on his world, there was a great diversity in the species there, especially in their shopping centres.'

'We are still in the infant stages of coming to terms with meat-eating races.'

'What about Federation One?'

'Why?'

'You want him to meet Ne´ and there is more diversity at Federation One. There are Humans, Ortea and Ambatta, all going through there with lots of different species.'

'That may be a good idea. I will get in touch with Ne´ tomorrow.' Darrick got up, 'I'm off to bed, catch you in the morning.'

'Night.'

CHAPTER 34

Charlie was up early and quickly out the door with a basket. The field was still covered in morning dew. He was hunting down some peas when he came across a rather forlorn figure.

Florina's eyes flew wide, 'Oh! What are you doing here?'

Charlie held up a basket, 'Isn't it obvious?'

'I see, don't you have a servant to do that duty?'

'I don't have any servants full stop.'

'I am afraid I don't understand that mentality.'

'Of course you couldn't.'

She frowned, 'What do you mean by that?'

'You are rich, you are Royalty, your head is so far up your own arse you can't see a damn thing.'

He spotted a green patch and made a beeline for it, but the pods were small and thin. He growled and looked around for more. His eyes zoomed in on a patch, and he moved on. When he arrived, Florina was only a few steps behind. She looked mad.

'How dare you?'

'How dare I what?'

'Say such things to me, and walk away from me when I was talking to you.'

'You want to try getting over yourself Lady,' Charlie peeled off the stalk and expertly cracked open the pod. With a thumb he slid the contents into his mouth. A large smile cracked his face. Florina looked mortified.

'That thing is unwashed.'

Charlie shook his head slowly, 'You are a joke, you and your kind. There is nothing finer in this world than shelling a peapod by yourself and tasting peas fresh. Yet you want it to go through a dozen hands before it gets into your mouth.' He offered her a good pod, 'Do yourself a favour, try it.'

'Disgusting.'

The Black of Space

'Then piss off out of my field.'

She stomped a foot, 'I will not.' She looked around, 'Why do you grow so much anyway?'

'I don't. I sublet this field to the locals, it is them who grow it.'

'Then you are stealing.'

'No, it's a part of the deal. My own garden lies behind my cottage. Thing is, the Modloch liked the vegetables that I was growing and stole everything in it. When I came home, I couldn't even feed myself. They had also stolen all of my chickens. So I had a right falling out with them. In the end I made a deal: they buy seeds off me, rent out the land, then I can have my pick of anything I want and they leave my damn garden alone.'

She snorted, 'You lease it out. You can't make much from it.'

Charlie looked down, 'Do you see that plant you are standing on.'

She looked down and stepped off the potato plant. 'What about it?'

'It is probably worth more than that dress you are wearing.'

'That is ridiculous!'

'As it stands, it is worth about an eighth of a silver bar. When it is fully grown, it will be worth about quarter to a half, depending on the size and quality of the leaves. If a Modloch gardener sees you standing on it he will probably kill you in rage. Why do you think I wear a weapon strapped to my waist so early in the morning?'

'You are serious about that?'

'I am deadly serious. One small leaf can give a Modloch male stamina for half an evening during the mating season. It is the most expensive plant in the whole of the empire. I ship in tons of the stuff from Earth every year. Our turnover at this time is about a billion Federation credits a year. It is all marketed by my company here.'

She was stunned for a moment then bent down to try

and repair the damage she had done.

'I am sorry, I never realised.' She stood back up, 'You aren't joking, are you?'

Charlie shook his head, 'Oh hell no. Anyway, try it,' he held out the peapod.

'I don't know how to.'

With a sigh of exasperation, he peeled and split the pod, 'Open wide.' She obeyed and the peas popped into her mouth. 'Chew.'

A strange sparkle came into her eyes and she placed a delicate hand in front of her mouth. Her head began to nod.

'Very sweet, delicious. Nicer than they are cooked.'

'These are very nice raw. There are loads of different varieties.'

She hung about as Charlie filled the basket. He moved onto a row of carrots, then the cabbage and lettuce.

'Why do you need so much?'

'Very little of this is for us, it is mostly for Darrick.'

She screwed up her face, 'How could he stay in a place so small?'

'He likes it, I also have a device that adjusts the gravity to the same as his home planet.'

'The gravity isn't too bad here. You don't seem to have any problems.'

'It is still less than Earth, my home-world.'

'What is Earth like?'

'It isn't much different from yours. Same kind of diversity.'

'I think your vegetables are nicer.'

'It would depend on where on the planet you were brought up and the vegetables available in those regions. Same goes for the fruit.'

'I see.'

She was quiet as she followed him around. It took her a

while to find her confidence.

'You don't find me attractive, do you?'

'You are a little too alien for my tastes, Princess.'

She looked around, then slid the dress off her shoulders and undid her bra. 'Look at me.' He did so. His eyes went down then up to her eyes. 'You don't like this?'

He turned away, 'No.'

'Nothing, nothing at all?'

He turned back, 'Get dressed, the gardeners will be here any moment.'

'That's it?'

He turned back to his task, 'Your breasts are impressive, and you are very pretty, but I don't find you sexually stimulating.'

'Any of my race?'

'No, I am only attracted to females of my own race.'

'That is very narrow minded of you. I know you and the Captain aren't in love. It is obvious that you are just fucking.'

'It is no business of yours.'

'As I was offered to you, I think it is.'

'We are happy together and comfortable. Love, that joyous wonderful feeling, is for the young. We are old, have shared many of the same battles. Our capacity to fall blindly and hopelessly in love with someone is long gone. What is important to us is each other's ability to empathise with the other. To understand the demons that lurk beneath the surface, the shared sorrow and pain of loss, and the ability to enjoy what little time we have together.'

'I don't understand.'

'Of course you don't. I wouldn't expect you to.'

'Because of my youth?'

'Your youth, your station in life.'

'I see.' She dressed quickly, 'If I wasn't a Royal…'

'You are still as alien to me as a Modloch female is.'

'You are very narrow minded.'

'I am the product of my environment and my life

experience. I had no idea aliens even existed until just a few years ago. Since then I have probably killed more than I have met. You were brought up knowing about other races. You no doubt have a way of judging them for suitability as a mate, one that was implanted into you from birth by those around you. I have no such thing.'

It made her think a little, 'The large black skinned man has no problems with an alien female.'

'So? I am not Lewis and you aren't Trinnie. They were both desperately lonely people at the right place at the right time. I would say it was more that their souls touched than their hearts. I am neither desperate nor lonely. I am happy the way I am. If anyone pisses me off, I will just return home to Earth.'

'Where no one can follow you.'

'Exactly, and don't think you can apply political pressure the way you would to the Modloch Emperor. My country has no God-like Emperor governing over us, only a few politicians who respect the rights of the individual. They would simply laugh in your face. We vote for our politicians, any subversion like the kind that happens out here all the time would never work. They would find themselves in jail and out of a job for life.'

'Your country? Ah, I remember, you are not one world politically, are you?'

'No. There are hundreds of different nations.'

'Ridiculous.'

'Aye, whatever. So, what were you doing here?'

She folded her arms across her chest, 'I couldn't sleep very well. I found myself awake. I came for a walk. I was curious about this parcel of land you were given by the Emperor. I simply didn't get it.'

'If the locals got their way it would be border to border potatoes. I stopped that. Now some of the other vegetables are selling really well and filling their pockets. They are happy enough, and I have enough food every time I come home to fill even an Emperor's stomach.'

Inexplicably she found herself laughing, 'All three of them.'

'Aye, all three.'

The basket was quite full. Charlie turned for home. She turned away, but he noticed the gardeners turning up for work and realised it would be safer for her to return home his way. They didn't know her and might well attack.

'Come this way.'

'It is shorter that way.'

'Maybe, but the gardeners are here, and they have no idea who you are.'

She noticed the weapons on his waist and how one hand hovered close, and realised he was trying to protect her.

'The Modlochs are aggressive?'

'They can be. This field is very valuable, and they attack intruders on sight.'

One of the gardeners saw them and raised an arm. Charlie mimicked the action as he waved in return.

'It's alright, they recognise me,' the tension went out of him and his hand returned to the basket.

'Have they attacked you?'

'A number of times for various reasons.'

'Did you have them executed?'

'There is only one person in this empire who is allowed to have someone executed, and it isn't me. Besides, it's normally me that gets into trouble over it.'

'How can that be?'

'Let's just say I have a peculiar way of dealing with it.'

'I don't understand.'

'There is a green board high up on my wall to the right of my door. Have a look when we get there.'

They reached the stile and she made it over on her own. It was by the door that she saw the green board. It took her a moment to realise what she was looking at; her hands went to her mouth. There were three of them.

'Are those what I think they are?'

'My wee collection of horns.'

'I imagine they are very fond of them.'

'You have no idea.'

Darrick appeared having a scratch. He lifted a leg and let off a huge fart.

'Is that my breakfast?'

'Your dinner.'

His eyes flicked over, 'Good morning Florina.'

She bowed low, 'Your Royal Highness.'

'How did you end up here?'

'I was out for a walk and bumped into Charlie.'

His eyes scanned the field, 'You are lucky he found you, or you him.' He looked upwards, 'I don't want to add whole heads to that wall and have to deal with your enraged father.'

'I did not realise the danger sire. I am sorry.'

'Did Glee not inform you?'

'I haven't seen much of her. She did say to be careful around the grounds.'

He snorted, 'It probably never occurred to her that you would wander as far as the field.'

Gord appeared from around the corner eating something.

Charlie growled. 'Have you bastards been munching out of my garden again?'

'Just the lettuce,' Gord admitted.

Charlie shook his head and Florina caught his eye, she looked amused.

'See what I mean?'

'He doesn't like the lettuce all that much anyway, and the greenhouse is locked up, so we can't get to the tomatoes.'

Darrick grabbed Charlie by the shoulder and dragged him close.

'You have tomatoes?'

The Black of Space

'What's it to you?'

Darrick puffed himself up, 'I am your Emperor!'

'Only because you made me one of your subjects. Against my own will by the way.'

Darrick bellowed, 'I want a tomato with my muesli.'

Charlie's mouth dropped open, 'You don't eat tomatoes and muesli together.'

'I am an Emperor; I will do what I want.'

Gord snorted, Charlie whirled on him, 'You bastard!' The emergency escape tool leapt to Charlie's hand and Gord howled in fear. He took to his heels, holding onto his horn. The rest of the guard fell about laughing. Darrick grasped Charlie's shoulder, 'Play later, go get my tomatoes.'

The tool snapped off. Charlie thrust the basket at Darrick.

'Fine! Take this in.'

With a triumphant laugh, Darrick carried in the basket. Charlie sulked all the way around to the greenhouse. Florina appeared at the door.

'You still here?'

'Just wondering what the fuss was all about.'

Charlie bit into a ripe red tomato. 'Have you got your tester?'

She stuck her arm out and Charlie dripped a tiny amount onto it. It cleared the tomato, so Charlie handed her one.

'Don't let one of those Modloch guards see you eating that, they will rob it from you.'

Charlie finished his tomato and picked a load of ripe ones, putting them into a small plastic tray. He discovered Florina leaning against the door with a look of ecstasy on her face, sucking the contents out of the tomato.

'I suppose that hit the spot.'

Her eyes had a dreamy look in them, 'This is wonderful. Can I have another?'

'Not if you want to live long. If Darrick suspects either

of us have eaten one of his bloody tomatoes, we will both end up on that wall.'

She finished her one, 'I have never tasted anything like that.'

'It's nothing special, just a tomato.'

'So refreshing.'

'You want to try a melon then, that's really refreshing.'

'Do you have a melon?'

'I have the seeds, haven't had the chance to try and grow them yet. This world is warm enough to grow both tomatoes and melons outside, but it is the bloody Modlochs, they nick everything.'

'Nick?'

'Steal. I had to buy this super secure greenhouse to grow my tomatoes. They will even eat them green, but it gives them a severe dose of the shits.'

She moved aside as he came out of the door and locked it up again. She pointed to a very trampled bare patch of soil.

'Was that where the lettuce was?'

Charlie sighed, 'Aye, I'm no very fond of the stuff, but it's good for you, so I eat a wee bit of it. Again, there's loads of different varieties.'

She seemed very amused. Gord appeared, still a fair bit away, but Charlie took a tomato and launched into the air. Gord caught it with a laugh and punched a hand into the air as a salute.

'You get on well with him?'

'Gord, aye, he is the head of the imperial guard. You two have something in common.'

She snorted, 'How so?'

'The first time I met him, I hung him off a balcony.'

It took her a moment and she laughed, 'I get it. You were hanging the Druac off a balcony the first time I met you.'

'Yup.'

She followed Charlie inside. Darrick was waiting with his bowl. With a howl of joy, he grabbed a tomato and rammed it into his mouth. Cookie came through enjoying his morning scratch. He gawped at the Emperor in wonder.

'Muesli and tomatoes, first time I have seen that,' he looked to Charlie, who just shrugged.

Darrick pointed to the plastic tray, 'Is this all there is?'

'It's all that's ready.'

'Damn it.'

'You could make a chutney,' Cookie suggested.

Darrick's head came up out of his bowl, 'What's that?'

Charlie was scowling at Cookie, 'Really, you want my green tomatoes too? Will I ever taste a tomato again?'

'Green tomatoes aren't good for you,' Darrick humphed, 'they make you shit.'

'Not if they are cooked in a chutney they won't.' He closed his eyes for a moment and a jar appeared on the table. Darrick ignored it. Charlie was scowling, but Cookie took a spoonful from the jar, grated some cheese from the fridge, and wrapped both into a lettuce leaf parcel. Darrick scowled at it, but the smell appealed to him. He reluctantly took it and had a small bite. His eyes popped wide and the rest disappeared.

'More!'

'You will give yourself a sore gut,' Charlie growled.

Darrick held up his hand, 'You are right, I am just being greedy. I will have that for my lunch. The tomatoes and muesli will do. Who makes this relish?'

Cookie shrugged, 'I do. Well, I make my own. You can buy it, but it isn't the same.'

'Do you have everything here to make it?'

Cookie looked to Charlie, 'Do we?'

'How the hell would I know?' Charlie shrugged.

'Green tomatoes, apples, sultanas, brown sugar, vinegar.'

'There's plenty windfall and green tomatoes. As for the

rest, you're on your own.'

'I think we have the rest of what we need on the ship. I can make you some.'

'Please do so, as much as you can make. I will pay you for it.' He looked to Charlie, 'I'm not paying you; I will take it as part of the tax you owe me.'

'I thought I was supposed to be tax free?'

'You make three times more through that small field and the company than a handful of my other Lords.'

Charlie growled, 'Whatever, see Glee. She does the books.'

'My accountants will. I hear she is making a tidy little sum as well?'

Charlie shrugged, 'I have no idea.'

'I am having her investigated. She had better be playing it straight.'

'She was well warned.'

'So you are denying all responsibility.'

'For what?'

'Clueless, bloody clueless,' he dug into his bowl with a smirk.

Charlie dragged Cookie outside. Cookie picked clean apples from the tree. They were looking a little worse for wear.

'I think he is after your balls Charlie.'

'Nah! He is just being a shit to me. He has no one else to pick on. Are these okay?' Charlie held up some windfallen apples.

Cookie glanced down, 'Aye.'

Mya appeared on the scene, 'The Emperor's in a good mood today.'

'He would be,' Charlie snorted, 'Not only has he eaten all of my ripe tomatoes, he has also found a way of eating my green ones.'

She giggled, 'No wonder he is happy. How did the Princess get here?'

'She was wandering about, I found her in the field.'

'He is giving her a lecture on how to rule an empire and keep the scum in line.'

Cookie looked down, 'That has to be you.'

'Nae doubt.'

A figure came running up, Merro, and he was out of breath, 'Has anyone seen Florina?'

Charlie jerked a thumb at the cottage, 'She is inside entertaining the Emperor.'

He sighed with relief, 'Thank goodness for that. Oh, Lady Glee said she will be down soon with the books.'

'Right, thanks.'

CHAPTER 35

Florina was laughing at Darrick when Merro came in.

'You are here! I was worried.'

'Good morning brother, I am having breakfast with the Emperor. This bacon, sausage and egg is divine. Common food I am told but fit for our father's plate.'

'I had some too. It didn't smell as nice as that though.' He ogled Darrick's huge empty bowl. 'How did you end up here?'

'I was simply out for a walk. Charlie found me; I think he rather rescued me. The gardeners can be very territorial it seems.'

Darrick pushed his bowl away, 'Since Charlie arrived here, there has been a huge increase in violence.'

'Oh, is it his fault?'

'It is.'

'Have you punished him for it?'

'I am taxing him where I wasn't before. Not that he even notices. It has been caused by the food he grew in his garden. The locals were stealing it. To rectify the matter, when I gave him that field, he rented out parcels of land to the same locals and sold them seeds. The price they get for their produce, which they have to sell through him, is astronomical.' Darrick picked up a small tomato, one of the few left and tossed it up.

Merro looked at it dubiously then sank his teeth into it.

'Oh!' he exclaimed, 'What is this?' He looked to the bowl for more, 'Where can I purchase these?'

'You can't. They don't last the journey from Earth. Charlie is the only person who grows them on this side of the barrier. He had to build that secure greenhouse to grow them in. As you can imagine, with so much money at stake, the locals have become very protective of their produce. Despite their agreement with Charlie that he can help himself when he is at home, a few have taken upon themselves to try and stop him. Didn't you notice the horns on the wall outside?'

'No…'

'I get complaints about it from the local authorities.'

'What about your local police force?'

'It would seem they were helping themselves as well; which led to violence. They had to have a restraining order put out against them.'

'What a strange predicament.'

'A strange but lucrative problem. Many are making enough money to give up their normal jobs, which is fine, because it has attracted more people into the area. However, once they are here, they too want in on the action.'

'Then there is a waiting list?'

'A big one I believe.'

'Have you a solution?'

'I may have. However, it means pushing Charlie a little harder.'

'You are contemplating giving him more land, which he doesn't want.'

'Correct.'

Merro laughed, 'It really is a strange predicament. Two nobles that don't want their titles or the responsibility that goes with it.'

'You have been talking to my Chief Engineer.'

'I have. He has a private income of some kind.'

'He has amassed a vast fortune, however he spends most of that money maintaining my city ship, so I have no complaints there.'

'I can see why. I believe that had something to do with Charlie too.'

'Everything he does turns to money. He is still employed by the PD Company of Earth, which he set up with the help of the Ambassador's mother. It his job to find new acquisitions, things that Humanity can sell on this side of the barrier. He helped the Ortea sell their bricks. He initiated that trade in fact. The Ambatta sell their asteroids to private buyers as a result of his input, and he helped set up the tourist trade.'

'On top of that, he has all of this as well. He just doesn't come across as that type of person.'

'If he was, it would be easier. He simply goes around finding solutions to problems, and they invariably turn out to be money spinners.'

'I see, his solution to people stealing from his garden was to rent out plots of land and sell seeds.'

'Now the produce from it is worth more than the grass in this whole valley.'

'Which puts more money in your pocket.'

'Of course.'

'Now you want even more money.'

'Of course. I can easily give up this whole valley, it would make no real difference to the supply of grass.'

'Yes, but it would mean a huge increase in your income from this planet.'

'Of course.'

'There is only one problem though…'

'Charlie, and of course the violence.'

'I get the feeling that is one of the reasons you wished to stop here.'

Darrick smiled, 'You are again correct. If you ever have to leave your own world in a hurry, look me up. I am sure I can find a job for you.'

'Why thank you.'

Charlie lugged a basket of green tomatoes into the kitchen. Darrick peeked over at them and Charlie scowled.

'Is that all of them?'

'Aye.'

Cookie appeared with a basket of apples. He looked to Darrick, 'Don't you have any of that imperial stuff to do, Your Highness?'

'Lots and lots and lots. I presume you need the space to work.'

'I'm going to need this whole kitchen.' He raised his voice, 'Mya!'

She appeared, silent as a wraith. Merro jumped. She bowed low to him then to Darrick, side stepped them and went to help Cookie. The Royals took the hint and went outside. Darrick sat on the bench close to the wall, where the gravity was still comfortable for him. They sat chatting for a while.

Lady Glee soon appeared with the Chief at her side, carrying their son. She had a large folder with her. They both bowed low.

Darrick stuck his arms out, and the Chief dutifully handed over the child.

'A fine son. Whom does he take after?'

It was Glee who answered for them, 'His father sire, they all do. They consistently take apart anything they can get their hands.'

'Then they may eventually serve their Emperor well.' He handed the child back, 'Your friend is in the kitchen.'
'Thank you sire.'

He hastily bundled up the child in his arms and disappeared inside.

Glee bowed again, 'I am also here to see him sire.'
'Sit down Glee.'

She hesitated. Florina moved up the bench a little and she sat down.

'I presume those are the books.'
'Yes sire.'
'Show them to me.'

She hesitated a moment then opened the folder. It was a large tablet with double screens. She placed it upright on the table between them.

'Show me what you have been doing Glee. I want to see the money the company has made you, your children and Charlie. I also want to see what my subjects are making.'

She began to take him through it. Every now and then

he paused her and asked her a question. He was impressed by her bookkeeping and by her honesty.

His smile when they were finished wasn't pleasant. 'You seem to be doing very well. All of you in fact.'

'We are sire.'

'How does it feel to be working for a living Glee?'

'At first I admit to being highly embarrassed, but Lord Noch Man Drich left me with very little option.'

'You sold off all his chickens I hear. He wasn't very happy.'

Her eyes lifted to the horns on the wall above.

'The passage from noble woman to merchant wasn't an easy one sire. I admit that, however, I have found something I love to do. It is so much fun. Hard work, yes, but rewarding.'

'I can see by your bank balance that it is rewarding. Are you enjoying the money?'

'Of course.'

'I also see that you are playing it straight for once.'

'I have no choice in the matter. I now have far too much to lose. I don't want to end up on Lord Noch Man Drich's trophy board.'

Darrick howled with laughter, 'How are you dealing with all the applications for plots of land?'

'It isn't easy sire. Some of them want to dig up the pathways so they can plant more. I fear the problem may well escalate. There is a lot of jealousy and rivalry.'

'How many people are waiting for a plot?'

'Twice what I have here.'

'You could fill another two fields?'

'Yes sire.'

'Do you have the seed to do it?'

'Easily.'

He looked across the table, 'Florina, could you fetch Charlie for me?'

She gave a small bow and shot off.

The Black of Space

Charlie was reeking of apples when he came out.

'What's up?'

'I am giving you another two fields.'

'Why?'

'To stop a war amongst the locals here.'

'Seriously? When will it stop, how many fields will you end up converting?'

'As many as I damn well please.'

'Make it three then.'

That took Darrick by surprise, 'Why?'

'I can order greenhouses from Earth of modular construction. Place them under Royal warranty. We can fill them with tomatoes, then employ people to work in them, let them garden in part of the field as a reward for their service. Then you can bathe in the damn things if you want and sell off the rest.'

'You mean I won't even have to pay them?'

Charlie turned to Glee, 'Pick the best gardeners. Do you think they would do it for a couple of extra plots?'

'They would do it for one.'

Charlie shrugged, 'There you go. Three years tax should about cover the expense. It won't cost you a penny. As Glee and her daughters will be doing all the work, give them five years tax free, and a fifty per cent reduction on their tax after that to run the place for you,' he stomped back inside.

The Behema were left speechless. Glee turned to her screen.

'I suggest these three fields sire.'

Darrick leaned forward, 'Yes, I approve. Send the details to the right department.'

'What just happened there?' Merro asked.

Darrick dismissed it with a wave of a hand, 'It is the way his mind works. You get used to it. Glee, write down the details of this deal as Charlie mentioned them, only you will get a thirty per cent reduction on your tax rate, not a fifty.'

She dipped her head, 'That is very generous of you sire.'

'I know. It also means you will be working directly for me. Don't even think about messing up.'

'I won't sire.'

He leaned forward, 'I may even lift some of the restrictions on your travel if you are a good little Modloch girl.'

He saw the hope in her eyes, 'That is really generous of you sire.'

His smile was again unpleasant, 'I foresee the day when I get to execute you, and I am looking forward to it with great pleasure. I am quite sure that the more room I give you to play with, the quicker that day will come.'

She went very still, 'It won't happen.'

'Why not?'

'Because I am happy. Happy with my life, my son, and even with that oaf in there. I have even got used to the gravity on this world.'

His eyes twinkled as he rubbed his hands together, 'We will see. Dismissed. I will tell Charlie that I have checked your books.'

She got up and bowed low. They watched her as she left.

Merro eventually turned to Darrick, 'Did you just manage to have a whole complex built, at no cost to yourself, and no running costs ever, for a massive future profit?'

'Yes. I think it has been a good morning's work.'

Half an hour later Merro escorted Florina back to the mansion. He was still having a problem coming to terms with what had just happened.

'Florina?'

'Yes.'

'If you don't throw yourself down naked in front of that man, then you are an idiot.'

Florina smiled, 'I already tried that this morning. I was prepared to throw myself onto the dirt floor and be taken like a peasant woman. I am afraid he didn't even twitch, let alone get excited. Alien species do not interest him I am afraid.'

'Seriously?'

'Yes, even though I was a total slut.'

'You must feel humiliated?'

'Strangely, no.'

'Not like you.'

'He told me I had lovely breasts and was very pretty.'

'Is that enough?'

'It will have to do for now. Do you honestly think the Emperor is going to simply let an asset like that walk away? Besides, he told me if he was pushed, he would return to his home-world, where neither we nor the Emperor can follow.'

'I see. I thought this was a simple matter, I have underestimated both Charlie and Darrick. Their bond is strong. I wonder what we can do to weaken it.'

'Nothing brother. Do not try and get between them. That could be a lethal mistake. Try and build a mutual bond with them. That would be far more effective.'

CHAPTER 36

Eragon screamed with delight as Charlie launched him into the air. Ten metres away the Chief caught him. He put him down and he toddled back to Charlie who launched him screaming back into the air. Steven and Komoru stood on the side-lines and shouted encouragement. A steady stream of officials had been coming and going all afternoon while Darrick held court at the picnic table.

Lewis appeared and Charlie passed the child to him. Lewis tossed him back. The pace picked up a little. Eventually the toddler collapsed.

Laughing, the Chief picked him up, 'Enough Eragon, you will be sick.'

A few minutes later he did so and the Chief gave him a bottle of water to settle his stomach. Five minutes later he was fast asleep. Komoru dashed inside past all the dignitaries and fetched a blanket. She handed it to the Chief who wrapped him up in the blanket and laid him on the short grass. The adults sat around.

'You need a back-door Charlie.'

Charlie looked up at Komoru, 'I think you are right. Especially when Darrick is here.'

She turned her attention to the Chief, 'How is home life?'

He seemed embarrassed, 'You must be disgusted with me.'

'No. I don't blame you for what happened. The Emperor manipulated you into this position knowing full well what would happen.'

'I am glad you see it that way. Frankly I am quite embarrassed over the whole situation. The Emperor teases me endlessly with lewd remarks.'

Charlie snorted, 'Don't try and act all hurt, you get three times the booty any other Modloch gets.'

'You are just as bad as he is.'

'Charlie!' Komoru admonished.

'Whit! You haven't seen the stupid grin on his face after mating season's over.'

The stupid grin reappeared, 'Charlie might actually have a point. I do leave here in a very good mood, but now I miss the children.'

'Well, he told Glee that if she behaves, he may well remove some of the restrictions on her and her daughters.'

'That is progress maybe.' He frowned, 'It also worries me.'

'Believe it or not she is actually enjoying herself. I don't think she really want to mix with her old friends either. There is a certain embarrassment being mated to the same person as her daughters, and all three having children to him.'

'Then I will trust in your word Charlie.'

Komoru flopped back onto the blanket, 'This is boring.'

'Revel in it.'

She caught Cookie nodding in agreement with Charlie's statement.

'How can you revel in boredom?'

'Would you rather be back against that wall of asteroids with everyone trying to kill us?'

'Of course not.'

'In my experience the boredom doesn't last for long, so relish it. Do the stuff you have been putting off for months. Take up that hobby you have been wanting to try. You might not get another chance.' Cookie was still nodding.

'I understand.'

At that the Bear appeared, 'I think that's all his work finished, but he has attracted a bit of a crowd. I think he is going to talk to them.'

He sat down and Charlie offered him a bottle. He took a drink and handed it back.

'I miss this place. It's nice and quiet here. Any more bother with the locals?'

'No for a while. The tally is still three.'

The Bear laughed, 'They seem to have received the message then.'

'I am quite sure some of them will forget soon enough.'

They heard a great roar of approval go up from the front of the house.

The Bear kinked his head, 'What's that all about?'

'He has probably just told them that he is making a couple more fields available.'

'Sounds like it went down well.'

'Aye, it would do.'

'Can I have a patch?' Cookie asked.

'Pointless, they would raid it. If you want to grow anything Cookie, do it in my garden. They don't come near it now. What do you want to grow?'

'I was thinking of kiwi, avocado, that kind of thing.'

'I got a catalogue somewhere. Fancy helping me with the beehives?'

'Didn't know you had bees.'

'Most of it is self-pollinating, but not all. I ordered the hives from Earth and Darrick gave me some bees. The locals are shit scared of them.'

Komoru lifted her head, 'I haven't seen a bee since I got here.'

'Sonic barrier, I canna be bothered with them myself when I'm here.'

'You got the gear?'

'Aye, in the back shed.'

'What about extracting the honey from the combs?'

'No need man. Fancy hives, all we do is turn a handle and walk away. We just got to rig up a couple of big tubs to collect the honey.'

'We need jars for all that relish.'

'Aye, and for the honey.'

'I can do a lot with honey.'

'If I can keep it hidden from Darrick, he's like Pooh Bear…'

'I wonder if Babes could make us stoneware jars like Pooh Bear had to keep the honey in.'

'Now there's an idea. That would be pretty cool. Nice one Cookie.'

Komoru sat up, 'I think I am going to go insane.' A few seconds later she disappeared.

They eyed the vacant spot for a moment. Cookie looked over at Charlie.

'I thought the Japanese had a thing for peace and tranquillity?'

'Dinna look at me.' He pointed to Stevie, 'He is the one who's bonking it.'

Steven growled at them, then vanished.

Cookie stood up, 'Now we got that boring pair out of the way, I think it's time for the beers.'

Charlie also stood up, 'We can do the bees tomorrow.'

'Sounds like a plan to me. Did you chill that load of beer that came in this morning?'

'In the bath right now.'

Jeb suddenly appeared too, he clapped his hands together. 'Is it on?'

The Bear stood up, 'Hell yeah!'

CHAPTER 37

Komoru stomped a foot. 'I can't believe they all got drunk.'

Steven shrugged, 'I don't know what to say. They all turned up as drunk as lords.'

'Lewis as well. Are we going to discipline them?'

'I don't think they care.'

'It is intolerable.'

'What is?'

'They broke our new rules already.'

'They weren't on the ship. No one who was on duty got drunk. I don't think we are in a position to punish anybody.'

She waggled a finger at him, 'They were scheming.'

'Probably,' Steven agreed.

'You don't care, do you?'

'Why should I? I already pointed out that they weren't on the ship, and none were on duty.'

'The rules are no drinking during the day.'

'I told you it was an unreasonable rule and it wouldn't work.'

'It is not unreasonable.'

'Not if we are going somewhere. No one drinks when we are working or travelling between planets. Let them kick back and enjoy themselves a little.'

'It is undisciplined.'

'Oh shut up!'

Komoru was stunned for a moment then turned and walked out. Steven groaned, 'Oh, why did I say that?'

'It was rather insensitive of you my heart.'

'Babes, I was just sick of it. I can't be bothered with it. She is too controlling at times.'

'You both spent a lot of time coming up with those new rules.'

'She cannot control what everyone does off the ship as well as on it. I already made that point clear.'

The Black of Space

'An order has just come through: we are leaving in three hours.'

Steven got to his feet, 'Beam me down then.'

Steven waded into the debris of what had obviously been a very large party. Dozens of beer bottles were stacked against a wall. Food scraps and partially eaten balls of hay lay around. It was hardly any better inside.

He found Cookie and Mya on their chair fast asleep. The Bear and Merro were sharing the couch. He went through towards the master bedroom, but a guard blocked his way. He scowled at Steven who retreated and went into the spare room instead. The ears sticking out from under the covers were unmistakeable. His heart skipped a beat, he dashed over and pulled back the covers. In a heartbeat he whipped them back over and made a dash for the door. He made it before anyone stirred. Confused, he asked Babes to track Charlie. She guided him to the back garden.

There he was, in a hammock, swinging between two trees in the morning breeze. Steven gave the blanketed figure a shake.

Charlie stirred, 'Hey!'

'We are moving out in three hours-time.'

'What's up?'

'No idea.'

'Our people?'

'Federation.'

'Ne´!'

'Yes.'

'Everyone is heading there in a couple of days anyway.'

Steven shrugged, 'I just about had a heart attack there.'

'Why?'

'Thought you were in bed with the little princess. I whipped back the sheets to discover the three ladies in it.'

'Lucky you never got caught.'

'I know.'

'That will teach you to go blundering in where you

aren't welcome. She would have had your nuts off.'

'I was seriously out of order, right?'

'Bang on there.'

'Komoru isn't happy.'

'So?'

'Man, you have no sympathy, have you?'

'With what, your stupid orders?'

Steven let out a long sigh and ran his fingers through his hair.

'I told her to shut up.'

Charlie chuckled, 'What!'

'She was moaning about it, this party, I told her to shut up.'

'I'm impressed dude.'

'No really! What should I do?'

'You've been in a relationship with her longer than I have been in a relationship with any woman. Why the hell would you ask me?'

Steven thought about it for a moment, 'Yeah, you might have a point there.'

'Damn tootin.'

'What would you do anyway?'

'Me? I'd consider that I was on the point of being dumped and go look for another chick to take the strain.'

'Right… I'm beginning to see where you have been going wrong all these years.'

'Listen to the one chick wonder!'

Steven burst out laughing, 'I have no idea why I talk to you.'

'Yes you do.' Charlie closed his eyes. Blood began trickle from his nose as he concentrated. Steven waited patiently. Eventually he opened his eyes.

'Well, she is still as mad as hell, but in a weird way, kind of turned on as well.'

'Oh God…'

'She thought you were very manly,' Charlie shrugged. 'Anyway, she isn't going to talk to you until we get there.

She is thinking of revising your new rules but is hoping you will make a start on it first.'

Steven sighed with relief, 'Thanks. Get everyone up will you?'

'No probs.'

A second later Steven vanished.

Charlie went to the next tree over. He shook Eddie awake.

'Piss off Murison.' A second later he was face down on the ground, the hammock above swinging idly.

'Up and at it. You got to do your sodger thing. The ship's leaving in three hours. Go wake your buddies.'

Eddie groaned, 'Man, is there no peace in this world?'

'Nope, no even when you retire.'

He lifted his face from the grass and keeked up at Charlie one-eyed.

'I'm no sure who I feel sorrier for, you or me.' He pushed himself up with a groan, 'Right, I'm on it.'

Charlie found Gord and told him what was happening, he also left him the key and the passcodes. By then the crew were stumbling out of the house. When they were all gathered together, they were beamed up.

CHAPTER 38

Steven and Komoru found themselves in Ne´s headquarters. There were a lot of people going to and fro. All were in Federation uniform. They had waited almost half an hour for a docking slot.

They were eventually ushered in. Ne´ waved at them to sit down while he read something on a tablet. He answered whatever it was he was reading before putting it down.

'How would you like another long trip Ambassadors?'

They looked at one another, 'What is wrong?' Steven asked.

'The Ambassador sent from Earth died of a massive heart attack on route to the Empire's main planet. The Behema Emperor has sent his condolences but requested that a replacement be sent straight away. We, of course, don't have one. You can also get there a lot faster than anyone else. In fact, he insisted on you two specifically. It would seem you have made a good impression on his son.'

'I am going to assume this is not a request.'

Ne´ smiled, 'Of course not. You will finish the tour with his son and then head off to visit the Empire. As for now, you have a couple of days of boring lectures to get through with your staff before you meet up with the Behema delegation on Federation One. Have fun Ambassadors.'

Ne´ got up and took them to the door. As he showed them out to the reception room outside the office, where Charlie was waiting for them, another door opened and a troop of Haspsopot walked in. The two groups met halfway across the floor. Four guards quickly surrounded their young Emperor.

He smirked at Steven and Komoru, 'Ambassadors. I am so glad to see that you are both safe. I am so sorry for what happened on my planet, I had no idea what the Albany were doing.'

'He is lying.'

Ne´ felt the blood freeze in his veins. The Haspsopot weren't supposed to arrive for another hour. Panic filled the eyes of his aide on the other side of the room. Ne´ was about to open his mouth, but it was too late.

'Who said that? Who besmirches the word of an Emperor?'

At a silent word of command, the two Ambassadors moved to the side and took a few steps back. Charlie came forward, with Lewis right behind him and slightly to his left.

'You have no honour, you're nothing but a common liar.'

He was infuriated, 'How dare a commoner like you talk to me in this manner?'

'I am the Ambassador's aide. I practice something called body language, I am an expert at it, probably one of the best my world produces. It is my job to tell him when someone is lying to his face. That is exactly what I am doing.'

Ne´ could feel chills running down his spine. The feeling of menace was heavy in the room, and it emanated from the two Humans facing the Haspsopot. The Emperor was oblivious to it but his men weren't, they visibly tensed.

'What farcical excuse is that to insult someone of my standing?'

'It isn't farcical. I will give you a demonstration if you want. Pick a number between zero and two thousand.'

The Emperor's eyes went cold, 'I will not play your games.'

'Why not? It may save your life.'

'You dare threaten me!'

'With no hesitation. Pick a number.'

The Emperor thought he could get the better of Charlie. He smiled coldly.

'There.'

'You haven't done it, pick a number.'

'I did.'

'You're lying, pick a number.'

A number flashed through the Emperor's mind, 'There.'

'One thousand five hundred and twenty-five.'

Despite himself, Ne´ was now intrigued.

The Emperor took a half step back, 'How… impossible!'

'It's quite simple. We all learn to count with our fingers. As you thought of the number, the digits in your hand twitched almost imperceptibly. It is a subconscious thing, very few even realise they are doing it.' The Emperor lifted his hands to his face instinctively. Charlie smiled, 'Now, I believe you owe the Ambassadors an apology for helping to have them abducted, then lying to their face.'

His fury returned with a snarl, 'I will not. How dare you threaten me. I am an Emperor.'

'And I don't give a shit what you are. Apologise.'

'Kill him.'

His guards had been waiting for the order, but so had the Humans. As the guard on Charlie's right lifted his weapon, he moved. His emergency tool sliced the guard into pieces. His scream of shock and pain was cut short. Charlie heard the hum of Lewis's emergency tool to his left. As Charlie turned on the Emperor, Ne´ screamed aloud.

'Stop this instant. No one move.'

Charlie froze, as did all in the room. His tool was only inches from the Emperor's face, who stepped back away from the heat.

'Lower your weapons and sheath them.'

The guards lowered their weapons, then Charlie and Lewis similarly followed the order from Ne´.

The Haspsopot Emperor was swinging wildly between terror and anger.

'You dare cause a war between our worlds, a no-one like you?'

'Our worlds are already at war.'

He was breathing hard, 'We are not at war with Earth.'

Charlie smiled coldly, 'Who said anything about Earth? Didn't I introduce myself properly? I apologise.' He gave a tiny bow, 'I am Lord Noch Man Drich, a Modloch noble, brother to the Great Modloch Emperor, member of the Royal Modloch household. As our worlds and races are already at war, I easily dare take your life. I know Federation territory is considered neutral ground. However, I am allowed to respond if provoked by violence.'

'Charlie,' Ne´ growled, 'Enough.'

At the mention of his title, the guards and the Emperor had taken a step backwards. Now the Emperor felt sick to his gut. The smell from the corpses wasn't helping any. However, Charlie wasn't quite finished with him just yet.

'You should know your enemies better than you know your friends, Emperor Ma Na Gach, first born son, born in the fifth year of your father's reign, twenty-seven years, five months, and twenty-three days ago. Your favourite colour is emerald green, which you indulge yourself with in your private quarters. You have an official wife and three concubines. Each of the concubines have a different coloured room, chosen by you. I believe you prefer pastel colours for your ladies.'

The Emperor began to shake. Just then Federation guards appeared. Ne´s aide had sneaked off. They now stood in a line between the two parties. A young guard began to vomit. It broke the tension in the room.

Ne´ growled at Steven, 'Ambassador, could you do your thing please?' When Steven turned to him, Ne´ lifted his hand towards the ceiling. It was obvious what he wanted. Steven nodded and seconds later they vanished.

Ne´ visibly relaxed. He skewered his aide with a look, 'Take the Emperor to the other waiting room. See to his needs. Then come back and see me. Also, get this mess cleaned up.'

'Yes sire.'

Ne´ returned to his office. It was obvious to him that Charlie had manipulated the Emperor into losing his temper. It had almost worked too. It was by a hair's breadth that Ma Na had survived the encounter. Ne´ correctly guessed it was retribution for the kidnapping of his friends, a lesson the young Emperor would not forget. He would get in touch with Darrick later, but knew Darrick would just howl with laughter at the encounter and curse him for stopping Charlie.

He also had to sort his aide out. The Haspsopot should have been taken to the alternative waiting room immediately they arrived. If he wasn't aware of the possible conflict between the Haspsopot and the Humans, then he had no right to be on his staff.

Steven and Komoru found the lectures as tedious as they had the first-time round. Only this time most of the information they were given was the information that they themselves had gathered. There was one difference: the Ambassador that had been sent after them had visited the Druac's home planet en-route. They were also sent the star maps of the route they were to take. That caused some excitement between the two, and they were soon on good terms again.

When they eventually arrived at Federation One, their companions of the past few weeks were already there. It was there that Merro saw the opportunity to get home a lot faster. It didn't take much persuading to have Ne´ agree to let them travel with the Ambassadors, but it meant that the ships would have to reconfigure themselves so as not to blind their visitors. Neither ship was happy about it. They refused to alter the engine rooms; those would remain off limits to the passengers. Steven's ship would hold the dignitaries while Komoru's ship would take their personal guards and aides, although only eight in total. The rest would travel back in their own ship. The only one who seemed really upset about the whole thing was Darrick.

Charlie and Jean managed to spend a last night together on Federation One, but the evening was strained. Charlie assured her he would turn his hormones off for the duration of the journey, but she didn't seem all that bothered.

Amongst all of this, Richard and Abby moved like wraiths. On Earth, their following was now bigger than any others. The translation equipment in their cameras and drones made sure that the people on Earth missed nothing. Small dramas on board the ships had been playing out for months at home. Shipboard romances were spotted and reported.

The crew were very quickly becoming household names and celebrities, although they were, for the most part, completely oblivious to that. Abby and Richard worked day and night. They even had some footage of the party. Abby had beamed down for half an hour. Eddie's pint pot had gone down a storm. What had been a little-known item on the PD Company's books became all the rage, especially in Scotland, and in Eddie's home city of Glasgow. It became the new official pint.

A large ceremony was held to send off Merro and the Behema Royals. When it was over, they were escorted part way by a Federation fleet and their own transport. Within a couple of days, two sleek ships accelerated away into the black of space.

CHAPTER 39

The journey began to stretch after the first week. Knowing the time they had on their hands, the crew turned to private projects and hobbies to entertain themselves. Charlie, Jeb and Steven were sitting with their feet up when Merro found them.

A huge grin split his face, 'So this is where all the cool guys hang out. Was that right?'

Steven laughed with the others, 'That is exactly right. What can we do for you?'

'I was bored and looking for company.'

'That's good, you can help Charlie and the team fill in the blanks on your charts.'

He clapped his hands together, 'Blessings. Something to do at last.'

'Take a seat then. Coffee?'

'A herbal tea if you have it.'

One materialised in front of him. 'I still find it hard to get used to this.' He took a seat, put his feet up and sipped at the tea. 'Perfect. So, what are we doing?'

'A little planning. We are going to be looking at the charts we received from your people and identifying the star systems that support life along our route. It is Charlie's team's job to try and estimate any dangers along the way. We simply haven't received all that much information.'

'I can certainly help with that.'

'Wonderful, where is Taylana?'

'I have lost her to the remarkable David.' He sighed heavily, 'They are designing dresses with matching jewellery, based on those they managed to procure on the Ambatta home world. She is in designer heaven.' The men laughed. 'The two girls are helping her. She says it will take three months to put an exhibition together. The ship is helping with cloth and making stuff. By the time we get home she will be ready to take the Empire by storm. She is looking for recruits amongst the crew to use as models.'

His eyes fell on Jeb and he smiled. 'She was wondering if the Lady Jane would help.'

Jeb went very still and guarded, 'You would have to ask her. You would also have to ask her properly. She is the sister-in-law of the King of England. Very old, very traditional.'

'Ah yes. I was afraid you were going to say that.'

The men howled with laughter.

Jeb put his cup down, 'You know, she has complained occasionally about modern design. She was born over a hundred years ago. Fashion has changed so much since then.'

'Ah! I believe I see what you are getting at. It may be old for Earth, but it is new and unknown in our world.'

'It was a time of great elegance.'

'Now you are talking Taylana's language. I will convey the message.'

A few minutes later the Lady Jane herself arrived. She looked at the men sitting with their feet up on the table. Her eyes fixed on the Royal, 'I see you are learning uncouth practices, Première.'

'I did learn a phrase Lady Jane: "When in Rome."'

'Well, they were quite barbaric.'

She decided to ignore them. She handed Charlie a folder and he began to flick through it. Rather than put it down, he finished his coffee and pushed himself across to his computer. Jane joined him and they sat and discussed whatever was on the sheets.

'I am so jealous, you all have something to do. The journey to your part of the galaxy was tedium at best.'

Steven put his cup down, 'You can join us in our diversions if you wish.'

'What would they be?'

'Five days of the week we have martial arts lessons – an hour in the morning with Commander Sato, and I take an hour in the evening. They are quite popular. The soldiers onboard have to attend twice a week. Many train every day.'

'What are martial arts?'

'A type of fighting style. Mainly hand to hand. There are a few specialist classes that teach the use of weapons. Swords, knives, that kind of thing.'

'That sounds quite interesting.'

'They are quite advanced classes, but you can sit in and watch if you want.'

'I would love to.'

'There are other projects on the go as well. Charlie, myself and our top engineers are going to come up with a design for a new freighter.'

'I'm out of my depth there, but it might be interesting sitting in on your discussions. We have many types of freighters.'

'The Federation only recognises one type, and it isn't ours. Right now we are restricted to unloading mostly at the Modloch city ship or at Federation stations. We are fighting that because we are so far away, and also no race from the Federation can actually reach our home planet.'

'I see. I saw one of your freighters, they don't look much like freighters either.'

'They are basically gutted out battleships. They are a lot faster than the standard freighter.'

'That's what I thought. How long would it take them to reach our solar system?'

'A normal freighter would take seven to eight months, a fast freighter, four to five.'

'It is still a long time. What do you hope to achieve?'

'We really don't know yet. We have no real goal in mind. We are going to try out different designs and configurations. What about your freighters?'

'I believe they are on par with the ones we have captured from our enemies.'

'They will be Federation standard then.'

'Interesting.' His eyes flicked past Steven, 'A little bird

told me you had some trouble at the Grand Commander's headquarters.'

Charlie looked round and caught his eye, 'There are too many little birds with big beaks around this ship.'

Steven grimaced a little, 'Charlie's right, it isn't something we are prepared to talk about.'

'I see.'

He could feel the tension in the room rise. He decided to make his excuses and left.

The next morning, he found himself embroiled in the Human's self-defence classes. He was simply fascinated and attended every class. By the time he arrived home, he would become a very keen martial artist.

A few days later, Taylana managed to waylay Jane in the canteen. She had been studying what she could about the roaring twenties and the fashion prior to that. She showed Jane some of the pictures she had found and asked about the kind of materials that they had used. It took Jane by surprise and she was drawn into the project. It kept her out of the men's hair.

CHAPTER 40

Abby rolled over in bed and handed the tablet to Richard. He in turn rolled into a more comfortable position to read it.

He growled and handed it back, 'Same old shit.'

'People are curious about him. Why was he made a Lord, is he really rich? What part does he play in the PD Company, is he an executive? Did he really almost kill an Emperor?'

'He still won't talk to us,' he picked the tablet back up. 'What else is there?' He grunted, 'Another interview with Taylana. Great, they really love the Behema. I know Aurora will be more than happy to talk, but the Princess is as bad as Charlie when it comes to an interview. We really need to crack those two.'

'How? We have exhausted every avenue. The moment you mention his name, everyone clams up.'

'Everyone seems to be covering up a big secret surrounding that man.'

'Only a few. The rest don't seem to know.'

He agreed, 'You're right. Some do, some don't. Those who don't talk with abandon about what little they know, while those in the know clam up tight. We need a different angle.'

His eyes swept over the pad. He put in a few search parameters that narrowed down the questions.

'Here is one that is interesting. What did Captain Gordon do during the assault on the city ship? Is it true that he fought in the campaign?'

'I suppose we could try and answer that.'

'Let's get to work then.'

It took them longer to find an answer than they expected. Steven was busy so it was Buzz who informed them that Steven had indeed led the initial assault on the city ship; he and Charlie had worked together to immobilise many of the big guns on it. It was Babes who proudly supplied them with the footage of the film crew's demise. She was very proud of the part her heart had taken in the assault and the amount of lives they had managed to save.

That evening, Amanda unwittingly gave Abby another small insight into Charlie.

When Abby had sat down at her table, Amanda was immediately on the defensive. More so when Charlie was brought up.

'Why will no one talk about that guy?' She eventually protested.

Amanda had put her cup down, 'Every member of this crew owes their lives to that man. He is a private person; he doesn't like to talk about himself. We respect that.'

'Seriously?'

'Yes, seriously.'

'You mean you aren't just scared of the guy?'

'No we are not. Do you know what he would be doing right now?'

'I don't know what you mean.'

'He retired from the army recently. He had saved enough money to get himself a small croft. He wanted to go to college and get himself a degree in archaeology. He wanted to spend his retirement going around the old battlefields, metal detecting, stuff like that.'

'Then why doesn't he?'

'Because the authorities won't leave him alone. Not long ago he spent a week imprisoned by our own intelligence community; they used physical and mental torture on him to try and get him to reveal details about the Modloch Emperor. He cannot return home.'

'No shit!'

'No shit Abby!!'

'Did they get away with it?'

Amanda shrugged, 'He had them all arrested the moment he was released.'

'Was that something to do with the city ship?'
'That's right.'
'Him and the guy they call the Bear.'
'That is correct. All Charlie wants is to be left alone. You should take the hint. Respect his wishes.'

Abby had a flash of inspiration, 'Why would he want to live on his own, on an old croft, wouldn't he be lonely?'

'You would be surprised by how many old soldiers, especially those who have seen too much fighting, do just that. They like the peace and solitude.'

'I see, I get it. Thanks.'

Ten minutes later she burst in on Richard, 'Charlie likes archaeology.'

Richard snapped upright, 'Really?'
'Yes.'
'Which means he also likes history.'
'More than likely.'

A few hours later they entered Charlie's office with the two boxes.

He glanced round, 'Piss off.'

'No,' Richard dug his heels in, 'We want your opinion on something.'

Charlie's eyes scanned the boxes and he was immediately curious.

'What you got there?'

'Artefacts from two different worlds. I heard you were interested in archaeology.'

'Battlefield stuff.'

'You'll like the box Abby has then.'

'Where did you get all this?'

Richard quickly explained. Charlie took the box from Abby and opened it. For him it was a treasure trove of delights. He studied the picture.

'We thought he might be a police officer of some kind.'

Charlie scanned the picture and it appeared on the wall

in fine detail. They were mesmerised as he zoomed in on something.

'No, this guy was a soldier.'

'How do you know?'

'Look at that symbol on his uniform. What does it look like to you?'

'Not sure.'

'A mushroom?' Abby suggested.

'No,' Richard disagreed, 'A bit like a parachute maybe.'

'Exactly like a parachute,' Charlie agreed. He isolated the symbol then more, very similar, appeared alongside it. 'These are ones from Earth. See the similarity?'

They both nodded their heads. Richard was genuinely excited.

'I think you are right. Are the others from Earth?'

'They are, different regiments from different countries.'

'Yeah, but all similar. I think you cracked it.'

They went through the entire box discussing each item in detail. Charlie was able to bring a different perspective to many of the items. They eventually came to the second box. Richard didn't expect much, but he was in for a shock.

Charlie lifted the lid, 'Gorgeous.'

'You know what they are?'

'Woodworking tools,' Charlie inspected the lid and pressed two corners. The pair gasped. A lid dropped down to reveal a host of different handles.

'How did you find that?'

'Didn't you notice how deep the lid is on the outside and how shallow it is on the inside?'

'Missed that. Wow, we had no idea they were there. You know what these are?'

'Carpentry tools.'

'I know they are wood working tools, but you sure they are carpentry?'

'Thought you were in the trade?'

'Builder, a little joinery, plumbing and electrical work, but no carpentry.'

'My uncle is a carpenter. I recognise a lot of these tools. What are you going to do with them?'

'We were going to donate them to a museum.'

'No way! I will buy them off you.'

'Seriously! What are you going to do with them?'

'I'm going to use them of course.'

'No shitting!'

'I love making things. My only A in school was in woodwork. How much do you want?'

'How much would we get at an auction on Earth?'

'Probably millions, but you said you were going to donate them to a museum.'

'That's true. What do you think would be a fair price?'

'Twenty grand apiece.'

'How about twenty grand apiece and that interview?'

'You know you are a bit of a dick, Dick.'

Richard laughed, 'You want them, that's the price.'

'Don't get personal, don't ask anything about the Modloch Emperor. Divulging any information on him is an instant death sentence.'

'Seriously?'

'In his mind, me telling you what he eats for breakfast makes him vulnerable.'

'If we cross the line don't get mad, just tell us.'

'Fine, give me your account numbers.'

'Babes has them on record.'

Charlie went silent for a moment. 'Alright, the money has been transferred. Or it will be when the signal reaches Earth.'

'I will take your word for it. When can we do the interview?'

'Just do it now if you want.'

'I'm ready. Abby?'

The interview took an hour. They never got anywhere

near as much as they wanted, but at least it was something, and a lot more than they had before.

CHAPTER 41

A couple of weeks later, Steven found Charlie in one of the hobby rooms. He was putting the finishing touches to a beautiful chest of drawers.

'I heard you sold your soul to the devil.' Steven looked closely at it, 'Wow Charlie, I never knew you were this good.'

'Forty grand and an interview.'

'They paid you forty grand?'

'No ye neep, I paid them.'

Steven was confused, 'What for?'

Charlie pointed to the toolbox, 'For that.'

Steven went over to the bench and inspected it, 'Tools?'

'They found it on the Ortea home world in an old workshop. Awesome piece of kit.'

'You made this with it…' Steven came back to the chest of drawers, 'It is beautiful Charlie. Honestly, I never knew you were this skilled.'

'I'm not. I mean, it's my augmented body and eyes. I can measure shit in real time. No need for a tape measure. I can work with a precision that I actually find a bit scary. I never get tired, worn out, sore muscles.'

'Where did you get the walnut?'

'It isn't walnut, not real walnut anyway. Babes made it. I upload my requirements and a few minutes later I get all the wood I need at exactly the right lengths. I use the tools to refine them, it has all the jigs you need to make drawers, glue that sets in a few minutes. Babes has some beeswax and dyes, and I can polish at a few thousand revolutions a minute.'

Steven's smile slipped a little, 'Did they take that without permission?'

'I would imagine so.'

'Doesn't seem right.'

'Didn't sit quite right with me either. But the simple

truth of the matter is, the owner died two thousand years ago.'

'Why aren't they a pile of rust?'

'They are not made from iron or steel, it's some form of super hard alloy that must be unique to the Ortea. A touch of oil and they were brand new.'

'I suppose you have a point. No relations either.'

'Exactly. They also have another box from the Albany world we were on. From a race that are long extinct.'

'I saw something about that. There was a bit of an outcry on Earth about it.'

'Bad?'

'Not yet. Still, if it gathers momentum, it might just get that way.'

'What's it about?'

'Objections to working with herbivores and the Federation. The way they wipe out whole species. People think we should align ourselves with the Behema and make an alliance with them.'

'I doubt they are any better.'

'We are a tiny little pebble in the bottom of a very big pond Charlie.'

'What's happening back on Earth, is your campaign working?'

'Yes and no. You already know the negatives, but the churches are no longer screaming blue murder at least. They seem to be changing their doctrine a little. The flat Earth society has basically disbanded. Those guys who tried to blow themselves up received life sentences. The closure of the hospitals and schools in countries opposed to us has caused a backlash against their rulers and religious leaders. Civil strife has broken out in many of them.'

'I spent half a lifetime fighting in those shitholes. I feel sorry for the normal people. Problem is, they have little say, no power. Unless they take it, they will never gain it. Other countries get involved for their own selfish ends, normally to help the regimes to keep civil order, and make sure the cheap oil and shit still flows through to them.'

'You mean the west isn't helping.'

'I have my own views on the matter Stevie, they aren't very pleasant. Bin it man.'

'If that's what you want.' He looked down at the chest of drawers, 'I wish I had somewhere to put this.'

'Aye, me too.'

'So what are you going to do with it?'

Charlie shrugged, 'Beats the shit out of me. I suppose Babes could just absorb it again. We could make something else.'

'That would be a pity.'

'Aye, I suppose.'

The door slid open and the answer they were looking for walked in.

'There you are Steven.'

'Hi Merro, is something the matter?'

'Just looking for company, I was told you were in a hobby room.' He stepped back suddenly, 'Are you hiding things Steven?'

Steven was a little flummoxed, 'What are you talking about?'

Merro moved towards the piece and ran his fingers over the top of it.

'How beautiful. Is this a wood from your home planet?'

'It isn't real wood,' Charlie confessed. 'Babes has just replicated it as closely as she could. If this was real it would be called walnut.'

'Walnut. Like the trees the Emperor Darrick has.'

'Aye, that's the stuff.'

'It makes such beautiful furniture.'

'Maybe, but it takes many years to grow to a point where it is worth harvesting. Don't ask me how long, I don't know.'

'Your ship is an artisan Steven.'

Steven frowned, 'The ship didn't make it, Charlie did. She just supplied him with the materials.'

That seemed to shock Merro. 'Amazing, how long did it take you?'

'I managed to stretch it out over a few days.'

'Impossible.'

'How so? It was easy. Babes supplied the wood at the correct lengths. All I had to do was glue it together then polish it.'

'There has to be more to it than that.'

'Not much. It would have taken five times longer if I had to work from the raw materials.'

'I see, you mean it was like fixing together a kit?'

'More or less. I had to make all the joints, but I have tools that make it easy. I was just trying them out.'

'It is still beautiful. How much, may I buy it?'

Charlie sniffed, 'How about a couple of beers when you get home?'

Merro laughed, 'Be serious Charlie.'

'Listen, if that was real Walnut, and I had taken weeks to do it from scratch, you would be looking at half a gold bar. It isn't real wood, it took me a couple of days to slap it together and a bit of elbow grease to polish it. Couple of beers anyway.'

Merro stuck his hand out, laughing, 'It's a deal.' He rushed off.

Steven and Charlie sat down at the work bench and Charlie took out all the tools. Steven recognised some of them, but not all. They were still at it when Merro returned with Florina. There were a lot of 'oh's and 'ah's. The next thing Charlie knew, Florina had come over and slapped him hard on the back.

'What!'

'You are supposed to be a Lord, a noble Lord. Why are you always showing your common side?'

'Eh? There is only this side.'

Merro howled with laughter. Florina shook her head. 'You really are common Charlie.'

'Aye… I know.'

'Can you make me one? Not like that, it is beautiful, but very manly. Something more feminine, more suited to a Lady.'

'I don't know. After all the abuse I get from you, it would be a big ask.'

'I will get you,' she thought it over, 'Twenty bottles of the best beer.'

'Sold.'

Stevie and Merro almost fell over laughing.

'You are so cheap!'

'You mean you would have gone as high as twenty-one bottles?'

She shook her head and left. Merro and Stevie were still laughing.

Merro was finally able to take a deep breath, 'You don't mind?'

'Oh hell no. Since we have finished interviewing you, I have nothing else to do.'

'Have fun Charlie.'

'I will try.'

Merro also left. Steven was still smiling.

'Can I help?'

'You're shit at woodwork.'

'True, but I am good company.'

'You could make something for Komoru. Maybe something small like a jewellery box?'

'I think she would like that.'

They bumped fists.

CHAPTER 42

It took the pair longer than they thought it would. Steven chose an ebony design that he found a picture of in the database. It was going to take a lot of intricate carving and inlaying. Charlie chose to make a dressing table with a lot of inlay as well. They decided to practice on a coffee table first. It too was black ebony. Steven did some of the more basic work, while Charlie took care of the carving and inlay. Charlie found a beautiful picture of a dragon and drew it onto the table first. He then used a couple of different highlighters to mark the areas that would have the wood taken away – one colour for areas that would have the wood removed for an inlay, the other for wood removed for carving.

When they had finished inlaying it they polished the wood. Then they discussed whether to seal the top in resin or cover it in glass. They decided to inlay a sheet of glass. When they were finished the piece looked stunning.

With Charlie's help, it didn't take him too long to finish the jewellery box. Steven then helped Charlie with the inlay for his major project. They used precious metals, jewels, and minerals for the piece. It only took a couple of days to build it but the inlay itself took them weeks. Charlie finished it off with a mirror and a padded stool. The two stood back and admired it.

'It is a work of art Charlie.'

'Bonny init?'

'Sure is.'

The piece was white, with flowers and roses, golden handles and beading.

Charlie cocked his head to the side, 'Is it too much?'

'No. It's just perfect.'

Charlie sighed. Steven frowned, 'What's wrong man? You don't seem very happy.'

Charlie shook his head, 'I just wish I had these kinds of skills when I was normal.'

'Are we falling back into that melancholy again?'

'Melancholy my arse, I'm depressed man.'

'Don't you feel awesome?'

'No I don't. At least I canna weld with my fingertips yet.'

It took Steven a moment, then he burst out laughing. 'What are you like?'

'Aye, but you get a guy like David who has natural talent, a bloody artist, who took a lifetime to perfect his art. Then along comes me with half a computer for a brain and artificial limbs that can do precision work at minimum effort. I'm sure he will be banging me on the back telling me how talented I am, and I will just feel like a liar.'

'That is the honest and good side of you Charlie. Let's get him down here and ask him.'

'Seriously?'

'Why not.'

It only took him a few minutes. When he arrived he was stunned. He looked at it front and back.

'Wow, you guys are amazing!'

'Charlie designed it and did most of the detail. I did a lot of the rough work,' Steven admitted.

Before he could say more, Charlie cut him off, 'Before you start gobbing off David, I was only able to do it because of my enhancements. I could never do anything like this before.'

David thought it over, 'I can see where you are coming from Charlie. It must be nice to be part machine.'

'Comes in handy sometimes.'

David knelt and slid open a drawer. It was as smooth as silk and lined in a red felt, 'Where did you get the design?'

'Bit of this, bit of that.'

'The ability of an artist is in being able to visualise a completed piece then take it to that point. If you had simply replicated something you had seen before, then I would agree with you Charlie, but you must have some good knowledge.'

'I suppose. My uncle is a carpenter. I spent a lot of time with him as a kid and it was the only thing I got an A in at school.'

'Then you have simply built on the basics that you were taught as a child. The artwork had to come from you. I have never seen anything quite like it.'

'I've seen similar stuff.'

'But this isn't a reproduction?'

'Not totally, no. The shape is slightly different to others that I have seen. The pattern is a bit of this and that.'

'It looks like you drew it out on a big canvas and then laid it on top.'

'Pretty much.'

'I love these roses. You even have purple ones. It all comes together Charlie. It isn't gaudy. It is a refined piece. I like it. Don't put yourself down for being half machine. It was the Human brain that devised it, the mechanics that refined it. You guys have both done a great job.' He looked around, 'What else are you guys hiding?'

He found the chest of drawers first, then the coffee table with the jewellery box on it.

'You guys are fricken amazing. I love this table. Can I have it to display stuff on?'

Steven laughed, 'We hadn't quite decided which one of us was going to take it. What do you think Charlie?'

'It will save us fighting over it I suppose. I don't think it is quite right for display purposes though.'

'You are right Charlie,' David agreed. 'How about adding silver corners and a silver bead all the way around here at the top?'

'I think that would finish it off nicely,' Charlie agreed. 'Give us a couple of hours.'

'I'll hold you to that.'

The two of them got to work. Charlie engraved some Chinese characters into the silver plates before folding them into shape to cover the corners and Steven, with the help of Babes, designed some silver beading. By the time Charlie had secured the corner protection, Steven had already began to lay the beading. It didn't take them long.

They stood back again and admired their handy work. Steven nodded.

'I think that finishes it off nicely. You still feeling depressed?'

'Nah. David was right I suppose, I did have the basic skills. You've done a good job too.'

'Cheers bud. I just hope with all this stuff on display, Komoru isn't going to think my small box is too shabby.'

Charlie looked round, 'You might want to give her it in private. It is really bonny Stevie, but, well… you know.'

'It pales in comparison to some of this other stuff.'

Charlie thought it over, 'It looks good on that table. Maybe you should show her it up in David's. See if she likes it.'

'Ah! See if she likes it first. If she ignores it completely, then we can just leave it in David's. Someone will like it and take it. Nice thinking Charlie.'

'You haven't told her you are making it?'

'No. It was going to be a surprise. We slow down tomorrow. She is coming over with Sato, he is giving Merro his new belt.'

'He is really taking to it, isn't he?'

'Do you think it has something to do with his species?'

'I don't know Stevie. We automatically assume that folk who look like cats will have cat-like abilities and reflexes.'

'The Ambatta do.'

'Aye, yer no shittin. It could well be similar. He is pretty damn fast.'

'Let's take this up to David.'

'Aye why not.'

They carried it up to his room. The girls were all there. They all stood around the table gasping. Steven had to give an explanation as to what a dragon was. David plucked the box from the table.

'It overwhelms it.' He put it on a pedestal, 'That's better.'

Steven had to agree. Florina cornered Charlie, 'Have you finished my piece? You seem to have had plenty time to do other things.'

'They were practice, and it is finished.'

She dashed off, while Charlie shook his head. Merro laughed at him.

'She has little or no patience. It was all I could do to stop her sneaking down.'

'That reminds me. Babes, you can remove that restriction on the door now?' Charlie grinned at him, 'I had a restriction put on the door just in case.'

'Did it turn out well?'

'We think so, but I have no idea what you people will make if it.'

'Us people…'

'Well, you are an alien, and she is female.'

'Watch who you are calling an alien.'

Laughing, they went to catch up with her. They found her sitting on the stool with tears streaming down her face. It was the first time Charlie had seen another race that could cry. He was quite shocked.

Her voice was very low, 'Come and look Merro.'

He walked over, his mouth hanging open, 'I don't think I have ever seen anything quite like it Florina.'

Charlie sniffed, 'You must have inlay.'

'We do Charlie, but these flowers are obviously not of our world. In that, it is unique. Dazzling.'

She got up and threw her arms around his neck.

'Thank you.'

He pushed her gently away, 'Glad you like it.'

'I love it.'

'Thank goodness for that. I suppose we had better get it all wrapped up for you then. I will go see if we have the proper materials. If you will excuse me.'

Charlie beat a hasty retreat.

They watched him leave. Florina sighed, wiped a tear, and sat down in front of the mirror.

'No progress?' Merro asked.

She ran her hand over a flower, 'Half the men on the ship are literally panting at the sight of me, yet he doesn't even seem to realise I am here. It is as though he has simply switched off all his feelings. Then me makes something like this. I hate it because it gives me hope, I love it because he made it.'

Merro sat down beside her and she give him a little room. He too ran a finger over the surface of the piece.

'It is simply beautiful. Taylana is going to flip when she sees this.'

A slow smile spread over Florina's face, 'What a good idea.'

Merro's head snapped round, 'Really? You are going to rub it in her face!'

'Brother, dear brother, we maidens have to take out our frustrations somehow.'

'She will nag me forever.'

'I know. I also know this was the last of the materials they have.'

'No!'

'Oh yes. Charlie told me last week, that if they make a mess of it, they don't have the materials to make another, they would just have to keep recycling this one until they were successful.'

'You are going to make her hate me if I can't get her one.'

'Oh dear. One of a kind from the man I love. Maybe he will help you make something for her when we get home.'

The words suddenly dried up in her throat, they had spilled out without thought. She clamped her mouth tight. Merro understood and got up, pretending not to hear.

'Please don't show it to her, she will kill me.'

Florina relaxed a little, 'Prepare to meet thy doom brother.'

A few minutes later Florina appeared in David's room. She smiled sweetly, 'Taylana, Aurora, come and see what Charlie made me.'

Both women were soon infuriated and both for different reasons.

CHAPTER 43

During the following week, both women went on a systematic hunt for Charlie. He had, however, moved on to a project with Steven and the top engineers. He was nowhere to be found. When they did catch up with him, it was to be told that there was no more material. They had to put up with a promise of him making something for them both on the trip home, if they could replenish materials on their travels.

When Komoru had visited David's the following day, she had spotted the jewellery box from halfway across the room. When she opened it, she had found a note addressed to her from Steven. She had even teared up a little. Two minutes later she found the coffee table. Steven explained how he and Charlie had made the table while she inspected it minutely.

It was a couple of days later, as Charlie was grabbing something to eat with his friends, that she was finally able to track him down.

He was surprised when she sat down. A scowl at the men surrounding him sent them scuttling for cover.

Charlie watched his friends depart, 'That wasn't very nice of you.'

'I wanted to talk to you alone.'

'You could have asked instead of giving them the killer look.'

'I see your eyes are beginning to show expression.'

'Getting there.' He took a sip of coffee, 'So, what have I done this time?'

'You made me something beautiful.'

'I did a little carving; Steven did most of the work.'

'I have already thanked him for the gift.'

'I hope it was pleasurable.'

'Very, thank you. I want a table like the one in David's. Although I want a round one with four dragon's head feet.'

An image flashed into Charlie's head. 'What, with like a ball in their mouths?'

'Exactly! You have seen one like that?'

'I think so. An image just popped into my head anyway. However, right now we don't have the materials.'

'So I have heard. There is no rush. Of course, Ico has some materials.'

'No! Please…'

She laughed, 'That's what I thought.'

'I have more than enough on my hands.'

'I know.'

'Why don't you come and help us?'

'I don't like the idea of designing a warship.'

'We have moved onto designing a luxury liner.'

'Oh! That's different. Yes, I would love to help you design it.'

'I personally think we need the aesthetic eye of a woman.'

'Why don't you ask Taylana?'

'Because I am hiding from her.'

'You still need to bring her in.'

'Later in the week maybe.'

'Alright, when do you want me there?'

'Come today if you want. We are still working on the hull and the engineering side of it.'

'I would rather help with the layout.'

'Probably Tuesday then.'

'Are we thinking luxury?'

'Not too flamboyant, but a high degree of comfort.'

'Thank you for asking. Are we friends now Charlie?'

Charlie looked at her, 'How about we don't raise any flags just yet. What about not being mortal enemies?'

'It is a start.'

'Fine.'

Matt McGuire was waiting for him when he returned.

Steven was seconds behind. They settled down to work, but Steven soon got fed up.

'Let's go back to the battleships.' They all agreed.

The design on the wall changed. 'The main problems haven't changed,' Matt reminded them. 'If we use the new Federation engines, then the Federation will jump on our backs. They are, however, twenty per cent faster than the standard ones we have available for the battleships. Babes won't share the design for her engines either, so that is still off the table.'

'You simply cannot maintain them properly,' Babes interjected.

'We know. I'm not having a go at you.'

'Charlie and I may actually have a solution,' Babes offered.

All heads turned towards him, 'What?'

'If you give her a chance, she'll tell you.'

Matt grimaced, 'Sorry Babes, that was rude of me.'

'Typically Human though. I have, in my data banks, designs for old engines made by my species. It was Charlie who thought of this last night. They are still more advanced than the Federation engines, but smaller. The problem is the mass of the ships. We would have to either upsize the engines or install a lot of them.'

A diagram appeared on the wall showing a small engine next to a larger one.

'The lower one is an old design, the one above is a standard battleship engine.'

'It is a quarter of the size. I presume they have the same thrust?'

'Yes.'

'We could install half a dozen of these easily in the same space.'

'Yes, but they use the same amount of fuel as the large engine.'

'Bollocks! What about upsizing them?'

'There is a major problem Matt. If you look at the

Modloch vessels, you will see that the engines are practically the same for all ships, it is just the size that differs. Larger engines are used for a larger mass of ship. The extra thrust you gain is lost in the mass of the ship.'

'So even upsizing them won't matter?'

'Not much, no.'

'So, it doesn't matter then, it was a waste of time.'

'Charlie, could you explain your theory please?'

'An engine is an engine, right? It is the way it converts the energy to thrust that counts, or more to the point, the bloody exhaust. I still remember my dad telling me that. You can change the exhaust in a car and drastically change the output of an engine.'

'It's not the same Charlie. The exhaust in these ships is the thrust.'

Charlie gave a silent command and the screen changed. 'Babes and I have gone over the schematics of the new Federation engines with a fine-tooth comb. Alright, they do have a little more output, but the biggest difference is in the design of the thrusters. Basically, they changed the exhaust.'

Matt laughed, 'Alright, I see where you are coming from. So what though? We still can't use the Federation design.'

'I wasn't proposing to. That wee engine is about two thousand years old now. It was the last engine that the Builders made which was completely managed by the crew. That is why Babes chose it. However, it wasn't the last one that used thrust exhaust technology. That changed about a thousand years ago.'

'Oh no shit!' Matt's eyes had lit up, 'I think I see where you are coming from Charlie – we use a later exhaust system with the same engine.'

Charlie lifted his hands up, 'Tada!'

'Do you have it?'

'Finished it in my sleep.'

'Seriously?'

'A couple of hundred thousand calculations, tried and tested. My other brain told me that it had to redesign it about a hundred times before it came out right.'

'How can you do that when you were sleeping?'

'I didn't, it was in touch with Babes. The basic idea and concept was mine, but she worked it all out. Here it is.'

The screen changed again. Matt and Steven both moved forward. Both played with the image.

Matt was the first to step back, his eyes gleaming, 'That is a thing of beauty. It looks longer than a normal engine though.'

'It's about half the length of one of the big ones.'

'This is a small one!'

'Then our design for a ship will be longer and thinner. The big question is, how much faster is it?' Asked Steven.

'We have calculated it at seventeen per cent faster than the new Federation models. At top speed of course. Now here's the thing: why are we building colossal ships anyway? To me it seems like we are just keeping up with the Joneses. Why can't we have smaller battleships more suited to our race? Let's take the modern firepower of a battleship and wrap it in something smaller. We don't need the cargo space of a Modloch war vessel. In fact we could quite easily develop a fleet based on the ships we know. This is just a concept that I have come up with.'

Charlie sent orders to the screen, 'To start with, I would like to compare the biggest aircraft carrier on Earth to a standard Modloch battleship. As you can see, the Modloch battleship dwarfs it. Yet that carrier has a crew of thousands, can go to sea for months without replenishment, and carries over seventy aircraft. The aircraft, however, aren't all fighters. They have helicopters, anti-sub aircraft, all kinds of shit. They can have them on the deck or store them internally.'

The picture changed to only that of Modloch battleship. 'The standard Modloch battleship carries a hundred fighters, fifty on each side. A dozen shuttles.

The Black of Space

What if we changed this design to that of an aircraft carrier?'

The picture changed again. Now they were looking at a sort of space carrier. Matt moved forward. The Modloch battleship was above. The space carrier was larger than a conventional carrier but still dwarfed by the battleship.

Matt wasn't sure, 'I don't know Charlie. What are the advantages?'

'It's about half the mass, and with four standard sized engines it is thirty per cent faster than the battleship. It also carries three hundred fighters and a dozen shuttle craft.'

That turned their heads, 'Three hundred fighters! How the hell did you manage that?'

Charlie got up and expanded the view until they were looking inside.

'With a carousel. There is no gravity, no turning into the wind. You can launch a fighter any which way you want. You can get three side by side on the flight deck. Fifteen banks of fighters gives forty-five fighters on the deck at the same time. Twenty fighters on each carousel and an empty space.'

'Why an empty space?'

'Jeez. Every fighter has its own piece of deck which it is attached to. It slots into the carousel. The empty one is to make the deck look clean. The first deck is the flight deck. The second the hanger. The third the maintenance deck. The fighters can be fuelled up while on the carousel. It is all automated. The front part of the carrier is the living area. Storage. The back is the engines, fuel and so on. It doesn't have the same heavy guns as the battleships, but it doesn't need to, it is a support vessel delivering masses of fighters into battle.'

Steven pointed to something, 'So the fighter lands on the deck. It is anchored. The deck falls away, the next one lands on the same spot.'

'Aye, the last part is automated. Damaged fighters can

land at the front of the ship out of the way. There are lifts there that go directly to the maintenance deck. There are no torpedoes or bombs to replenish. It all saves space and time turning them around. A fighter will drop below deck, into its cradle, be refuelled and back out in under five minutes. You can do multiple refuels on any carousel you want. Put a fresh squadron up at the same time. Ach, work it out for yourselves. The important thing is that those engines will propel this thing faster than the new Federation vessels.'

'What else have you got Charlie?' Matt asked.

'Okay, I got battleships and destroyers.'

Charlie went through a host of different ships. Matt and Steven were both dumbfounded. Matt held up a hand to stop his explanations.

'How long have you been thinking of this Charlie?'

'Dunno.' He turned to Steven, 'When did you tell me to start designing ships?'

The question took Steven by surprise. It took a moment, but the conversation popped into his mind.

'Oh! Quite a while a go.'

'There you go. Quite a while.'

Steven suddenly burst out laughing, 'I thought you told me to do it myself.'

'Did I say it nicely?'

'Yeah, I think so.'

'Then I must have liked the idea. What I never had were the engines to do anything with them. Most of these ships are a quarter the size of their Modloch equivalent, but they were built with the same specs. So, there is no advantage to them. They have the same shields, same firepower, they're a little faster because there is less mass, but that's about it. Now we have a different powerplant, that shakes things up a bit. We got better output to the shields, power to spare. We can upgrade the weapons and we will be a lot faster than anything else out there.'

A thought crossed Steven's mind. 'What if we put them

into our existing ships?'

'It all comes back to mass. These engines are a lot smaller than the Modloch powerplants.'

He held up a hand, 'Right, I got it. Not much then.'

'Better, but not by much, less than ten per cent.'

'Ten per cent is still good.'

'Aye but still slower than the new Federation vessels. Do you want to see my fave?'

Steven did, but Matt gave him a funny look. He didn't like the sly smile on Charlie's face much.

'You mean we haven't seen them all?'

'I got another dozen I haven't developed, but this one is my particular favourite.'

The screen changed. Steven got halfway to his feet. 'Woah! That is so cool.'

Matt felt himself break out into a cold sweat, 'What the hell is that Charlie?'

'I got a few variations,' the screen changed and the grin on Charlie's face broadened.

It was now apparent to Matt exactly what Charlie had been trying to devise. 'That looks like a chisel blade on the prow. Seriously? You want to ram them?'

'Seemed like a good idea at the time. The major problem was field harmonics. The shields are like a bubble. To burst through another ship's shields would also compromise your own. We had to fit the shields around the ship, skin-tight, which is hard to do.'

'Impossible.'

'No it ain't. We managed it when designing the shields on my robot body, remember?'

'Aye, I do. Right enough. The shield had to conform to your body. You did that with nanites though. Is this different?'

'Aye, the shield projectors are usually on the outside of the hull. We just brought them inside, retracted them until the bubble was close to the skin of the ship then rotated the ones at the front and back to make it almost skin-tight.

It seems to work in theory. The problem then was that the shields weren't as effective, about a quarter of their strength.' The scene changed and Charlie played a demonstration. 'Now here was the thing that scuppered the whole idea. You could plough right through the middle of a battleship, but as the ship folded itself around you while you passed through…'

'It crushed you,' Matt stated flatly.

'You win the major prize. So it was a bust. But Babes has been playing with these since we got the specs for the new engines and output. This is what would happen now.'

The battleship cleaved clean through its opponent. Matt pulled over a seat and sat down.

'The shields now have the power to stop you being crushed. Where the hell did you get this idea from?'

'A film. Ramming speed.'

'Which is?'

'Two hundred miles an hour. Two fifty to be really sure. The shield doesn't extend to the front. The chisel point, or ram if you will, is forward of the shields. No much good in a ship to ship action, but in a fleet to fleet action, where they can't manoeuvre all that well, it's deadly.'

'You have a horrible mind Charlie.'

'I just love a challenge.'

Steven glared at him, 'Didn't I ask you to design a passenger liner?'

Charlie glared back, 'Do I look like a pool princess to you?'

'No.'

'Then ram it.'

'I don't like you anymore.'

'Aye well, tell that to someone who gives a shit.'

Matt burst out laughing, 'Any other problems you have come across Charlie, can we use these engines in a liner?'

'No, nor a freighter.'

'Why not?'

The Black of Space

'You gonna send out defenceless liners and freighters that can outrun everything any other race has? How long before they start disappearing along with the passengers and crew?'

'Good point.'

'There is one other problem.'

'What's that?'

'No one has a clue how to maintain the buggers. So all we are doing here is giving our brains a little pleasant stroking.'

'Man, you are a shit!'

It was Charlie's turn to laugh, 'Just pointing out the obvious.'

'You know we have some pretty solid guys now.'

'It's still three or four generations ahead of what they are working on now.'

'There would be no harm in building a prototype or two. Let our top blokes loose on it. See what they can do.'

Charlie shrugged, but Steven was mulling it over.

'We can't even put the Dents to it. Could we put this new exhaust system to work on the vessels we already have?'

Babes felt she was the only one capable of answering this question.

'Yes my heart. It will improve the top speed of the vessels. The second generation of ships built by us have a smaller mass than the original designs, so they are already faster. This should enable them to keep up with the new Federation ships at cruising speed, although I am quite sure the top speeds wouldn't match.'

'Because no one ever cruises at their top speed.'

'It is the nature of all machines my heart. The harder you work them, the quicker they wear out and break down.'

CHAPTER 44

A few days later, Steven was alone looking over designs of Charlie's ships when Merro walked in and caught him by surprise. He took one look at the picture on the wall.

'A fleet carrier. That's a nice design.'

Steven's hand started reaching for the control, but he hesitated and smiled.

'Do you use them too?'

'Of course. I do like the design. How many fighters does it carry?'

'Three hundred.'

Merro frowned, 'Why so few? Our smallest carriers carry five hundred.'

'Big ones a thousand?'

'Yes, medium around seven hundred. Why so few?'

'This was one of the first, more or less a prototype.'

'I see. Some of the older vessels were truly works of art themselves. Was it fast?'

'I don't know much about it; I just use the picture as a screen saver.'

'I don't blame you; it is a nice one.'

'What is it I can do for you Merro?'

'We are getting close to home now. I think it is about time we sent out my recognition signal.'

'We are still a few weeks away.'

'I know, but we have vessels that patrol the black space. No point in getting into trouble.'

'Just go and see Sid on the bridge. He will do whatever it is you require.'

Merro looked around, 'Are you busy?'

'No not really, just going over a few files, waiting for my Chief Engineer to arrive.'

'Still trying to design a new liner?'

'We are.'

He shook his head, 'Well good luck.'

As soon as Morro left Steven asked Matt to come and

see him straight away.

Matt walked in and looked at the screen, 'What's up?'

'Merro walked in and saw that.'

Matt smiled, 'What does it matter? It doesn't exist, never will.'

Steven took a deep breath, 'It might well do.'

'I thought we had more or less agreed to bin it? Weren't you making a final decision on it today?'

'Merro knew exactly what it was.'

Matt came over and sat down opposite him.

'You mean these guys use them.'

'He was shocked to hear it only held three hundred fighters.'

'I can't believe you told him that.'

'I took a chance. Their smallest ones hold five hundred. Medium seven, and large ones a thousand.'

'Holy shit!'

'That is exactly what I was thinking.'

'Did you tell him it was only a concept?'

'No, I told him it was an old ship, a prototype.'

'That was quick thinking. You know this means we are going to have to start building them.'

Steven slumped forward and laid his head on top of his arms for a moment. 'I know. Federation vessels are fairly evenly matched. If imperial ships have carrier fleets, they can launch thousands of fighters at once, which would put them at a sever advantage over any federation vessels. Babes, can you tell Charlie what has just transpired?'

'Of course, my heart.' A full minute passed, 'I have told him, my heart.'

'Did he say anything?'

'Yeeha.'

Matt laughed, while Steven lifted his head and smiled, 'I am out of my league with this military stuff. I was about to say no, and it turns out we will need them. Who can we talk to about this?'

'There is only one person I know of who can properly

understand all of this sir: Admiral Baxter.'

'Of course, why didn't I think of that. What time is it back home?'

'You mean home or the city ship?'

'Ah... city ship.'

Babes supplied the answer, 'It is three in the afternoon there.'

'Ask Sid if he can get in touch with him. We need to talk. Tell him it isn't urgent though.'

'I will my heart.'

Steven was surprised when five minutes later Admiral Baxter appeared on screen drinking a cup of tea.

'Ambassador Gordon. How can I help you?'

'I hope I am not disturbing you Admiral.'

'You are lucky, you caught me at tiffin.'

Steven laughed, 'Is that a real thing?'

'Military tradition for hundreds of years.'

'We need professional help here. Can I send you a package?'

'Please do.'

'We have been trying to design our own ships. We have a few concepts. One of those is for a fleet carrier.'

Baxter held up a hand containing a biscuit, 'I have often thought about that, but no one here has them. We don't really need them.'

'That's what my thoughts were. However, the Première caught sight of our design for one today. His people do use them.'

Baxter was frowning now, 'You mean this new Empire uses them?'

'Yes.'

'Did he let anything else slip?'

'We designed our one to carry three hundred fighters. Their smallest carries five hundred, largest a thousand.'

'Wait a moment Ambassador. Your package has arrived. Let me have a look at it.'

'I will take the opportunity to have a coffee.'

Two cups appeared in front of Steven and Matt, and both men took sips as they waited. Baxter was sitting up now, Steven could see his eyes gleam.

Eventually he got back to them, 'Some of these concepts are amazing Ambassador. Is that your Chief Engineer there, did he design these?'

'Matt McGuire sir, I didn't design them.'

'No,' Steven interrupted, 'It was a collaborative effort between my ship and Charlie.'

It didn't take Baxter long, 'The Captain? The infantry bod?'

'That is him.'

'I told you he shouldn't be galivanting around the galaxy. I don't care what you say Ambassador, when he returns from your little trip he is coming to me.'

'He is no longer in the armed forces sir. He is also a Modloch citizen. You haven't a hope in hell in getting him anywhere near Earth either. The last time he came into contact with your people he was arrested and held for five days without charge, tortured with sleep deprivation and starvation, all to get information about the Modloch Emperor.'

He frowned, 'Were those the ones the Emperor arrested?'

'That's them sir.'

'So he was the Modloch citizen they arrested. I am sorry, I heard something of the incident in passing, not the full details.' He let out a long breath, 'The idiots. Would he be prepared to work with our people on this side of the barrier'

'I don't know sir. There isn't much he can really do on his own. As I said, it was a collaborative effort between him and my ship. Charlie provides the concept; she builds it for him. All we can do is hand the details over to you and your people. You can either reject them out of hand or ask for a proof of concept. We also have new engines for those and for upgrading our existing fleets.'

'Of course, it isn't like you can leave your ship with us, is it?'

'No sir, I can't.'

'Alright, leave this with me. I presume you want me to go over these plans with my experts and choose which ones we want to trial?'

'Yes sir. How important is it that the Empire has fleet carriers?'

'It is a game changer, Ambassador. A concentrated attack from even three hundred fighters can seriously compromise a ship's shields, making it vulnerable. Imagine a thousand. In a fight with equal numbers, three of these carriers would easily tip the balance in their favour. I will also need to speak to the Grand Commander about this. Do you mind?'

'No, of course not sir.'

'If they have carriers that can hold a thousand fighters, then we will need the equivalent. However, what you have here at least proves the concept. We can trial it to death with a ship that will probably be more suitable. Speak to Charlie and the ship and see if they can come up with a design for a larger ship. Did you say a thousand fighters?'

'There are three carrier classes: five hundred, seven hundred and a thousand.'

'If you get an opportunity, then get us some footage of those carriers Ambassador.'

'I will try.'

'I would also appreciate a courtesy visit from your crewman when you all get back.'

'I can but try.'

'I appreciate this Ambassador, I will be in touch.' The screen went blank.

Matt turned to Steven, 'We may well have thrown the proverbial cat in with the pigeons.'

CHAPTER 45

'Did it have to be him!' Ne´ was on his feet, 'Seriously Admiral!'

Baxter was surprised by the outburst, 'I sense that you two have a history?'

Ne´ sat back down, 'We do. I dislike the man intensely.'

'Why?'

'I feel like he is always hiding something about himself.'

'Aren't we all allowed to do that?'

'It goes deeper than that Admiral. I dislike anyone who seems to know what I am thinking before I do.'

'I have had a small dose of the man myself. It wasn't pleasant. I did, however, look into his background. He was a good soldier but nothing remarkable. Then he found an Albany after a great battle that could talk English without a translator.'

'Ah! The one you made Human, who is in charge of foreign affairs?'

'That's the one.'

'When Charlie was a young soldier on his first mission, he came across two intelligence officers who had just perpetrated a crime. He reported it to his senior Commanders. The report was buried, but the crime caused a wave of violence that cost many lives. Years later, who do you think he was told to hand over the Albany to?'

'Rhetorical question Admiral?'

'Indeed sir. It was the same two men who had perpetrated the crime years before. The sergeant, as he was then, realised that the Albany was too important to hand over to a pair of brutal murderers. He took him away, but not without violence.

'His own CO refused to hand either over. The Albany was picked up instead by Ambassador Gordon and the sergeant incarcerated for disobeying orders. While on manoeuvres, the intelligence officers managed to get their hands on him. He was then systematically tortured and sentenced to death. It is here that reports become a little vague. According to some testimony, he shouldn't even be alive. One said he was blind, every major bone in his body broken, without eyes, feet, hands. Of course, I find that difficult to believe. There would be some disability and the man looks as robust as an ox.'

'Was it not the Ambassador and his friends who rescued him?'

'How on Earth do you know that?'

'He told me a little of his story himself, and of course the Modloch Emperor knows the full story, he is my best friend.'

'I see.'

'I didn't believe either of them myself, I found it hard to comprehend. The Builder ship apparently saved his life, replacing his limbs and eyes. I once saw him pull a rebar from a block of concrete with his bare hands. A frightening man.'

'Is that even possible?'

'Obviously it is. The Builder race is generations ahead of the rest of us in technology. You are lucky to have two of their ships.'

'If it wasn't for those ships, none of us would be here now. Still, this is getting us away from the matter at hand.'

'That is true. I chose not to believe the Captain as he was then, but if this is from your own intelligence community, I cannot do anything but believe it.'

'It is difficult to comprehend.'

'Very. Yet to move forward, we need to believe, and learn to trust this man. This revelation has indeed changed my views on the matter, and these concepts are startling. They propose a new engine, one that is faster than our newest ships. I don't suppose we can have some of these.'

'What good would it be for only Humanity to have these ships? This threat comes from outside the Federation. We have no idea of the size of their forces, their capabilities, or how many of these carriers they have.'

'I think we are going to need a lot more from Humanity than just these ships. No Federation force has ever worked with a carrier force before.'

'I know some fantastic fleet officers who specialise in just that.'

Ne´ smiled. 'I think it is time for Humanity to take another step forward. Get those men into the Federation, I need them to begin teaching. We need this carrier as soon as possible. We need it to train with. We need to rethink and reform out battlegroups and strategies.'

'We have some great literature on that.'

'Translated into every language please.' He sighed, 'Now what else do we need?' He flicked through the files. Baxter who was mirroring his actions suddenly burst out laughing. Ne´ glanced over and swiped to the next page. He opened the file and soon burst out laughing too, 'Oh, I need a whole fleet of these.'

'Exactly what I was thinking sir.'

'What carnage we could create. Alright, could you ask the Ambassador to build the carrier and at least one of these to start with?'

'I thought about keeping these for the Human fleet.'

'Don't you dare tease me Admiral.' They both laughed and settled down to look over the rest of the files.

CHAPTER 46

Charlie was enjoying a coffee when the call came in from Ne´. The two sat contemplating the other.

Ne´ was the first to break the ice, 'I suppose you want me to call you Charlie.'

'Call me what the hell you like. It doesn't have to be nice.'

Ne´ barked a laugh, 'Do you know what I am calling about?'

'For you to call me at the arse end of the universe, it has to be about those designs. I can't see you calling me up because Lady Glee has failed to send your potatoes.'

'She hasn't. I appreciate your thoughtfulness.'

'It isn't me just being thoughtful, it is an apology.'

'One I accepted. Although it still gets under my skin.'

'I can tell. How can I help you Grand Commander?'

'We need you to design bigger carriers. We need information on their fleets, their makeup and tactics.'

'On my to-do list already. I believe Stevie has already sent orders to start building your carrier and one battleship.'

'Why weren't they sent to me first?'

'I bet you can think of a hundred reasons yourself.'

'You know, it is considered polite that when someone of my status asks you a question, you answer it properly.'

'I am nothing more than a glorified bodyguard. I am paid by the Ambassador, not the Federation. I didn't design those craft for anyone, it was just a bit of fun in my spare time. They were impractical until I was able to come up with an advanced power source. As it is, they are still impractical. Those engines are more advanced than anything anyone else has at the moment.'

'Don't worry about that side of things. If I had the power to, I would haul you back here in an instant.'

'Just as well for me that you don't. I have already given a lifetime of service. Even if it wasn't to the Federation.

You can't touch me.'

'I can if there is a war.'

'If there is a war, I will either be with the Ambassador or at Darrick's side. Catch me if you can.'

Ne´ laughed, 'So you are determined to stay retired?'

'I most certainly am.'

'What fighters were you proposing to use on those carriers?'

'After talking to the Ambassador, who talked to Admiral Baxter, I changed the design slightly to accommodate the latest Federation Fighter. I am also playing with the design to see if I can fit any more fighters into it.'

'Don't bother redesigning that one, design another specific to the task. I wanted to ask you about storage space.'

'It was designed around Humans. However, you will find extra storage space in what was once the ammunition bunkers. When they told me it was going to be used by the Federation, I added an extra deck to the bottom of the ship. Five bales high the entire length and breadth of the ship.'

'That should be more than adequate. Can you send me the new design?'

Charlie did something on his computer, 'On their way.'

'You added to the other ship too?'

'I added length to that, rather than bulk. I also finished a design for a freighter that can keep up with the fleet.'

'Is it designed on a Modloch battleship?'

'No, it is a totally new design, but you would recognise it as a freighter.'

'Send the design please.'

'Already have.'

'How the hell can you tell what I am thinking from so far away?'

Charlie looked surprised, 'I thought about all of this a week ago. You're the one who is playing catch up here.

They are bigger than standard freighters, but nowhere near as big as the battleship ones we use. They can carry the same amount though.'

Ne´ took a deep breath, 'I am sorry, that outburst was unwarranted.'

'You aren't the only one with a brain Grand Commander. I also have a ship here that is smarter than all of us put together. She has been guiding me, especially on what a crew of herbivores would require. We added headroom in all of the designs, extra storage space for food, larger latrines, and a hundred other damn things. It was she who insisted that a freighter to keep up with the fleet was a must. I simply thought you might like to look at these designs at some point, so I included them in the package.'

'That was thoughtful of you, thank you.'

'I don't know what it is that gets up your nose about me Grand Commander, and I don't really care either, but if you want to work with me on this stuff then you had better pull your head out of your arse and stop over-reacting to everything I say, or over-thinking things. Either that or get a liaison. I am seriously trying to be as nice and respectful as I can towards you, but if things go south, I will simply just stop.'

'I did apologise.'

'You did, and I accept that. So why don't we clear the decks, start afresh. I have the utmost respect for you and also hold you in the highest regard, but that will never stop me from speaking my mind.'

'Alright, let us put the past behind us. There's far more to you than it first seems. My first priority is always the Federation and you are helping us for no reward. I can respect that. Your package has arrived. If you don't mind, I wish to look at it.'

'Just call if you need anything.'

'I will.'

The screen went blank and Steven put his cup down on the table. He had been out of sight of the Grand Commander the whole time and had kept quiet.

'Did you really just tell the Grand Commander of the entire Federation to pull his head out of his arse?'

'I suppose I did.'

Steven shook his head, 'One of these days you are going to say that kind of thing to the wrong person.'

Charlie spun in his seat, 'I don't care who these people are Stevie. I had a lifetime of bullshit while I was in the army. I didn't kowtow to officers there either.'

'It must have got you into a lot of trouble.'

'It got me demoted as well,' Charlie sighed. 'Maybe I do over-react a bit now and then.'

'Now and then!'

'If you are going to get uppity, you can piss off as well.'

Steven laughed, 'You know, they picked the designs I would have dismissed.'

'You don't have a military mind Stevie. You made the right decision. I didn't realise any of them would ever be built. Just goes to show!'

'Sure does. Now the liner.'

Charlie growled in exasperation, 'Do we have to?'

'Afraid so. The ladies will be here as well, so be nice.'

'I'm always nice.'

Steven wasn't very sure if he had actually heard him right.

CHAPTER 47

The months had flown past for Taylana, even though she had been dreading the return journey. The ship shimmered below her feet and they all gasped as she saw her home world come into sight. It wasn't the first time she had seen it from space, but it was the first time she had seen it as if she was actually floating in space.

Over the last few days they had been tidying up all of the projects. It hadn't really been long enough, she mused. The fashion world was holding its breath for her return from the Federation. Her adversaries would have been having fun in her absence. It was time now to put them all firmly back in their place.

She had a hundred photo shoots with Florina, considered the most beautiful woman in the whole Behema Empire. Aurora had also turned out to be very photogenic. She had also used a variety of the Human females. She was sure Himari and Komoru would appeal to the men of her race, but some of the other women were also beautiful and exotic.

The person she was going to miss the most was David. She sighed as she thought about it. She loved Merro with all of her heart, but her soul yearned for someone like David. They had spent three wonderful months together. She had never before gelled so well with any other person. It was as though he knew exactly what she wanted and he created to perfection all that she needed. Indeed, many times he exceeded her expectations. There was never any chance of a physical relationship. She didn't feel for him in that way. Yet she would be devastated by his loss.

She prepared herself mentally for what was to come while a small camera buzzed somewhere close by. She ignored it.

Merro's hand closed on her shoulder, 'Wow, it is difficult to walk when it is like this.'

She laughed, 'I am not trying to walk.' His smile was

radiant. 'You are happy to be home.'

'Of course, but I can see that you aren't.'

'Of course I am.'

'You have been in design nirvana for three months. You are going to feel lost.'

'Nirvana? You are picking up more Human words. You are right though. From the jewellery to the dresses, the perfumes to even designing a starship. How wonderful was that Merro?'

'It has been an extraordinary journey. Of all the journeys I have undertaken, this is the one that will stay with me the longest.'

'How long do we have them for?'

'Five days, then they have to head to the central planets.'

'I am going to miss them all so much. I wish we could visit their world.'

'So do I.'

She gave him a strange look, 'I hope we aren't going to go to war with these people Merro.'

'I am not recommending it. I liked the people we met. Even some of the herbivores. Especially the Modloch Emperor.'

'Let us make the whole crew welcome Merro. Both ships. If we go to the summer palace, we can have both ships land.'

'That is a good idea.'

The walls began to reappear, and the breath-taking view of the planet disappeared. Their escort for the final half light year began to break off. Merro went over to Sid and asked to be patched through to their space control centre. It didn't take him long to get permission. They were met in orbit by a shuttle and guided down.

When they landed, Komoru and Steven gave permission for all their crews to go out and stretch their legs. The air was fresh. Through an avenue of strange trees, they could see a large complex. Men and women stretched, took deep lungs full of air and began to move away from the ships. Some lay back in the well-trimmed short grass. Hailey lay on her back with her arms spread wide, running her hands through the grass. She opened her eyes and smiled as Sid sat down beside her.

Richard and Abbey were away inspecting the unusual trees. There were also wildflowers on a thin verge, which were similarly inspected minutely. A shuttle raced in and landed close by. A number of armed guards ran over but they caused no real consternation. When Steven saw Charlie relax and turn away, he also relaxed.

One of the guards bowed to the Première, then the guard split up a little, spreading out. Another shuttle shot overhead. Merro wandered over to Steven.

'Not to worry, it is just the guard.'

'I figured that,' Steven smiled. Those that had been on Komoru's ship went over and mingled with them. Some were soon laughing. 'They know one another?'

Merro looked round, 'Yes of course. None of my staff are here right now. The palace is big enough for the whole crew; however, the rooms will have to be prepared. In the meantime, I must go and speak to my father on our secure communication line.'

'I would imagine he is dying to get his hands on all the intelligence you have gathered.'

Merro laughed aloud, 'Of course he is, he and all of the other rulers of the Empire. I will catch you soon.' He looked around with a smile, 'I can see the crew is already enjoying themselves.'

Steven looked around, 'It is a lot like home. Just different. Would you like your furniture offloaded here as well?'

'No, could you please drop that off for me at my normal residence. Florina's too, before you leave.'

'Not a problem, we have five days to do it anyway.'

'On your way back home, can you stop for a few days? I want to show you and the crew more of our world. We have some really fine holiday spots.'

'I think we can do that.'

'Wonderful, but right now my father is waiting.' He went over to Taylana and let her know what he was doing. A couple of guards stayed behind, but the rest went with Merro.

Florina wandered over to where Charlie was standing with one of his friends. The friend was doing something with a strange box. He handed a white cylinder to Charlie. Then he made one for himself. The were both out of uniform in the clothes they called jeans and t-shirts, attire the crew often wore when they were off duty.

To her surprise they put the cylinders in their mouth and lit them. Smoke was drawn into their lungs and expelled.

'What are you two doing!'

'Having a fag,' Charlie confessed.

'A what?'

'A cigarette. It is tobacco. Comes from a plant, very addictive. An old habit the pair of us haven't quite kicked yet. The nanites in our system have killed the addiction, but we still like a smoke now and then. We rarely get the chance these days.'

'I would take a bet that it isn't good for you.'

'You would win, but it isn't an illegal substance or anything like that.'

She glanced across, 'That would be why Amanda is scowling at the pair of you.'

'Exactly why.'

She shook her head, 'You are the strangest person I have ever met Charlie.'

'Well, I am an alien.'

She laughed, 'I know lots of aliens, you are still strange.' She glanced at Eddie, 'So are your friends?'

'Don't say that in front of him, he will think it is a compliment.'

She thought that was even funnier, then paused a moment, 'You could stay here with me you know. You could indulge every passion you have for the rest of your life – build your furniture, design ships, anything you want, or simply do nothing if you wanted to.'

'No thanks, but have a happy life Florina. I wish you the best.' Her face fell.

'Stop being such a dick Charlie.'

Charlie scowled at Eddie, 'You know I can pick you up by your nipples don't you?'

'Aye, and I will kick you in the balls while I'm hanging in the air. The lassie has done you no ill man, be nice!'

Charlie sighed in exasperation, 'It would seem my conscience has spoken.' He thought it over for a moment, taking inspiration from the clouds drifting overhead, 'Would you like to be stuck in my small cottage, with a husband who is only home for about a month in the year, with no friends, no family, and surrounded by strange aliens?'

She shook her head, 'No I wouldn't.'

'Neither would I Florina. I have a purpose here, friends, family, a job. I like my life the way it is. Living here with you would bring me nothing but misery, I simply couldn't take the lifestyle.'

'I understand. Thank you at least for the gift.'

'It wasn't a gift, you asked me to make it.'

'I will perceive it how I wish. I want to go say goodbye to some of the others.'

She had almost turned away when she caught a blur out the corner of her eye. Aroura had sped past, leapt up on Charlie and planted a huge kiss on his lips. Her arms were wrapped tightly around his neck and her legs his waist. Charlie had to literally rip her off.

'Aurora! How dare you!'

Aurora allowed herself to be detached from Charlie.

The Black of Space

She looked up at Florina in a way only one woman can look at another when they know they have gotten the better of her.

'What?'

Florina's eyes changed, 'You little macca!'

Aurora simply smirked and skipped away. She paused for a few seconds, 'My parents are heading over to pick me up Charlie. I will see you some time,' she waved.

Charlie burst out laughing and waved back, 'Bye Aurora.'

Florina went after the skipping teenager with murder in her heart.

The two watched the women go as they finished their smoke.

'What was that like?'

Charlie thought it over, 'About the same as snogging a woman with moustache I would imagine.'

'You must have done a few of them in the past.'

Charlie scowled at him, 'Whit?'

'You're getting that look back.'

'Right now I am contemplating how far across this park I can throw ye.'

'Was it nice?'

'No, it was itchy and minging.'

Eddie looked at the backs of the retreating women, 'Ye've din a lot worse.'

He managed to dodge the friendly punch.

CHAPTER 48

Merro locked himself into the secure room. They had all gathered. Merro felt his gut tighten. It was rare the rulers of the Empire would gather together to listen to one person like this, and you could never tell how things would go or what they would ask.

'Welcome home Merro.'

Merro bowed low, 'Father, honoured leaders.'

'Did you enjoy your trip?'

'I believe I did.'

'Did you see any of their fleets?'

'No, they were kept out of sight. We had a small battlegroup accompany us on our journey. It was well led, very effective. The ships were all built by the Humans. Good effective fighting ships, but nothing we couldn't handle. According to our data scans, we would most likely have the upper hand in a ship to ship combat. Their fighters have virtually the same specs as ours have.'

'So in reality, it is just their numbers.'

'I believe so.'

'Did you find out the structure of their armed forces?'

'The Federation has a core of professionals, as we thought. Each race supplies battlefleets proportional to the size of their empire. The Modloch Empire is the biggest, with twenty-two planets under their control. Almost half are recent acquisitions and they are simply paying tribute. They smashed the fighting forces of three different races in a recent war, one race of which is now struggling to survive.'

'Not someone we want to get on the wrong side of by the sounds of it.'

'You would like the Modloch Emperor, Father, as I believe most of you would. He is a very strong, decisive leader. He looks after his people. They are willing to die for him. His forces are well led, professional.'

'Did your sister manage to seduce his Human brother?'

'No, I am afraid not. I don't believe the Emperor is willing to give him up either.'

'I am disappointed in her.'

'Don't be. He already has a companion. Wait a moment please,' he took out his pad and found the pictures on social media that some of the girls had posted. He cast it to the screen. Jean in her swimming costume walked across the screen and dived into the pool. He then found the footage of the shooting competition, where she displayed some of her skills.

When the screen cleared, he found all of the Emperors sitting forward. It made him smile.

'She is a Captain with the Federation and works with one of their best Admirals. She is also a favourite of the Federation's Grand Commander. I believe she is earmarked to go very far in her career.'

One of the other Emperors found his voice first, 'Are those tits for real?'

They all burst out laughing, his father the hardest.

Merro found it hard not to join in, 'They are very real.'

'This is the woman that Florina was competing against?'

'Yes it was.'

One of his friends leaned across and grasped his arm. 'Do not be too harsh on her, that woman must rate as a beauty across the whole galaxy. Would you stray if you had such a woman?'

'I never thought I would see the day when Florina was out classed and out matched. You're right Baal, there are few who could stand up to that one. I will not be harsh on her. Still, I feel a little insulted that my daughter would be rejected. Is he here, this man?'

'He is Father.'

'Then I will meet him one day and see if he was even worth her hand. Do you like him Merro?'

'I do Father, very much.'

'Let us move on then. Would it be worth our while

attacking this Federation?'

'No Father. We may win a few battles, but we would lose the war. Our biggest problem is their biggest problem: resupply. Thus far there are only three meat-eating races in the Federation. All three planets are untouchable. Earth is protected by its own star, the Ambatta live on a world that is surrounded by a vast asteroid field. Most of them live within that field. They have slaughtered every adversary that has tried to take them on. They can control the asteroids, open pathways, close them, in seconds. With billions of asteroids, it is impossible to winkle them out.

'The last planet that could supply us is the Ortea. They live in vast underground cities that are, I have to say, wonderous to behold. They held out against the Federation for two thousand years. We don't have the technology to locate those cities. We don't have the manpower to assault them. It has been tried many times.

'Every other planet is completely devoid of life, other than the superior indigenous species of that planet. To survive, we would have to eat the natives. It would be an impracticable expectation to keep our supply lines open. To make such an action feasible, we would have to secure the help of all three meat-eating races.'

'We herbivores would be fine though,' stated another of the Emperors.

'It isn't outwith their ability or mindset to sanitise an entire planet. Indeed, the Modloch Emperor did exactly that to expedite his latest victory. He sanitised all of the Albany's planets, causing a huge refugee problem that crippled his enemy's resources, armed forces, and infrastructure. He didn't kill the people, just their food source. Within days the populations were starving.'

'A formidable foe indeed.'

'I am not the military man that many of you are, yet I can see it would be futile endeavour.'

His father took over the questioning again, 'What if they came here?'

'Again, they would have the same problems as we face, their biggest being that their supply craft aren't as fast as their main battlefleets. They can't stock up enough food to make the journey in one go. They would have to wait for their freighters. They aren't equipped or prepared for this type of long-distance warfare. Once here they could forage for food, but that would also make them vulnerable. They could sanitise planets as they passed, but then they too would starve. These people fight in space, they aren't used to protracted ground wars. Only Humans have that kind of experience, and there just isn't enough of them.'

'Give us a few minutes Merro,' the screen went blank. With a sigh of relief, Merro walked over to a corner where he prepared himself a hot drink. He sat in the only chair in the room and drank it. He was finished before the screen came alive again. He stood and went to the centre of the room.

'Merro?'

'Yes Father.'

'Please submit all that you have through the normal channels.' He smiled, 'You did a wonderful job my boy. I am proud of you.'

His praise raised Merro's spirits, 'Thank you Father, I am unworthy of your praise.'

'No you aren't my boy. We are all impressed. We agree with your assessment on military matters at this point. What about profit and trade?'

'We have opportunities there. Trade within the Federation is strictly controlled. However, there is no restrictions on trade outwith the Federation. For example, the Humans can trade no metals or rare minerals, and they have an untapped solar system that is rich in just about everything you can imagine. They have planets and moons that have never been properly explored. I have sent a report on what I have been able to gather. I think you will find it mind boggling the resources they have at their disposal, but which they have no idea how to exploit or even use.' He threw his hands in the air, 'We can have our pick of whatever we want. The Ambatta have a whole asteroid field that they can do nothing with.'

'What do we have to offer them?'

'Technology, materials, whatever they want. The Federation has everything going through a single Human company called the PD Company of Earth. Everything is filtered. Companies on Earth are screaming for access to the stars. We can supply that access. We can sell them old ships and old technology. Not warships, but freighters. We can sell them new ones if we want. They also deal in gold and silver as currency.'

'So, the Federation has bottlenecked trade through a single company... interesting. No doubt that is to prevent trading in illegal metals and minerals. Any idea who owns it?'

'Believe it or not, it's the Ambassador who I returned with. He and his family own everything. They build their ships, war fleets, freighters.'

'Then he must be immensely rich and powerful.'

'To be honest, I don't think he fully realises that or cares. All he wants to do is sail across the galaxy meeting new people and going to new worlds.'

'Alright, I think we need a much better handle on this person and the dealings of his PD Company.'

'I have a brochure.'

His father laughed hard, 'It is a start. We of course don't want the Humans flooding our galaxy with rare minerals either, we don't want our profits to crash. We may want to deal with this PD Company ourselves. Let's not kick the door down only to have it slammed in our faces. Let's start some sort of regular trade first. Thank you Merro.'

The screen went blank and Merro went to his room. He looked out of a window as shuttles flew overhead. His staff were arriving. Time for a long bath and a change of clothes.

The Black of Space

The crew of the ships were still loitering on the great lawns. A flock of birds flew overhead and gave them great entertainment. Others walked around the trees, some hand in hand. Over them all small drones flew here there and everywhere as the news was sent back to Earth.

CHAPTER 49

Charlie sat on the couch opposite Steven and Komoru. They had called him in to get a brief on what Merro was thinking and the things he had done since arriving home. Their week off was quickly coming to an end and they were trying to get their business heads back on straight before being hauled up in front of the council of Emperors.

Charlie explained everything he had picked up. Merro had made daily reports and matters had been on his mind a lot. They were relieved to know that the Empire was no longer thinking of pre-emptive action against the Federation, but were alarmed to discover that they were prepared to sell ships directly to individuals on Earth.

When Charlie left, Steven and Komoru talked about everything at great length. Babes helped them sift through all the guidelines and Federation rules and regulations. They discovered that there was nothing preventing such direct sales from happening. They both made up a report and sent it on to his mother. Mary read the report in utter disbelief. She called in Brian and then they sent it onto the President.

It wasn't long before Steven and Komoru received a request to find out as much as they could about the Empire's intentions. They refused any and every effort to be courted by local business and political leaders. They were, after all, supposed to be resting. All requests were politely guided back towards their administration.

Florina had left after a couple of days to go visit her friends. When she returned to her normal residence, it was to discover her mother sitting in front of it, running her hands over the piece of furniture that Charlie had built.

Florina was immediately on the defensive, 'Can I help you?'

'Florina! They said you were going to be longer…'

The Black of Space

'You aren't getting it Mother.'

'Is this not a gift for the Royal family?'

'No, it was a gift to me, for me.'

'Don't be silly Florina, this is far too valuable for a child like you.'

Florina advanced on her mother, her eyes blazing and her fur standing on end.

'It was made for me by the hands of the man I happen to be in love with. I will totally destroy it before I allow anyone else to possess it.'

Her mother was alarmed, she had never been talked to by her daughter like that.

'You fell in love with a commoner?' Her mother snorted. 'You!'

'Yes, me.'

'You were supposed to fall in love with a noble Lord.'

'Lord Noch Man Drich is a commoner. He was born a commoner, and he built me that with his own hands. Merro has one too, go steal that.'

'One like this?'

'No, nothing like it, but it is still a beautiful piece.'

'Do you know what this is made with?'

'Precious metals, gems, some of which don't exist in our Empire.'

'That would make this piece priceless. The craftmanship is also exquisite. I don't suppose I could purchase it from you?'

'No, nor order it handed over. I told you I will destroy it first.'

'I believe you are serious too. Your father is not amused that you did not achieve your goal. Didn't you try to seduce him?'

'I stripped naked in front of him mother. I did nothing short of throw myself on the ground and open my legs. He wasn't interested.'

'Is he queer?'

'No mother, he isn't queer, but he does have a

companion. One far more beautiful than I.'

'I find that hard to believe.'

Florina had access to the same files as Merro did. It didn't take her long to find them.

'Oh!' Was about as much as her mother could think of to say.

Florina put the tablet away. 'As you can see, I am outclassed. He also isn't used to other species. He isn't attracted to them.'

'That is a little racist!'

'I don't think it is intentional Mother. Humans didn't even know other species existed until a few years ago. They just aren't used to them.'

'You had a three-month journey, his woman wasn't there.'

'He just looked right through me as though I wasn't there. I made friends with one of the women on board, one that works with him. She is very beautiful and in love with him too. She has been trying for years without success. She says that is just the way he is. She had never known him to look at any other woman either. And, in his world, he is considered a plain looking man.'

'I see. He finally landed himself a beauty, and now refuses to look at any other woman.'

'That is the impression I am getting.' She lifted a hand and ran it gently over a rose, 'Then he makes me something like this, with his own two hands. It takes my breath away, fills me with hope. How can anyone make something so beautiful for someone else if they simply don't care?'

'What are you going to keep in it?'

A strange smile played across her lips, 'My underwear of course.'

In the crystal-clear glass of the mirror, her mother could see the look in her daughters' eye and knew she had it bad.

CHAPTER 50

Steven and Komoru were both very nervous. It had taken them another three weeks at top speed to reach the central core of planets. They found not one, but three inhabitable planets, all orbiting the same sun.

One was dry, another was very wet, and the third a harmonious balance between the two. Three planets, three entirely different species. Three planets in perfect synchronisation. Three species that had gone to war more times than they could count. Three species that eventually had to learn to live together. They had formed an alliance and brought other worlds into it. They had learned that honest trade was far more profitable than war.

Their shuttle took them down to the planet's surface. They docked in what seemed to be a normal spaceport. A guide was waiting for them. He escorted them to a vehicle. Two hours later they were still travelling. It reminded Steven a lot of cities in America – a grand metropolis but with strange buildings and strange vehicles. The four Humans were communicating directly with their minds. Beaver and Colonel Howe sat directly opposite the Ambassadors.

The journey had begun to get tedious before they arrived at a huge complex. There were a lot of security measures and a double gate system. They were checked in through both. They saw grand houses through stands of trees, perfectly tended lawns. Flowerbeds poked through the trees with a splash of colour. The road split up onto many different paths until eventually it joined a main thoroughfare. It took another twenty minutes to reach the main building, which looked more like a university than a place of government.

The security was insane. Their weapons were impounded, and an armed escort provided. Other people were being escorted similarly. Male and females worked within the building. The array of different races was mind boggling, and it was easy to spot the meat eaters from the herbivores.

They went through check point after check point. Steven finally lost his patience.

'How many more of these are there to go?'

'Excuse me?'

'I am completely fed up of this bullshit. Take us to where we are supposed to be going right now, or we are leaving.'

'We have to go through the proper security measures sir.'

'We have been through more security measures than I would ever have believed possible. The only thing you haven't done is ask me to bend over so you can look up my arse. We have been body searched by a dozen different scanning devices, and we are not going through anymore. Take us to where we are going now, or we are leaving.'

'You will still have to go through all the security checks again on the way out.'

'You think so do you? Watch this space.'

Komoru held up a hand to stop Steven, but a few seconds later they were back on the ship. The weapons that had been removed from them appeared a second later.

Howe and Beaver thought it was hilarious while Komoru was furious.

'That was stupid Steven!' A second later she was back on board her own ship.

'What are you doing Steven?' Her voice was loud in his head.

'I am not in the mood for a lecture. As soon as our shuttle gets back, I am leaving. You can stay if you want,' he cut communications to her.

Thirty minutes later the shuttle docked and Steven prepared to get underway. An urgent communication came in. Steven was in his chair.

'Ambassador, you are on your ship. How did you get

The Black of Space

there?'

'Who are you?'

'I am the senior advisor for visiting dignitaries.'

'How I got here is none of your damn business. You can convey to whoever is in charge that we will not be visiting your planet again. We are leaving forthwith.'

'Why?'

'What do you mean why? I am an Ambassador to the Federation yet I am being treated like a pizza delivery boy. How many bloody security check points do you have in that damn place? It is ridiculous. You subjected us to hours of driving, then another hour of security checks. Who do you people think you are? If any of the Federation's Emperors come here to visit, and you treat them like you did us, and you will have a bloody war on your hands. I have heard of paranoia, but that is well over the top.'

'It is just how it is here sir.'

'I don't care, I will not be treated like a piece of shit.'

'Ambassador Gordon...' it was a voice out off to the side. A hand appeared and the official got up, bowing as he went. A very dignified person sat down.

'Please calm down Ambassador.'

'Why would I calm down? Our systems are full of nanites, it is how we communicate with each other and our ships. Every time you scan us, it causes severe discomfort. I will not calm down.'

'I am Morro's father, the Grand Emperor, Terrie Macdoe. I can assure you we had no idea our security measures would cause such pain and discomfort. It would seem, however, that out security measures are quite pointless against your people if you can simply vanish into thin air like that. What do you call that?'

'It is called matter transportation.'

'I see, we have theorised about it here for generations, but no one has proven the science yet. It also renders every security system we have here useless.'

'Of course it does. Didn't Merro tell you about it?'

'No, that was something he failed to report. I suppose it stands to reason that if you were hostile, we would all be dead by now. If I give you coordinates, could you meet me there? It is my own private residence.'

'If you give us an hour of your time, we will. Right now, I am very hungry.'

'Have your lunch Ambassador, and I will see you in an hour.'

'We will see you soon, Your Highness.'

It wasn't long before Komoru came stomping through.

'Have we calmed down a little?'

Steven looked up from his bowl of soup. 'A little. But if you are going to start on me while I am eating, I will have you beamed back off the ship.'

Komoru became concerned, 'Are you all right?'

'No. I have a massive headache that the nanites aren't coping with.'

'Maybe you should go see the doctor.'

'Babes is analysing the problem.'

'I see, then I will join you for soup.'

She returned quickly with a bowl. She wasn't fond of the thick broth many of the Scots ate with gusto, however she was very hungry and knew it would be filling.

They had almost finished by the time Babes completed her analysis.

'Steven, some of the nanites in your body were destroyed by their equipment and they have lodged in your brain. I have had to reprogram them. Ico is analysing Komoru now and I am going to check on the Colonel and Beaver.'

'Thank you Babes.'

It wasn't too long before Steven began to feel better. His headache began to recede, and his temper settled down.

Charlie and Lewis appeared. They grabbed some soup

and sat down.

'How is your little mission going guys?'

Charlie tore a chunk off a loaf and dunked it in his soup, 'It's going well. It was good of them to stick a nice fleet our there for us to analyse.'

'It was indeed. What about that carrier?'

'It has to be one of their biggest. It's a completely different system to the one I envisioned. Makes me feel like a complete bannock to think I had the audacity to even try to design one.'

'It's a bit late now Charlie. They have started work on it.'

Charlie shrugged, 'Que será, será'

'Don't worry, it is only proof of concept. But it is going to be a lot smaller than that one, isn't it?'

Charlie blinked a couple of times, 'If my calculations are correct, you could fit about eight of my design into that one.'

'Then yours is a lot more effective.'

'How do you make that out?'

'What's eight times three hundred?'

'Two thousand four hundred. Alright, I get where you are coming from. Doesn't mean to say I am right. These guys have been at it for thousands of years.'

'Look at it another way Charlie, you had no preconceptual ideas about what it was supposed to be like.'

Charlie turned to Lewis, 'You got to really love his use of fancy words. Any idea what he is gabbing on about?'

'Ain't got no idea. I just blow shit up.'

'You got a good job. Blown anything up lately?'

'Been a while.'

'What do you think it would need to take out that carrier?'

'A nuke, from inside.'

'That's what I was thinking.'

Steven shook his head, 'Are you pair ignoring me now?'

Charlie sniffed, 'Sorry, I only talk to people who know

how to talk proper like.'

Komoru suddenly started to laugh, Steven wasn't long behind. It was what he needed.

'You guys going back up there?'

'Aye, I'm scanning and recording, Lewis is sorting the information, trying to make sense of it. What we need is a navy guy who has served on carriers.'

'As soon as you think you have something sorted out, send it to Baxter.'

'Will do. How did your meeting go?'

'Steven took a tantrum and beamed us home,' Komoru answered. 'We were just about to leave.'

Steven scowled, 'They were pissing us around something terrible. It took hours just to get to the place from the spaceport, then we were another hour going through the security checks. It was ridiculous.'

'I bet they near shit themselves when you beamed out.'

'There is no way you can go down there Charlie. They will probably think you are some kind of bomb and shoot you. Their scanning devices killed a heap of nanites in our systems.'

'Looks like you are on your own again. I'm busy anyway.'

'Merro's father has invited us down to his private residence. We are going to beam straight down there. You were right though, they did just about shit themselves when we beamed out.'

Charlie stood, taking his empty plate with him, 'We had better get back to it then. It won't take them long to figure out we can beam a nuke on board their precious carrier.'

'Do you think they will leave?'

'Well I would.'

Lewis stood as well, 'Charlie got a good point. Let's get to it man.'

They dropped their plates off at the wash point on the way past. The dirty plates vanished, only to reappear in the clean pile a few seconds later.

The Black of Space

Komoru squeezed Steven's arm, 'Maybe we should get going too.'

Steven stood up, 'I am going to have a coffee first.'

CHAPTER 51

Steven felt his irritation rise the moment they beamed down. Two guards rushed towards them with strange devices in their hands. He was just about to kick the nearest in the balls when Beaver and Howe acted. The two guards found themselves flying through the air.

'Enough!' A growl came from the shadows. The Emperor was even more imposing in person than he was on screen. He walked over to someone and roasted him in front of everyone. The officer slinked away and took his men with him.

Steven felt himself calm down a little. His irritation had risen again for some reason, and obviously Howe and Beaver were feeling the same effects.

The Emperor came over, 'Your men act quickly and efficiently. However, you need to be careful. The guards around here are hired independently from all over the Empire. They are very highly paid and notoriously twitchy. Over the centuries, we have experienced a lot of assassinations and attempted assassinations. It wouldn't be the first time someone from off world had disguised themselves as an Ambassador from a different planet. Nor, unfortunately, the first time an Ambassador has been killed by mistake because of a misinterpreted gesture.'

'You people must spend a lot of time fighting.'

He gestured towards a seating area, 'Please come and sit down, Ambassadors.'

They crossed over to semi-circular seating that faced a small fountain.

'I am very happy that you have made such a long trip. My son speaks very highly of you all, and his companion is at this moment taking the Empire by storm.' He smiled, 'It would seem that our race and the Human race have a lot in common.'

Steven returned the smile, 'She is also taking our world by storm. We have received word from Earth that the ladies from our world are crazy about her fashion. Our PR team also sent her broadcasts back.'

That delighted him, 'I believe we also have a common currency. I firmly believe that will help trade. I also believe that you are the person to talk to about it. Are you not the owner of the PD Company of Earth?'

The question caught Steven a little by surprise, 'I am indeed, but I am more of a figurehead than anything else, it is my parents who actually run the company. My other duties give me very little time for the family business.'

'I have over a thousand requests from interested businesses who wish to trade with your planet. None of your goods are on any prohibited list here. Some are suggesting a free trade alliance. However, we are aware that your solar system virtually remains untapped. That is a very rare thing indeed, Ambassador. We propose to set up a team to identify what we don't want to be flooded with.'

'Humanity isn't in a position to flood anyone with anything. My company are the only ones who are, at the moment, capable of mining anything off world.'

'So, you have the whole thing sewn up tighter than a Druan's arse. I am impressed. You must wield a lot of power on your world Ambassador.'

'I disagree your Royal Highness. My family aren't in it for profit. In fact, my parents' home would fit into this courtyard.'

'Seriously?'

'We are in it to save Humanity. We aren't an advanced race like you are. As a species, we had never travelled further than our own moon until a few years ago.'

The Emperor sat back, 'Pray tell Ambassador. I think I know some of the story, but as we are going to be trading with your world, I wish to know it all.'

The story took a while to tell. The Emperor had many questions for Steven. Snacks were brought and all were fed.

'I think I have the full picture now Ambassador. So you and your family have been scrambling to keep your world safe. Now you have achieved that, you have come under huge pressure to hand it all over. The Federation, however, have prevented that from happening.'

'That is right sir.'

'Federation technology, our technology, would do your planet little good if it is so backwards. Also, your technology would be considered little more than junk here. The way our power is generated and the amount we use is just not compatible. The Federation's Grand Commander is very smart. He must have picked up on that straight away. I presume you have large power companies on Earth?'

'That is correct.'

He shook his head, 'Is your power fed to homes by overhead cables?'

'Yes, that is right.'

He laughed, 'I would love to see that. We have had nothing like that for thousands of years. I enjoy a bit of history Ambassador; I have seen pictures. One of the hardest things to do was to break the monopoly of the energy companies. It caused so much conflict back in its day. It took imperial edicts and laws to stop them. Those in power, those with money and power, are not prepared to give it up lightly. Your troubles are just beginning.'

'You do not fill me with enthusiasm sir.'

The Emperor laughed, 'I don't suppose I do. Every home here has its own power source. A day's sunlight is enough to power a home for a month. The power companies now make their money from selling technology, the batteries to store the power, the coatings that are sprayed onto the houses to collect that energy, the converters, that sort of thing. We could of course sell you all of this, but without the knowledge to develop or maintain it, or the materials to produce it…'

'I understand sir. We aren't there yet.'

The Black of Space

'What a quandary you have given us. Some are ready to sell ships to your people if they have the money.'

'There are plenty who have the money, but none who could pilot or maintain such a vessel.'

'No one at all?'

'No one. Right now there are thousands of people being trained up, but all are part of the military. They will eventually filter down and join civilian life. At home our aircraft are sub-sonic and fly on fossil fuels.'

The Emperor thought that was hilarious, and it took him a while to gain his composure.

'I would really love to see one of those.' He nodded to the two men behind him, 'Your weapons are also chemical based. In some ways that isn't a bad thing.' He thought things over for a moment, 'I really need to talk to the other leaders of the Empire.' His eyes swept up and he looked over Howe and Beaver. 'I would like to ask you one thing: I am aware that the man who rejected my beautiful daughter's hand in marriage isn't here. May I ask where he is?'

Steven rubbed his temples, the pain in his head had been getting steadily worse. He closed an eye.

'Right now he is about to start a war with your people.'

'Excuse me?'

Steven tried to stand, but his legs gave way. Komoru cried out in alarm. Barely a second later there was a familiar hissing noise and a terrified scream came from the shadows.

CHAPTER 52

Charlie rolled onto his back in relief. It had taken over an hour for word to reach the massive fleet that had been circumnavigating the planet below.

'Man they are bloody slow.'

His answer was a grunt. A second later pieces of plastic flew over his nose. Charlie snapped upright. Lewis was smashing the tablet he had been working on into fragments.

'What the hell Lewis?'

'Useless junk,' Lewis grunted. His eyes were badly bloodshot when he looked at Charlie. 'Man I got de sore head.'

Charlie opened his mind and was flooded. He cut it off.

'Babes, what the hell is going on?'

'What do you mean Charlie?'

'How many of the crew have bad headaches?'

'I don't know.'

'Why not?'

'I don't know. Steven had one earlier.'

'Patch me through to Ico.'

'He is listening.'

'Ico, how many of your crew are suffering from headaches?'

'None that I am aware of Charlie.'

'Start scanning the area for outside interference.'

'I will ask permission from the acting Captain.'

'Who is it?'

'Sato.'

'Patch me through.'

Sato came on, 'Yes Charlie?'

'Any of your guys showing signs of headaches?'

'No, nothing, we are all fine.'

'We aren't. Half the crew seems immobile here, including Babes. She isn't working properly. Start scanning the local area for anything you can find.'

At that, Charlie just happened to look out the window. The fleet was moving away steadily. Two ships however, of a different configuration to the warships, had remained stationary. 'No scratch that Sato, scan those two ships that aren't moving.'

Charlie helped Lewis out of the observation pod and made his way to the bridge.

'Charlie, they seem to be using scanners on Babes.'

'It isn't directed at you.'

'No.'

'Get your shields up.'

'Alright.'

Ico wasn't so sure it would work, 'I don't know if it will be effective Charlie. It is a very strong signal, not one we are used to.'

'It will work, or it will once I reach the bridge. I will tune Babes' shields to the same frequency as mine. I am completely unaffected.'

'I understand Charlie.'

Charlie was passing members of the crew sitting on the floor nursing their heads. 'Sato, I have no idea what these people are up to, but I want you to get a couple of boarding parties ready. My guys look goosed.'

'Is that wise Charlie?'

'No, but it is a lot wiser than letting them get away with it.'

Sato hesitated a moment, 'Alright. I am on it.'

The bridge crew looked lethargic. Sid seemed asleep at his station, Buzz had slid halfway down in the big chair. He only seemed to half notice Charlie, who made his way to the security station. His fingers flew over the console. A few seconds later the figures around him began to revive a little.

Buzz sat up, 'What the hell is going on?'

Charlie answered him, 'We have two ships off our port

quarter. They are bombarding Babes with beams. She has lost thirty per cent of her capabilities. We are almost crippled. Red Alert, action stations.'

'Oh shit, Stevie is going to kill me.'

Babes had been trying to speak to Steven. 'Charlie, something is wrong with Steven.'

'Can you scan the area Babes?'

'No Charlie, I'm sorry.'

'Sato, are you listening in?'

'Yes, scanning the area now.'

Lewis walked in, belting on his personal weapons. He came to stand by Charlie. His eyes were still bloodshot, and he looked pissed.

Sato got back to him, 'Charlie, there is someone using a device down there. It is emitting the same kind of beam and I think it is aimed at Captain Gordon.'

'On the count of five Sato, beam Lewis right down beside that guy.'

'Roger.'

'Lewis, get down there and take care of it.'

A huge paw slapped Charlie on the shoulder and a millisecond later it dissolved.

'I think they realise they have been rumbled Charlie; they are preparing to leave.'

But Charlie was well ahead of him, 'Patch through control of your guns to me Sato.'

'Done.'

'Get ready to assault. Secure the bridges and weld the damn doors shut.'

'On your order Charlie.'

Two thin beams of light streaked out from both ships. They cut through the vessels' skins in a surgical strike that rendered the engines inoperative. They slewed out of control.

'Go Sato.'

'On their way.'

Buzz tried to stand, 'What the hell is happening Charlie?'

'Try and get your head in the game Buzz. We were attacked by those two ships. Get as close to them as you can. We need stealth mode and faster than light speed. Get to it.'

'Damn it, right man.'

Charlie talked to Ico and his gear appeared at his side. He strapped it on. Charlie looked around. 'Sato, these guys are totally goosed, can you send over your spare shift to get this ship up and running?'

'Already getting themselves together Charlie.'

'Awesome, now beam me aboard that ship on the right.'

A few seconds later, Charlie arrived on a bridge filled with gun smoke. There were a couple of bodies lying around. A second look told him none were dead. His eyes quickly scanned the room. The majority of the crew were made up of lizard-like creatures. To him they looked like something out of the old TV series 'V'. Charlie walked up to the nearest and punched him so hard in the face that he flew across the room. The creature hit a wall and slid down unconscious, blood pouring from what Charlie suspected was a nose. The attitudes of the others changed drastically.

He went over to a console and looked it over. It was locked. He waggled a finger at one who looked almost Human.

'Put your hand on here,' Charlie ordered.

He stepped back, 'No.'

'It doesn't have to be attached to the rest of your body son. I just need your hand.'

His repeated no was accompanied by a scream of agony. Charlie picked the severed hand up off the floor and placed it against the pad. He quickly searched its data banks for the information they had gleaned from the ship. Satisfied, he deleted all the data, then took his emergency escape tool through the terminal. He caught a stray thought and disappeared, re-appearing in an isolated part of the ship. He ripped open a panel and ripped a large box from inside it. He then repeated the process on the second ship.

'Sato, get everyone back to the ships. Lock onto the hardware I have in my hands and take it on board your ship, then send me down to the surface.'

'Can I ask what you have done Charlie?'

'I have destroyed their local memory and stolen their hard drives.'

'Will we be able to access it later.'

'Play later Sato.'

'Roger that.'

The devices vanished from his grip and he appeared on the surface next to Lewis, whose eyes weren't as red as they had been. In one massive fist he held the half-conscious body of an alien species Charlie didn't recognise, but who was wearing the same uniform as they had been on the ship. He also had an arm missing. Lewis held a device in his other hand.

'Make sure you take that with you Lewis. You can dump the body though.'

The figure dropped to the ground. Charlie crossed to where Komoru was kneeling beside Steven with his head on her lap. Tears were beginning to form.

'Get him to Ico, Sato and I will take care of things.'

After a silent order the pair disappeared. Charlie turned on a figure standing by the fountain.

'Did you have anything to do with this?'

'I don't know what you are talking about.'

'Liar.'

'Who are you to call me a liar?'

'I am the man who holds your life in his hands.'

'You are the one, the one who refused my daughter's hand in marriage. It is a shame.'

'You almost killed my friend, and our ship. What were you after?'

'I don't know what you are talking about.'

'Did you kill the previous Ambassador just to lure us here?'

'Again, I have no idea what you are talking about, we would never do anything so crass.'

Charlie stepped closer, 'Did Merro never warn you about my abilities?'

'To what are you referring?'

'My ability to detect lies. You are lying. Let me guess: you quickly realised that we have a superior technology, one far superior to the Federation's or yours. Like many before you, you thought you could steal it. So you assassinated the Ambassador and insisted that we were sent as a replacement. You have been trying to scan our ships. When that didn't work, you tried to disable one of them and her Captain. I bet you were really looking forward to the post-mortem. Had you thought up some ridiculous disease to blame our demise on? What a shame, our people could have become great friends. You have your life, thank your son and our friendship for that.'

As Charlie stepped away his eyes detected forms rapidly approaching, all were armed.

'We need to go guys.'

A moment later they vanished.

Grand Emperor Terri Macdoe slapped a teapot with his hands. It sailed through the air, smashing off the wall. There was a feminine scream.

His temples throbbed, 'Lady Aurora Malinci, what are you doing here?'

'I was with Princess Florina, Your Highness.' She looked around, 'Where is she?'

He shook his head, 'She was never here. Leave.' She bowed hurriedly and almost ran. Guards rushed onto the scene. He pressed a button on his communicator.

'They have discovered us, surround those two ships.' He listened to the voice in his earpiece. 'What do you mean the fleet was withdrawn? Who ordered it?' He sighed, 'Idiots! Send someone to detain them. Order a couple of squadrons back.'

He paced back and forth for a good ten minutes before flying into a rage. The ships had got clean away. He ordered a thorough search before leaving to tell the others in person that their plan had failed.

CHAPTER 53

Charlie was aware that time was of the essence, 'What is happening Sato?'

'Babes can go into stealth mode, but for now only has sub-light speed.'

'Then we need somewhere to hide. This whole thing was a huge setup to get the Builder ships into the Empire's hands.'

'No shit!'

His eyes flicked over the three men, 'Stations gentlemen. Colonel, would you like to take command of the ship?'

'I am only half aware of what is happening Charlie. Carry on please.'

'Lewis, can you stay for a while? We need you here.'

'Sure man. We uh… got another problem.'

'What?' It was then he noticed the hands digging into Lewis's shoulders, and the red splotches of blood soaking through his uniform. A small head popped out from behind his shoulder. Charlie was stunned.

'How the hell did you get here? Ico, beam her back to the surface.'

'Wait, please. I know somewhere you can hide.'

Charlie felt a wave of anger wash through him for two reasons. Firstly she was right, secondly she would come in handy as a hostage. It was a situation that Charlie hated immediately.

'Colonel, escort her to the bridge.'

They rushed towards the bridge. Florina was almost blinded. The deck beneath her feet shivered and disappeared. She had seen it before so wasn't frightened, but she was disorientated.

Lewis picked her up and carried her like a teddy bear under his arm the rest of the way.

Buzz got up from his chair as they arrived. He looked

terrible.

'Got word Stevie is OK, but take over man. I feel like shit.'

'Go rest Buzz, we will need you on your feet as soon as possible.' He turned, 'Florina, where is this place we can hide?'

'On the third world.' Lewis put her down. 'There is a region there that is famous for its electrical and magnetic storms. For centuries it was where everyone attacked them from.'

Howe interjected, 'You just told us everyone knows about it, it will be the first place they look.'

'Normally yes, but they don't yet know that you know about it.'

Charlie thought it over, 'She has a point Colonel. Where is the nearest asteroid field from here Florina?'

'At sub-light, a few days I think.'

'That is where I would look for us.'

'And it is heavily populated.'

Charlie looked straight at Howe, 'I would take a chance on the Princess's first choice. We won't be able to stay long, but Ico says we need to replenish a lot of materials. If there are strong magnetics down there it could be a good choice. It's up to you though. I will go with your decision.'

Howe smiled and regarded the Princess, 'If you think she is playing it straight.'

'She is.'

'Let's do it Charlie.'

Charlie looked over the unfamiliar bridge crew, 'Follow Ico to the third planet. Try to keep up.'

They acknowledged him and turned to their work.

Long range visuals showed that they had escaped before they could be surrounded. The screens showed traffic coming and going. A swarm of destroyers arrived at the planet behind them. They soon began a complicated search pattern. It wasn't long before they increased the size of the pattern. More ships arrived and spread out in two different directions. Some went to light speed and shot past them. The crew calculated their trajectories. Some were headed for the asteroid belt while others were taking a direct line back to Federation space.

'Sato, can you prepare a communications probe? Get in front of those search ships and launch it. Tell home what is happening, what the Empire have done and tried to do. Send it in clear, don't use code, I want them to know exactly what we have told them. I want them to think it is us and we are heading for home. Stay long enough to make sure they have taken the bait then have the probe self-destruct.'

'You mean you want them to think the probe is us.'

'Of course I do. They won't know what is in the signal at first, but they will hear it and be able to track it. Be quick in case they have contingency plans.'

'On it.'

Ico streaked away at faster than light speed. It took them a couple of hours to get far enough in front of the search ships to send the probe onwards undetected. Sato waited until the imperial ships pass before he ordered the probe to transmit. The signal was immediately picked up by the pursuing ships. They increased speed. Other ships were called in from lots of different vectors. Sato sat for half an hour watching their signals bounce back and forth through the black, until he was satisfied the probe had done its job. It was time to go back and find Babes.

They were approaching the third planet as they picked up her beacon. What would normally have taken Babes minutes had taken hours. There was a great sense of relief on both ships. At Charlie's request, Sato made planet fall first to do a reconnaissance. There were signs of recent activity in the vicinity of the great storms.

Sato's pilot looked dubious, 'Are you sure you want to

take us down there sir?'

Sato wasn't too sure himself, but he shook his head, 'We don't have a choice, take us down. Once we are in, turn on all of our sensors, we may have to guide the other ship down.'

'Yes sir.'

Sato instincts had been correct. The ground below was a warren of huge canyons and dry desert. The ship was rocked by the elements. It took them an hour to find a suitable spot to do repairs. They came back up out of the storm clouds. Babes was waiting patiently for them in orbit and he guided them down.

Docking was conducted manually. Lewis was one of the first across, with Charlie hot on his heels. They found a red-eyed Komoru sitting with the doctors.

She reached up for Lewis's hand, 'I'm glad you are here.'

'Where is de Captain?'

She pointed to the floor, 'It was bad. Ico thinks it will take a day to completely heal Steven. Most of his nanites have shut down, others are causing him damage. Ico is flushing them out now. He has had to send in hunter nanites to kill them. Once that is completed, they can fill his system with new nanites and repair his body. Ico says that Babes will not function properly until he has fully recovered.'

She turned her attention to Charlie and stuck out her hand, 'Thank you.'

Charlie hesitated for a moment, then took it.

'You got us out of trouble again.'

'Right now we are deeper in the shit than we have ever been. We have them fooled for now, but it won't last forever. We have to come up with a cohesive plan. Ico will need to grab what Babes needs to heal herself. The navigators and military guys need to come up with a plan, and you need to coordinate all of that.'

'What will you be doing?'

'I stole their hard-drives, I need to break into them.'

'Why would you do that!'

'How much of your brain is a supercomputer?'

She held up two fingers and held them a slither apart, 'Teensy-weensy bit.'

Charlie laughed; she had spoken in English. He held up a hand with his fingers open.

'I got this much, that makes me more suited to the task. I will still need the best hackers we have to help though.'

'We have a starting point then.'

'Is there anything I can do to help?'

Komoru's head cranked around, her mouth falling open, 'What is she doing here?' Her eyes narrowed and she made a move. Lewis swept her up off her feet.

'Princess Florina, she done tell us where to hide, Miss Komoru. She on our side.'

Komoru's eyes flicked towards Charlie, 'You will never have him. Do you know why he isn't interested in you or any other woman? It's because when he isn't with his big boobed Captain, he turns his hormones off.'

'Here we go!' Charlie threw his arms into the air, 'As soon as you get mad, you tell everybody my wee secrets. Will you ever learn to shut your gob?'

Komoru went very still. She calmed down quickly and squirmed out of Lewis's grip.

'I'm sorry Charlie. I've done it again.'

'That isn't healthy.'

Charlie's eyes swung towards the pretty Japanese doctor.

'What's it to you? It isna like you would be able to take it anyway.'

She was alarmed. She and Charlie had never really met, nor had they ever been formally introduced. He was a patient that Amanda never shared anything about. His reputation preceded him though, and she knew it was not wise to cross him or talk about him openly.

'I meant no harm; it was simply a professional observation.'

Charlie snarled at her, but Florina distracted him, 'What are they talking about Charlie?'

He bit back the retort that was on his lips. 'Florina is on my team. Could you make a room available for us to work in?'

'Yes of course,' Komoru flushed.

He walked over to Florina and dragged her inside. He shoved her in front of the doctor.

'Give her nanites.'

'Is that wise?'

'We can take them out later.'

She sighed and took Florina by the hand. She yelped when they were injected. Charlie grabbed the hand that wasn't in pain and dragged her out of there. Ico guided him to the room that was being readied for them.

Komoru sighed, 'One step forward, three back.'

CHAPTER 54

Florina's eyes were watering quite badly, and her mind was in turmoil. Charlie took her over and placed her hand on a table. He pulled a few chairs over and sat her down. He sat down opposite her and threw his legs up onto the remaining chair.

Florina was gawping as things began to take form around her. It was different to what she was used to. This was what the ships really looked like in their world. Her eyes finally fell back on Charlie, who knew the signs and was simply waiting for her to adjust.

'The ship looks different.'

'Of course it does.'

Her mind flipped back, 'What were they talking about Charlie, why do you have a computer in your head?'

He had been waiting and preparing for this question. He pulled back his sleeve. She screamed at the sight. All she could see was the bare muscles in his arm. Then her mind kicked in.

'That isn't tissue? What is happening?' She watched, horrified, as metal probes appeared and peeled back the muscles. She recognised what she was looking at. Her eyes looked wounded.

'Charlie, are you a robot?'

'No, not quite.'

She was mortified as the muscles closed together and the skin began to stitch itself back over the hole of his arm. It only took a few minutes. He flexed his hand and pulled the sleeve back down.

'A few years ago I was, let's say, in a very bad accident. There wasn't much left of me, I was dying. Stevie saved my life. He and the ship. She built me a new body. A body that requires its own operating system, one that is tied into my real brain. I eventually became one with the machine. My internals are Human, my extremities are machine. I no longer sweat, but I do have a cooling system. I have two hearts, one mechanical, one biological.'

'So that is why you are so strong!'

'That is why I am so strong.'

'I don't know whether to laugh, scream or cry.'

'Neither would be appropriate at this time.'

She had a flash of inspiration, 'So your computer brain can help control your Human body! That is why you can turn your hormones down.'

'You got it in one.'

'Will it kill you?'

'No, in fact the exact opposite is the truth. It is a very sophisticated system. I don't need to eat as much as normal people, I have no wear and tear. The normal life span for a Human is about eighty to a hundred of our own years. Those with nanites in their system can expect to live for about another twenty years or so. My life span, we have calculated, could be as long as five hundred years. It will really depend on my mind.'

He thought it was quite cute the way her ears flattened. A stream of thoughts cascaded through her brain all at once.

'You would… can you still have children?'

'Yes, and yes I would outlive them all, and my grandchildren, and their grandchildren.'

'That is not natural, not normal Charlie, it isn't right, it isn't fair. You would have to watch them all die.' She sighed, 'It is no wonder you control yourself. You have feelings after all.'

'Of course I have feelings, I am still Human, still a person.'

Her ears snapped upright, 'Does that Captain use you as a sex toy?'

'Oh, for God's sake! Why is it all you women always ask the same damn thing? Why are you all so obsessed with sex?'

'I am not,' she was embarrassed now. 'It was just…'

'A random thought, right? I genuinely like Jean, and she

me. We aren't planning on getting married or having a family. She understands and accepts me for who and what I am. The relationship won't last Florina, both of us know and accept that. One day she will return to Earth and I won't.'

'Alright Charlie, I think I understand better now.'

The door opened and his new team walked in. Himari had one of the hard drives and another Japanese girl carried the other. They were both surprised to find Florina there, but they kept their mouths shut and set to work. Florina helped translate much of what they were seeing. It only took them five hours to crack the hard drives. Charlie's initial estimation had been right. They had gleaned very little data from Babes. Their backup plan had basically been to kill her, and her Captain, then dissect both. There had also been a plan to kill Ico and his crew. Florina had been shocked and depressed since discovering that. She counted the crews of the ships as her friends.

Charlie called an emergency briefing and presented his findings. They had in their possession a map of the whole Empire, its worlds, military installations, patrol routes, its dangers, all the latest intelligence. Everything they would need to get home.

Komoru found herself clapping, and some of the senior staff joined in.

'Wonderful work Charlie.'

'Just doing my job, the same as the rest of you. Any word on Steven, what is happening now?'

'Ico has all the materials we require to fix Babes. She was badly hurt and requires Steven's input to repair fully. He is past the worst and is now on the road to recovery. Once he has woken up, it will take another twenty-four hours for us to get Babes back to full health. After that we will be ready to leave. There are problems, however. We don't have the stores for a long journey. In fact, we have about a month's worth of food left. I suggest that for the moment everyone gets some rest. You must be tired.'

'Shattered.'

'What about the Princess, is she a security threat?'

'No, and she won't be as long as everyone treats her with respect. Leave the Princess Florina to me.'

'In that case all we have to do is wait for Steven to wake up.'

The meeting broke up. Charlie found Florina and escorted her back to her room on Babes. He watched from outside as she fell onto her bed. He saw tears stream down her face and read her thoughts. He was content she would be no trouble. He then made his way to the observation room. It was pitch black outside, but Charlie watched the storm with inhuman eyes. Strange colours raged across his vision, and the swirling patterns of electricity and magnetism kept him entertained until he slipped off into a deep sleep.

Printed in Great Britain
by Amazon